With Very

A RAKE OF LEAVES

Olga Merrick

Olga Merrick

chadgreen books

First published in 2016

Cover Image: Marie Banks

ISBN-13: 978-0992957759

chadgreen books
are published by Chadgreen Publishing
Telford, Shropshire, United Kingdom

Printed and bound in Great Britain by BookPrintingUK,
Peterborough, Cambridgeshire

DEDICATION

I dedicate this book to Danny Charles DeBanks (1937–2000) and his five wonderful children.

A Rake of Leaves

1 AUTUMN

Bob Shackleton stood by the graveside as they lowered the coffin, a very plain, unadorned woodchip casket, into the dark, gaping hole. A hole that had been dug in the furthermost part of the cemetery, practically a field, far away from the gentle dead, good people who had led blameless lives. It was all she deserved after her evil deeds. He was sure Tilda and Danny, her twins, were fine about it, judging by the detached looks on their faces.

A skein of geese flew over, interrupting the flow of the vicar's intonation. Leaves dipped and whirled from the surrounding oaks, beech and ash trees as a soughing wind blew across this far corner. Bob shivered, but not from cold or fear, more from the loathing he felt for his dead wife.

Looking down at the cheap coffin he knew some would accuse him of penny pinching. He couldn't give a toss: she was not worth spending money, effort, or time on... had not been for these past ten years. Money should be spent on the living, he reasoned, and given to those still grieving: like the widow and orphaned children of P.C. Gerry Sinclair. Delia's last violence, before her permanent incarceration in the asylum, was to bite a chunk, Hannibal Lecter style, from Gerry's cheek, and cause his premature death when septicaemia set in.

Bob barely listened as the unfamiliar vicar intoned the funereal passages from his prayer book, ignored the chill breeze that caught in his close-cropped hair, and tried not to look at Delia's family who were also present at their mother's and grandmother's final departure. The delectable Stella, the wife of Phil, Bob's old police buddy, stood slightly apart from Delia's twins. As did Denzil and Jessica Black, Delia's next door neighbours from Birchington. He watched his step-grandsons fidget and kick at some loose turf. So what? They were young and had only ever known the vicious bitch, their grandmother, by name.

Someone stepped up to him, one of the funeral attendants, and held out a handful of dried earth as the vicar repeated the words, 'Earth to earth, ashes to ashes.' This was the cue for Bob to scatter the handful onto the lowered coffin. He felt like throwing it into the wind and spitting on the plain wooden box containing the remains of a serial killer. *May you rot in hell, you evil bitch.*

Bob had chosen burial over cremation. He wanted her to rot and be eaten by insects and maggots: scattering the remaining fired crystals under a beautiful rose bush would have been far too good for her. Undeserved and inexcusable. Seven unjustified murders, eight counting Gerry's death – an even more indefensible loss of life.

He was aware that people were moving away

from the graveside. Danny and his partner, Ray, each took one of his arms. 'Time to go, Bob.' He nodded and allowed himself to be led back to the waiting cars, conscious of the others following. Relieved now that they would soon be at the hotel where the reception would be held. He refused to look back at the freshly-dug grave being filled in, refused to feel any sense of guilt at the lack of wreaths and flowers that normally decorated a new grave. At least until the stone masons carved an eternal reminder of the dead person's lifetime. There would be no headstone for Delia, no weekly, monthly or annual pilgrimage to lay flowers on this plot. In time, Bob guessed, it would be merely an insignificant hummock in an otherwise deserted field. He almost nodded to himself as he mouthed the word, 'Good.'

Travelling in the warm and comfortable, black limousine, no-one spoke. No matter: he knew everyone's tongues would be loosened once inside the hotel, where sherry and wine would be handed out as soon as they shed their outer garments. Bob maintained the silence: let them have their own thoughts for the next ten minutes or so. He, too, delved into his memory of a week ago. He recalled replacing the phone onto its base after saying 'thank you and goodbye' to the person at the other end. It was as if a great weight had been lifted from him: he sighed with the relief. The news was what he had been waiting for, hoping for, these past ten years. Yes, she was dead, really dead, not just in his desiring mind but clinically dead. Bob breathed another sigh of relief, gratified that it was all over. Well... almost. There was the funeral of course to arrange; people to contact, things of hers to collect.

Not that there would be many of those after ten years of her being shut up in that awful place. He shuddered again. Must be nigh on that number of years since he had last seen her, nine anyway. Strangely though, he had never divorced her, never wanted to remarry: that once was enough. It was during his one visit, not long after her incarceration, when Delia had acted so violently, it had taken three members of staff to restrain her. He could hear her now, that maniacal screaming, 'I'll get you, you bastard. I'll see you in hell.' He could see her foaming, spitting mouth with its bared teeth, and those blood-shot devil's eyes. Hard to believe now that she was the woman he had married only a few months before that visit.

Bob shivered with the memory, not only of that day at the institution, but the weeks before it, when he and his pals at Margate police station had finally pieced together the murders Delia had committed. Seven of them, eight really – counting P.C. Gerry Sinclair's death from septicaemia after her murderous bite. It had subsequently festered, left Gerry's wife a widow and orphaned his two young children.

Seven she had murdered, including three husbands and two friends of Danny and Tilda. Later, she'd arranged the death of her alleged best friend, Manda, (*at our wedding,* he recalled) followed by that of old Mrs Casey, their next-door-but-one neighbour. *Could have been more... bloody hell... I could have been her next victim*, he mused.

Bob never went back to see her, preferring instead to keep in touch with the institution by phone, email, or letter, informing them – when the time came – of his moving away from Kent to Highbury, London, where his step-daughter Matilda and her husband Mike lived. And not so far away, in Highgate, lived Danny with his partner Ray and their two sons.

Anything Delia had needed he provided, by parcel-post or transferal of money to the hospital's bank: he couldn't face going to the madhouse a second time, bad enough hearing her insane invectives the first time, and having to listen to the screaming and shouting of other inmates. Afterwards, after the fearsome confrontation, he had sat in the comparative privacy and security of the Head Nurse's office, almost squirming in his seat and wishing he could be anywhere but there.

His life now was one of keeping other people safe, much as he had done during his years with the Kent Police force. Today, though, his job was in a private capacity, working as a security adviser/consultant for Hogarth International, a global security firm, who advised and counselled companies on the prevention of violence in the workplace, industrial espionage, and anti-terrorism. Not so different from the crimes he had to solve or prevent all those years back, just in a more regulated capacity.

Following the phone call, he had walked through to his kitchen at the back of his apartment. It overlooked a small garden that belonged to the occupants of the basement flat below. They kept it well tended, with floral borders around white gravel and a central fishpond where water plants sheltered several huge golden carp. He watched as a few orange-coloured flashes rose to the surface and disappeared again, into the inky blackness of the pond.

Time for some coffee, he was thinking, although he could have killed for a large scotch. No chance tonight: he was on standby. He filled the kettle from a filter jug and listened as the water gurgled and bubbled inside the stainless steel kettle. He spooned instant coffee into a poppy-decorated mug and added a few grains of demerara from a stainless steel container. When it was ready he moved back into his front room, overlooking Highbury Fields, and sat at his desk in the window recess. He stared unseeingly, his mind elsewhere, not on the few joggers out for their early-evening run clad in high-viz jackets and thick-soled running shoes. Or the dog walkers cocooned in hooded fleeces or padded jackets also occupying the park, with shoulders hunched against the chill wind that blew among the plane trees. The first few leaves of autumn were already dislodging in that nippy breeze, making Bob shiver in sympathy as he suddenly focused on the joggers and walkers on the other side of the road. He watched traffic go by with dipped headlights, despite it being only four o'clock.

Perhaps he ought to ring the twins at their respective homes? Or contact a funeral director: but where, which one? Maybe he could find one in Canterbury, near the psychiatric hospital where Delia had been incarcerated? He didn't know and couldn't be motivated yet. *Leave it till tomorrow, ring the kids instead.* He smiled with no amusement. *Hardly kids anymore, both of them forty*, he thought. Mike was gone now, divorced and replaced by Tilda's older, second husband,

Freddie. Danny and Ray's boys, Alfie and Simon were in boarding school. They must be nine and ten. He'd lost count. Even after knowing Tilda and Danny these past ten years, being there for them, giving his advice when asked, comforting them, doing whatever was expected of him, he still didn't feel he fitted the role of stepfather. Such different twins: Tilda, in some respects, not unlike her mother. Not too much like her though, he hoped. Danny was the gentle one, a good father to his and Ray's boys; more approachable, Bob thought.

He must contact Phil and Stella: Phil, his ex-police buddy, and Stella, 'the delectable'. How long since he had seen them: a couple of years? They would come to the funeral of course. If not for Delia, they'd come to support him. Also, Dez and Jessica, Delia's next-door neighbours in Birchington, if they were still living there. For sure, they must be, he told himself: they exchanged Christmas cards with him every year.

Bob's mind raced on. *Go on Robert, be positive. Pick up the bloody phone and ring Tilda, or Danny. But you already know, don't you Tilda? You were there with her as she choked on the chocolates you took to her. You and the nurse watched her die. How come? Could neither of you have helped her? Done the Heimlich Manoeuvre, or stuck your finger down her throat?* Not that Bob wanted his homicidal wife to be alive still. Anything but that chain, weighing him down for another ten or twenty years, if he had such time left.

He made another decision: he really could drink that scotch now. He picked up the phone again.

'Hello, Martin? Listen mate, I've had some bad

news today. My ex-wife has died.' Bob didn't say where or how, just 'Could you hold the fort for me tonight? I'm only on standby, but better if I'm not, tonight, if you know what I mean.'

Martin agreed, and uttered a few platitudes before Bob put the phone down again. With a half-smile on his face, he hurried through to the kitchen. From the cupboards, he pulled out a crystal tumbler and a new bottle of single-malt whisky, and poured a generous measure of the amber liquid... it tasted so good. He sauntered back into the front room, noted that darkness had crept in among the trees and was only held at bay by the street lights and the forever-moving traffic. A glance at the carriage clock on his mantelpiece told him it was five-thirty-five: still early, so why so dark? The rain, he supposed.

Wonder why Tilda hasn't rung? Why did I have to receive the news from the asylum? Wrong word, Robert: they say hospital nowadays.

He took another sip of his whisky, enjoying its warmth and flavour on his tongue and the strange feeling of numbness on his gums. His thoughts went back, past the ten years of Delia's incarceration, to when they had first met on the plane, both en route to holidaying in Portugal. This was followed by a rapid courtship, their wedding day and belated honeymoon: a honeymoon delayed through her friend Manda's untimely death from choking on nuts. And the irony that Delia had suffered a similar fate. *Is that what they call Karma?* He found out, later, that Delia knew all along about Manda's nut allergy, only she chose not to tell her friend about the hidden, crushed almonds in the first course of their wedding feast.

Gotta admit it, Delia, you found some innovative ways to kill off your victims.

He was in the kitchen, pouring another scotch, when the phone rang again. He picked up the extension. 'Bob Shackleton.'

'Hi Bob, it's Tilda.'

About time too: I wondered when you'd ring. 'Hi, sweetie.' He paused, enabling her to tell him what he already knew.

'It... erm... you've heard the news... from the hospital?'

He so dearly wanted to feign ignorance, but no. *Let's hear what she has to say,* he told himself. 'Well, yes. Head Nurse Johnson rang me. He said you'd been there... are you ok?'

Bob heard her sigh. 'Yeah, yes I am, but it was an almighty shock. I didn't know what to do... neither did the nurse with Mum and me; it all happened so quickly. She crammed her mouth full of chocolates, like she hadn't eaten in days.'

Again he heard Tilda breathing, as if she was trying to control her tears. 'Terrible for you, sweetie,' he soothed. 'I don't suppose there was anything either of you could have done.' *Liar, what about the Heimlich Manoeuvre?* 'She's probably better off now, at peace and everything.'

Such a platitude... He heard the relief in her voice as she continued. 'She didn't know me, Bob. And she looked ancient.'

So would you, sweetheart, stuck in a hell hole like that.

He let her talk on, answering in more platitudes, and told her he would organise the funeral. He'd let her know the details as soon as... and yes, he would be grateful if she'd contact Danny and Ray.

Strange you didn't ring your brother first.

He put the phone down, went through to the front room again, after pouring another measure of scotch, and took time to think what to have for his dinner. He was tempted to go out and celebrate the good news. Might even ring Tilda back, ask her if she and Freddie wanted to join him, maybe Danny and Ray.

On the other hand, maybe not... if he went to the Turkish restaurant in Upper Street there was bound to be someone in there he knew. If he went to The Alwynne Castle first, there was always someone there to talk to at the bar.

The meal, however, was substituted by Bob taking a pub crawl; a pint in The Railway Arms, two in The Alwynne and a small swift one in The Hen and Chickens. There were one or two faces he recognised but couldn't put a name to, a couple of guys in The Railway that he felt sure were near-neighbours of Tilda and Freddie. On the way home, he picked up a portion of fish and chips to eat indoors, ate half of it and threw away the rest. Not as good as his 'Kent-On-Sea' days, he decided. He sat in front of the TV, with another large scotch, until it was time for bed... determined by the time he spent viewing versus the time he spent dozing. When the dozing overtook, Bob finally decided it best to go to bed.

Next morning, he woke up early, head fuzzy from last night's scotch and beer and a stale mouth from the second-rate fish and chips. Time for a swift shower and prolonged flossing, before coffee and toast drizzled with honey. The phone rang as he stepped out of the shower. *Damn it, let it ring, I'll pick up in ten minutes.* He half-heard the voice but hadn't identified the caller and the message seemed garbled anyway. It could wait till after he'd showered. Once shaved and dressed, he went through to the kitchen. The green light flashing on the phone base reminded Bob of the incoming call. He picked up the receiver and immediately recognised the quiet but strong voice of Head Nurse Johnson. 'Hi Mr Shackleton, I've had your late wife's belongings packed up and will send the parcel off to you this morning. There are a number of written works… our librarian encouraged Delia to write short stories… some of which are good, very good.' There was a pause, during which time Bob guessed the guy was conversing with a member of staff. 'Sorry about that… anyway, erm, I've included these stories, you might find them interesting.' *The hell I will. Tilda might, though, or Danny.*

The rest of the day was taken up with more phone calls, arranging the funeral, contacting those who might attend, and booking a venue for the reception. George Blomfield, the funeral director, was helpful and recommended The Hunters Manor Hotel, quite close to Barham and the church adjoining the cemetery. Bob booked five rooms: one for himself, one each for the twins and their partners, one for his step-grandsons, and one for Phil and Stella. *Looking forward to seeing Stella again… I've always fancied her. She's enough to make the sap rise in any man.* If Dez and Jessica decided to stay on after the reception, which he doubted, he had been assured by Matthew and Penny, the hotel owners, that another room would be available, particularly at this time of the year. Not much going on till the Christmas Season, they informed him.

2 DELIA'S DEPARTURE

The funeral service had been short and, almost, indecently impersonal. They were all relieved, Bob thought, to get out into the thin sunshine again: away from the sepulchral music and the damp, churchy smell. Then onto the cemetery and Delia's final resting place, *in a far forgotten corner*. They, all three of them, had decided against a headstone; she didn't deserve to be remembered every year with flowers in a vase.

Once back at the hotel, Bob stood there, Tilda and Danny at his side, as he greeted the other attendees. Dez and Jessica, looking distinctly older than when he had last seen them, with Dez's hair thinner and wispy as it blew, undisciplined, in the stiff breeze. His ex-policeman buddy Phil, and his wife Stella, stood next to them. *God you're still a looker; I could still fancy you.* Both sporting tans... probably just back from some exotic holiday, he thought.

Ray stood next to them with his two sons, handsome boys and very individual, not physically alike. Some feat of science had enabled two surrogate mothers to take both Danny's and Ray's sperms and create these boys a year apart. Tilda's husband, Freddie, stood a little away from the rest. Bob thought he looked ill, older than his sixty years. In fact, the more Bob observed him the more he was sure that Freddie *was* ill. *Why did you marry him, Tilda? He's so much older than you. Got money has he?* He wouldn't know, having had little social contact with either of them since their marriage.

Head Nurse Johnson was there, to represent the asylum (hospital, remember, they call them nowadays), and finally, the vicar who had conducted the short service. He had stumbled on saying the name Cordelia, calling her Cornelia instead. The name reminded Bob of the film, *Planet of the Apes*. Wasn't one of the apes called Cornelia? Appropriate in some ways: Delia *had* behaved like an animal. A shame to liken her to an ape, though.

Thirteen of us, Bob thought, to say our goodbyes to her. *You, evil bitch, don't deserve us all here. In one way or another, you damaged the lives of us all... except for the vicar. One thing's for sure, you won't reach Heaven, if there is such a place.*

At the graveside, they had bent down in turn to examine the floral sprays, pitifully few. Not one from Bob, though. He couldn't be that hypocritical.

'D'you want the cards, Bob? Or shall I take them?'

'Oh... erm, didn't think of that. Erm, no... I mean yes... you have them, Tilda.' He stood up and wrapped himself around Stella who had moved towards him. He could smell her perfume and imagined the rustle of silk underwear beneath her black suit. *Would that be black too?* he wondered.

'Are you ok, Bob?' She examined his face, giving him full view of her skin, still near-perfect.

He smiled, a warm one, reluctant to let her go. 'Yeah... I'm fine... well, ok, anyway.' He sighed. 'It's been a long time coming. A pity really she hadn't died years ago. Can't have had the best of lives, locked up in that place.'

'No. True.' Stella hesitated. What else could she say? She had never liked the woman, always suspected there was something very weird about her. Delia's seven murders more than justified Stella's suspicions.

Bob had arranged a buffet reception at The Hunters Manor Hotel, conveniently situated on the outskirts of Barham, and a couple of miles from the cemetery. All but the vicar was able to attend, including Head Nurse Johnson. Bob was pleased about that; he liked the guy, admired him for what he did for his inmates, and was looking forward to spending a little time with him in the more relaxed atmosphere of this reception. He had also arranged dinner, overnight accommodation, and breakfast for those who wanted it. Obviously Head Nurse Johnson wouldn't be staying and, as Bob had anticipated, neither would Dez and Jessica.

'Gotta get back sometime tonight, not too late,' said Dez. 'We've the dog to be thinking of.'

Bob thought Dez looked a bit like a dog himself, but which? *Gotta be a basset hound, with those loose jowls and long ears.*

'Sure, I understand. Not the same dog as when we lived there?' He grinned.

'No... we've had a couple since then. Got a little

schitzu now, a rescue dog. We call him Doogle, like that dog as was on 'Magic Roundabout' all those years ago.'

Bob nodded. He had never had children so didn't have a clue what Denzel was talking about.

'Don't like leaving him on his own for too long.'

'No, I understand. It was good of you to come today.' He was about to add that Delia would have appreciated it, but thought it best not to mention her name. Especially as it had been Denzil Black, in a way, who was responsible for Delia being arrested and charged with old Mrs Casey's murder. He had seen her leaving the old girl's house not long before the body was discovered, crumpled at the bottom of her long flight of stairs, her neck snapped in two. Well, it would be, after Delia had pushed her.

Bob apportioned himself among the small company, accepting their awkward condolences and the odd glass of red wine from passing waiters, until he reached Head Nurse Johnson.

'My name's Johnny, by the way,' he said and laughed. 'I know, Johnny Johnson: hard to believe what some parents inflict on their offspring.'

Bob smiled back. 'Yeah, I know the feeling, Johnny. People have been referring to my Antarctic expeditions, and a maritime aircraft named after me, for as long as I can remember.' To the blank stare he added, 'My surname is Shackleton.'

'Of course,' Johnny Johnson laughed. 'Delia was never sure of her name, apart from Delia.'

Bob laughed too. 'Understandable... she'd had four husbands.' He grabbed another two glasses of wine from a gliding waiter and stood there with the last man to see Delia alive. 'Anyway, thank you for coming today, much appreciated. And thanks for sending those papers.' He had declined any other personal effects of his late wife, suggesting they were given to a charity or something: if not, thrown away.

'Have you had time to read some of her work?'

Bob scratched his head, rubbing his short, bristled hair under his fingers. 'I glanced at one or two,' he said, 'Quite well-written, really. She had a bit of flair, didn't she?' *She put her talent into extermination instead of creation.*

They spoke for a few more minutes until Bob excused himself. 'Sorry, Johnny, I must go and circulate.'

'Of course.' He put out his hand. 'In any case, I should get back soon. I'll go and grab a plateful of food first... looks appetising.'

Bob watched as the man took his large, powerful frame away towards the well-laden buffet; noted that since he'd last seen him, Johnny Johnson's dark, tightly-curled hair had collected numerous flecks of grey in it. *Well, none of us are getting younger.* He gritted his teeth, prepared to spend an afternoon speaking in, and receiving, clichés about the dear-departed Cordelia... *the Bitch.* After half an hour of keeping a fixed half-smile on his face, he decided to go outside, grab some fresh air and walk the hotel grounds before daylight faded completely. He sighed and pulled wearily at his cheeks, like they were thick, elastic bands.

'Want some company?' It was his old police-buddy, Phil.

'Sure, why not.'

Together they strolled along the well-swept pathways that interspersed a huge lawned area surrounding the immediate hotel. Cedar trees and

English oaks gave shelter from the south-east-coast winds that blew inland from only a few miles away. Beyond these were acres of meadowland where rare-breed sheep grazed and white cattle that Bob had never seen before. They gave off, he thought, a blueish haze in the approaching darkness.

'You ok, buddy?'

'Yeah, I'm fine, Phil. I'll be glad when the day's over. Quite looking forward to dinner though... bit of roast: Kent lamb or something. How about you and Stella? You both ok?'

'Yeah, we're good. Just back from a holiday in the Seychelles.'

Bob laughed. 'Wondered where the tan came from.'

A sudden gust, bringing rain and a fresh fall of leaves with it, caused them to rush back inside. Bob was glad in a way: he was finding this particular social-gathering bloody-hard work. Wished he was back in Highbury and Hogarth International. *Not much longer, Robert. Just hold on...* He thought about the next few weeks, the several events that Hogarth's was arranging security for, during the pre-Christmas and Christmas season, including New Year of course: always a headache, that one. And later, there would be the top-security to arrange for the big, literary festival in Shropshire, due to be held in April next year. Earlier, he had caught a look on Tilda's face, a fleeting glance, which made his blood run cold. Someone or something had annoyed her. He did not know who or what. Only that she had looked, for a brief instant, the image of Delia: the bad, evil Delia. *Don't tell me,* he thought, prayed even, *her mother's genes have been passed on. Not that.*

3 WINTER

What to do with the ashes? Matilda sat in her high-backed leather chair staring at them, perched as they were on the book shelf in the alcove next to the fireplace. She wrinkled her nose, somewhat in disgust. The container, she thought, looked like one of those old-fashioned sweet jars, except it was chocolate-coloured and, worse, made of plastic.

When you consider,' she said out loud to herself, the container, and the ashes inside it, 'how much the bloody funeral cost, you'd think they' (they being the funeral directors), 'could have provided something a bit more tasteful.' She shuddered at her own use of the word 'tasteful'. Wrong choice. She mentally slapped herself. The plastic, chocolate-coloured urn stared back at her, silent, unmoving, and unmoved by her words. It made her think of the box of chocolates that had killed her mother, only three months before.

'Still,' she said in a brighter tone. 'At least you're all done and dusted, Freddie; just like her. Nothing the police can examine or find suspicious now.' She thanked the stars above for dear, old Doctor Van

Tuten, over-worked, over-aged and run off his medical feet. He had declared Freddie dead, patted her hand in gruff sympathy, and written the necessary death note for her to take to the registrar. All in the space of his half-hour visit.

'You look worn out,' she had said to him, in reciprocal sympathy.

He mentioned something about the flu epidemic that was taking its toll on his elderly patients and, on top of full surgeries every day, his house visits. She nodded, adopted a sad smile that shared her newly-widowed grief with his work load.

Freddie hadn't had flu. Doctor Van Tuten had been treating him for a bad case of bronchitis: double-strength antibiotics, expectorant cough medicine, and (with a sweetly mischievous and twinkling smile) the odd glass of cognac to ease the patient's sore throat. Matilda had done the rest. Two or three pain killers – ok, four or five, maybe more: she had lost count – crushed up and mixed in with the cough medicine. And when Freddie went into his deep sleep she had leaned lovingly on his pillow, the one that covered his face. By the time she called the doctor, Freddie looked quite peaceful, and dead: very dead.

'Will there have to be an autopsy?' she had asked, her voice quavering and her eyes brimming with unshed tears. 'I can't bear the thought of my darling being cut up.'

'No, my dear,' she was reassured. 'Mr Meadham, Freddie, has been ill for...' he paused. 'Well over three weeks now, almost four.' He barely glanced at the body in the bed but gave a swift look at his watch. 'I'm afraid this terrible winter is having its toll on a huge amount of the population.'

With almost shameful haste he put his stethoscope back into his bag. Both looked like they had been around for a century, or at least as long as the aged doctor had. Matilda reckoned he must be in his seventies, well past retirement age *and* working himself into an early grave. His problem not hers. Her problem was now solved: Freddie dead, soon to be fired up in the crematorium cauldron, and the precious piece of paper clutched in her hand that made his death legal 'from natural causes'... and the bronchitis.

She had let the doctor out into the freezing cold, waved him goodbye and tearfully wished him *A Peaceful Christmas* as he climbed stiffly into his car. She watched him drive away before shutting the street door against the grey, cold day. Back inside in the warm, she gave a little jiggle, waved the signed document about as if it was a small pennant, punched the air, and shouted 'Yes' to the empty room. Freddie, or what remained of him, was upstairs, his face tactfully covered by a sheet and the duvet, thanks to the doctor. Time for a swift glass of rosé, she thought, before ringing the undertakers. And switch on the computer to look for holiday resorts. *Portugal or Spain? Portugal, that's where Mum and Bob went for their honeymoon years ago.* Also where she and Freddie had holidayed once. *Maybe the Canaries then? Somewhere warmer than here... that's for certain.*

Matilda brought herself back to the present. Stared up at Freddie and the chocolate urn. *Plastic, mastic, drastic, fantastic. Yeah, all of those. 'You're a problem. You know that, don't you? I should have left you there at the Crem, in the garden of remembrance, smelling of roses. Only not this time of year. They're all dead or dying or sleeping. Like the ashes scattered around them, feeding their roots. Like yours should have been instead of you and them laughing at me up there on the bloody shelf.'*

Bob had attended the funeral, of course, along with Danny and Ray. Not the boys: too young they all agreed, even though they'd gone to their grandmother's funeral, the grandmother they had never known. Matilda remembered what a disaster that was, two energetic boys running around the hotel afterwards; not much discipline she thought. In any case they hardly knew Freddie. She also hadn't bothered to contact any of Freddie's family; there were only distant cousins anyway. Kept it quiet, small, just her immediate family, to console her in her grief and wipe her tear-swollen eyes. She hadn't liked the look in Bob's eyes; a kind of accusing stare she thought. Oh well, it's all over now. Time to book that holiday for after Christmas. Danny and Ray insisted she spend the festive season with them. They had asked Bob as well, but he declined she remembered. 'Phil and Stella have invited me to join them in Westgate. Besides,' he had added. 'I ought to have a look at the property to see if there are any repairs needed. Haven't been down there for nearly two years.' (He still owned a large house in Westgate, on the North Kent coast, where several of his police associates lived).

Tilda wished she had declined her brother's invitation too. Christmas was not her favourite celebration; all that present giving, putting up dust-collecting decorations and the wearing of silly paper hats throughout a gigantic turkey lunch. Danny and Ray made theirs a lavish one: said it was all about the children. Well, she didn't have any, nor wanted any. Let them celebrate Christmas and indulge their two boys. She'd give the kiddie-winks money to buy whatever they wanted: that way, they would not be disappointed.

Spring

Bob Shackleton relaxed in Danny's and Ray's comfortable Highgate lounge. It was a large, high-ceilinged room with two long windows that overlooked a small square. These were furnished with heavy, cornflower blue, drapes and delicate white muslins that ruffled slightly in the breeze coming in from the half-opened windows.

He sipped at a generous measure of malt whisky and considered how his stepson had handsomely matured where his twin, Tilda, was aging in an almost tarty way. Danny's expertly cut, thick dark hair shone, and Bob considered his square-cut features could have graced the front page of any fashion magazine. Ray, in contrast, had grown a little fleshy under his mop of still-blonde hair, but a permanent, gentle and engaging smile played about his face. Bob could see why their relationship had endured and why the two boys, Alfie and Simon, adored their two parents, Daddy and Pops. The older man had long got used to this same-sex parental relationship, and their boys, who called him Granddad, had never known anything else.

‘Lovely malt this,’ Bob said and licked his lips in appreciation. The other two nodded in agreement.

‘So,’ said Danny. ‘I gather you’re concerned about my sister.’

‘Well, yes. I am.’ Bob glanced slightly guiltily at his glass. ‘I think she’s drinking too much and,’ he hesitated, ‘I can’t... I don’t know... exactly what it is.’

‘D’you think she’s like Mum?’ Danny came right out with it, but there was a hint of anxiety in his forthrightness.

His stepfather drew in a quiet breath and exhaled slowly. ‘What do you think, Danny?’

‘I think you’re passing the buck,’ but he said it with a smile.

‘Yeah, sorry, I suppose it did come across a bit like that.’ He sighed again. ‘To be honest, I can’t quite put my finger on it. It’s... er... I noticed a look in her eyes at your mother’s funeral, a split-second look: that Dr Jekyll into Mr Hyde moment. I wondered, might she be bipolar?’

Ray got up and replenished their glasses. As he crossed the room, his fingers brushed lightly at a framed photograph of their two boys on the mantelpiece.

‘You know,’ Danny said, ‘we’re going to a business symposium next week? Well we asked Tilda if she’d mind looking after the boys for a couple of days.’

‘How come? I thought Alfie and Simon were boarders?’

‘They are, but it’s their Spring Holidays, they’re off for a couple of weeks, but they don’t want to come to the Symposium with us: made their own plans, apparently. Anyway,' he added, 'we'll only be away a couple of days. But she said she couldn't manage it, said she was going away again: to the Algarve or somewhere – sounded a bit confused, actually.'

'She's been away a lot, since Freddie died. Kind of restless, isn't she?'

Danny nodded agreement with his stepfather. 'Yeah, that's what we think, don't we Ray? Anyway, it doesn't matter now; the boys are staying with friends instead. Just up the road from here, in fact.'

Bob shifted in his chair, crossed one leg over the other, and scratched his ankle. 'I shall be off myself then. Our firm's doing the security for the Teme Literary Festival this year. They want me to stay up there, the whole ten days.'

'Nice one,' said Ray. 'We went there a couple of years back. The chap who runs it...' he paused, 'Caius O'Neill... gets some pretty famous names up there: authors and the like.'

'Yes, I know what you mean. Had a look at the program for this year, several top names included. Not just authors either: international politicians, film and stage stars... quite an eclectic mix, you could say.' He sucked in his breath and licked his teeth; placed his empty glass on the small table beside him. 'Chap from Highbury designs the program, you know: Aubrey Penhaligon. He and his wife run an art gallery, in Upper Street.'

'We know him,' Danny said. 'Bought one of his paintings a while back... a portrait of Bryn Terfel in his role as Sweeney Todd. Scary but colourful,' he added. 'Got it hanging in our office.'

'I've been told the Penhaligon man paints very colourful portraits. Not much flesh colour in them either.'

Danny grinned. 'Sounds about right.'

There was no more talk about his stepdaughter and Bob thought it prudent to leave it. Perhaps his worries were groundless anyway. He said his goodbyes to the two men and made his way home to Highbury. Nevertheless, on the journey back, he thought about Freddie and his sudden death. The death certificate had recorded Bronchitis. *Strange coincidence,* he thought. *Gerald, the twins' father had died from a chest complaint: pneumonia... or from exposure to opened windows and turned off central heating. Thanks to Delia, now herself the late departed. It would have been interesting to have had an autopsy on Freddie. Bronchitis? Or a pillow over his head?* Bob had no idea how close he was to the truth.

Matilda stood up. She was all packed and ready to go... again. This was her third holiday in as many months. Boredom: what else to do with her time? Maybe she'd think about getting a little job when she got back from this trip... maybe? Or get another dog. Freddie hadn't liked dogs, so she had given her two to Mike as part of the divorce settlement. She missed not having dogs around the house. Maybe she'd get a little dog, a Toy Poodle or Bichon Frise, and take him walking in the little park over the road from her, just like she used to. Funny to think, she and Mike had lived next door to Freddie until they divorced. Selling their house was part of the divorce settlement: half each of the balance after the mortgage had been paid up. It had given her and Mike almost thirty thousand each. He got the dogs and she had a new life with

Freddie. And what a disappointment that had turned out to be. She couldn't remember now what had caused the break up between her and Mike. Was it just a drifting apart? Boredom? Or '*ennui*' as the French call it? So Mike had gone, along with the dogs, Shame and Scandal. They had moved to Shropshire, so she was given to understand. Wasn't that where Ray's parents were from? Anyway, her two lovely boys would have room to roam. Much better than the little park here, just over the road. It had never been big enough for her two mad Dalmatians, except for their nightly pee or whatever. No way. They needed space to run, like when she took them to Highbury Fields, or down to Mum's when she lived by the sea. A little dog would cope with the small park by the railway fence... next to where the old dear, Queenie, lived in the basement flat.

The poor old thing had that awful scar covering half of her face. Rumour had it her folks' house was bombed during the war, killing her parents and a little brother. Queenie alone had survived, but her face had been carved up by shrapnel *and* scalded from a boiling kettle. Matilda shivered, thinking about the ugly old woman, glad it wasn't her.

Her suitcases were in the hallway. They, and herself, were waiting for the taxi to take her to the airport. Mike had taken the car as well as the dogs as part of his settlement. She hadn't bothered to get another, especially as Freddie didn't drive, hadn't driven. Plenty of public transport here. Nowhere, really, to park in London anyway unless you had a resident's pass, and they cost an arm and a leg. She had hired a car to go and see her mother on that fateful day, when she watched her cram her mouth full of nutty chocolates... and choke to death on them. Her stomach churned at the memory. *Forget it, and her... that creature, the aged old crone who was supposed to be your mother. And Freddie, he who died of bronchitis and natural causes... plus a soft pillow on his face. But we don't talk about that, do we Tilda? No, of course we don't.*

Eighty quid's worth of taxi, but, so what? It's only money, she mouthed to the dust-covered urn. Three months it had taken her to get everything finally sorted, the will, the bank accounts, changing stuff over to her name and all that. But she had managed two short breaks in the Canaries, and they were, she had to admit, a bit of fun. Very wearing though, staying up half the night dancing and drinking all those exotic cocktails. She'd had her fair share of men to dance with, and to drink with... and the rest of the shenanigans. Time for a slowdown holiday, less booze and, definitely, less men. Now she was on her way to a bit more sunshine... and rest, she supposed.

Moving into the hallway, she shrugged into her coat and wound a '*pashmina*' round her shoulders, just as her phone gave two swift rings. The cab driver... Sure enough, when she opened the door, a shining, black taxicab was purring away outside. Its driver was decent enough to get out, open the door of the cab for her to clamber into the back, then fetch her two cases and load them into the luggage space.

'Gatwick, innit?'

'Yes please.' She sank back in the seat, enjoying the feel and smell of real leather and the sight of the back of the cabbie's head. She hoped he wasn't one of the chatty types; she had no need of trite conversation. She wanted to imagine what Portugal was like at this time of year: warm, maybe lightweight-sweater weather, but not all muffled-up-against-the-cold weather. It would be a better springtime over there than here anyway. She had chosen Salema, on the Algarve: had been holidaying quite near there before, a couple of years ago, with Freddie. Hmm. Well, he wasn't coming this time. He could stay in the chocolate urn, look after the house again until her return, until she decided what to do with him: where his final resting place would be. *Dead Fred,* she thought and smiled to herself. *Dead Fred. Silly*. Then, *Damn... damn, damn. What an idiot*. She had just had a brainwave; she could have brought him with her this time, flushed him down the aeroplane toilet and out into the clouds at 30,000 feet. What an end... he would have enjoyed that: the spectacle, the drama. Why hadn't she thought of that before? Ah well, too late now.

'Going anywhere nice?'

'What?'

'I said, are you going somewhere nice?'

'Erm... yes. Portugal, down on the Algarve.' She saw him grin in the rear view mirror.

'Bit warmer out there, then?'

'Better be.' She sank back into the seat again, hoping he didn't prolong the conversation.

'Been there before?'

'Erm... yes, I have, couple of years ago, with my husband.'

'Not going with you this time then? Your husband? Killed him off, have you?' He laughed, at his own joke.

'No. He's not coming with me this time, and yes, he is dead: died three months ago.'

'Oh... Sorry love.' He fell silent, shrank into the driving seat and concentrated on his driving.

Don't be sorry, she said to herself, *I'm not. Glad to be rid of the old bastard. I'm really starting to live again.* Nevertheless, she spared a thought for her husband: *RIP Freddie Meadham... yes, you there, in the urn.*

The cabbie paused at the junction with St Pauls Road while the traffic howled by. Idly, she watched a gardener rake some left over leaves, the last of winter. The trees opposite were now all in bud, some with the fresh, green leaves of spring and, at their lower trunks, daffodils waved in the chilly, late-March rain. Matilda sighed, yawned, and looked forward to flowering hibiscus and trailing bougainvillea...

Her two-week break passed slowly in one big disappointing yawn. The average age of the visitors must have been nigh on eighty. Ok, so she had a brief fling with Rodriguez, the owner of a '*tapas*' bar, where she met up with half a dozen keen golfers, who were oblivious of the older tourists but nicely aware of her. They were probably all married. Not her problem if the wives were all back in the UK. Two of the guys showed her a little more than moderate interest and another, well over moderate: he was the one who shared her hotel bedroom for three nights. Sadly, they all went home after that, leaving her wandering disconsolately about the small fishing town, dodging in and out of shops and bars when the spring rains fell again, and waiting for the tapas bar to open its doors at seven in the evening. Even that proved to be a disappointment: Rodriguez' wife suddenly showed up and insisted serving Matilda herself, while talking over her fat, black-draped shoulder to her extremely-slim husband. At least, Matilda had the grim pleasure of seeing him look sheepish and, definitely, coming across as the hen-pecked husband. *I'll be glad when it's time to go home. Enough holidays for now.*

Matilda was pleased when the plane finally sped down the runway and rose into the air. She consoled herself with glass of prosecco, a hot, filled Panini, and a mild flirtation with the gorgeous hunk across the aisle. Pity they were not sitting next to each other but that's life, she thought.

Freddie was furthest from her mind during the flight; however, when she went to the toilet, she remembered the chocolate urn that would be there to greet her upon her return to Harbourne Road: imagined flushing him down this airborne lavatory. Damn again...

The silent and unfriendly cab driver did not bother to get out of his cab when they drew up outside the house, and ignored her struggle with the luggage. She paid him by card, a credit card, and made sure *not* to leave a tip... ok, just five pence on the £79.95 total. He was not amused and she thought he swore at her in some foreign language. *Big deal*, she thought, as if she cared...

And yes, he/it was there to greet her: Freddie, silent and lifeless, just so many crystals inside the chocolate-coloured, plastic container. 'Did you miss me?' she asked. 'I didn't miss you.' She went through to the kitchen and switched on the central-heating boiler. Despite it being the beginning of April, it was freezing cold inside the house.

'I'll unpack you later,' she shouted to the two suitcases languishing in the hallway. 'Going out for a while, shopping and that.' They didn't acknowledge her words and she didn't expect them to. She was dying for a coffee and a bite to eat. A bare fridge and cupboard told her both would have to be purchased, unless she fancied a bit of mouldy cheese? Nah! She unhooked a couple of shopping bags from the kitchen door, locked the front one behind her and headed up towards St Pauls Road, to the little deli not far from the Alwynne. Gabriel Braithwaite from number four passed by her, obviously in a hurry to get home, armed with a big package of some sort, and obviously not in any kind of social mood: he barely managed a gruff 'Good Morning' as he scuttled by her. *Funny bloke*, she thought. *Wonder what he does with his life? Never seen him with a girlfriend, only sometimes with that crippled brother of his*. She knew they went to The Railway Arms a couple of evenings a week. Not a bad boozer. Maybe she'd start going there regularly, now Freddie couldn't tell her what to do. *And the Alwynne. Might even try the Hen and Chickens Theatre bar,* she thought, *though it might be a bit cliquey... maybe, maybe not*.

She needed to meet up with people, especially of the opposite sex. Matilda wasn't the type of woman to go without male companionship. This time around though, she'd look for someone younger. She remembered what old Mrs Casey used to say (years before Mum murdered her), 'Better to be an old man's darling, Matilda, than a young man's slave.' Well she'd been the old man's darling; now she quite fancied a bit of 'slavery' with a guy of her own age. After all, forty's young now, the new thirty. Her thoughts took her back to her two holidays in the Canaries. Yeah, definitely younger men from now on. She smiled to herself at these pleasant memories.

Matilda reached the deli, nodded at the owner's son behind the counter, picked up a wire basket and walked up and down the aisles of the narrow, well-stocked shop, fulfilling her needs and wants. She ignored the wine rack: plenty of Portuguese *'vino'* in her luggage, cheaper than Ali's prices for sure. Finally, she added a Daily Mail and the free local paper to her filled basket and struggled with it up onto the counter.

'There you go, sunshine.' She couldn't remember his name, then yes, she could: Rasheed, his brother Saeed, the two eldest sons of Ali. He smiled at her, displaying beautiful white teeth. He really was a handsome lad, she thought. Bit young for her though, still in his teens, but he was already sporting a scant beard. *Wonder if he's betrothed... or whatever?*

Rasheed took her bags and carefully packed them with her purchases, handing her each bag as it filled. 'That's forty-five pounds and twenty-three pence,' he told her. 'And would you like a chocolate bar, for our special price of seventy-five pee?'

'No, ta love. Gone off chocolate lately,' she replied, thinking of the chocolate urn. *Really must get rid of it now. Maybe I can empty it over the railway fence, one dark night?* She gave the boy a fifty-pound note, pocketed the change and replied to his 'Good morning' with a 'ta-da'... time now for that much-needed coffee with croissants and blackcurrant jam. She barely looked at the A-shaped notice board on the path outside the shop, only just glimpsing the name 'Darwin Harrison-Forbes'. Not one she was familiar with... or was she? She vaguely remembered Freddie talking about some guy with a double-barrelled name, someone who used to visit just around the corner, next-door-but-one: the late MP, the Braithwaite boys' uncle. *Funny that*, she thought. *Didn't he have a double-barrelled name as well? Yeah... Hartley-Edwards*. That was it, Norman Hartley-Edwards. Not that she had known him... a bit before her time.

Then she thought about the other dotty resident, Mungo Dickson. How was that for a name? Mr Dickson lived between her and the Braithwaite brothers. Mad as a sparrow in a net, he was. Matilda had heard he dressed like a rainbow and played with toy soldiers (or did they call them model soldiers in his world?) *Wouldn't know for sure... never set foot in the old boy's house. Well, not that old, has to be in his sixties though.*

She dismissed these thoughts, anxious to get back indoors, hungry and chilled to the bone. Plus, it was starting to rain. *Roll on spring*, she thought, letting herself back in to the house, now much warmer and cosier.

4 MUNGO DICKSON

Mungo Dickson, or Dickie as he preferred, rather than his other nickname of Chubby, was quite mad. Not in any dangerous sense, or in a sinister context. Probably a kind person would describe him as eccentric. A cheeky street urchin would say he was batty, or as nutty as a bar of chocolate. He did not mix overly much with people, enjoying just a few, well-chosen acquaintances. His precious collection of model soldiers were his friends and his family (although he did have a girl cousin in Hereford called Vivacity). The few friends he had, like him, enjoyed these military games, these re-enactments in miniature.

He loved his antique regiments, with their colourful uniforms that he frequently repainted: all of them from time to time. He had hundreds of these soldiers: each and every one had been lovingly handled by him, and placed many times in various strategic and fighting positions during his war games. Those who were not currently in battle were carefully placed in their original, though somewhat scruffy, boxes. Not much he could do about the boxes, most of which had been previously owned, often stuck away for years in attics, and purchased at auction houses throughout the country. Dickie had given each regiment a pet name to suit their former prowess in whatever battle they had fought, whichever campaign they had battled so bravely in. Some had fought in the battle for Rourke's Drift, others in the Napoleonic wars.

His dining room, or 'the officers' mess' as he preferred to think of it, was frequently attended by one or the other regiments, when he arranged a celebratory dinner for the latest victory gained. The crockery, cutlery and glassware were miniature (except for his own place setting of course), but they were a glorious facsimile of Mungo's rather expensive tableware. The napkins – the ones he used himself – were monogrammed with the appropriate military companies. Sadly, he could not acquire the miniature version for his 'officers', they would be too small to embroider with the emblems.

Mungo loved attending and organising his 'military dinners', the serving of fine food and wine, the military banter across the table (yes, even with his lead facsimiles), and – of course – the toast to the Queen from his fine crystal decanter filled with the best vintage port. He withdrew from the table after enjoying the port, into the lounge, to smoke a Havana cigar and to accompany it with an excellent VSOP cognac, just for himself. His fellow officers offered silent rebukes and remained quite straight-faced when it came to him smoking his best Havana cigars. He supposed because they were on permanent duty, had to keep fit and healthy.

Nevertheless, after such a sumptuous mess dinner, at least five courses, Mungo enjoyed relaxing in his favourite leather chair in the bay window that overlooked the narrow road and the railway cutting beyond, with a table beside it large enough to accommodate his fellow diners. The distant rattle of moving trains reminded him of troops being transported, brave young men going to fight for Queen and Country in some far off land.

Mungo would carry on the conversation after dinner with these wonderful, tin and lead soldiers of high rank, the lesser ranks and others being consigned to the kitchen for their celebratory dinner. His favourite officer enjoyed the same name as himself. They had both been named after a distant ancestor, Mungo Park, the late eighteenth century Scottish explorer of the African Continent. It was reputed that one of Mungo Park's sisters had married a William Dickson, a seed merchant from London. Mungo was convinced he descended from them. So, he supposed, Mungo Park was a many-times great uncle and William Dickson a many-times great grandfather. Pity it had not been the other way around, he quite liked the idea of having a great, great, great grandfather explorer who he had been named after.

Mungo's soldiers often took up residence on every window sill, every shelf, and every spare armchair and sofa in his three- storey house in Harbourne Road, Highbury. They occupied his antique Pembroke table that lived in the hallway and, at day-to-day mealtimes, they often joined him at the dining table. They drank pretend tea, or fizz when they and he were in party mood or celebrating the latest victory. For afternoon tea, they ate pretend dainty sandwiches with the crusts cut off, and exquisitely-decorated cakes, served on miniature china, and they used silverware of the very best quality. These soldiers were Mungo's best friends and were treated accordingly – with admiration and respect.

Unfortunately, it was they who encouraged his obesity, though he never admitted to being overweight, except his own collection of uniforms no longer really fitted him, not unless he breathed in as he tried them on. As one of his model officers, Colonel Mungo, a fine looking member of the Royal Scots Guards, frequently said 'An army marches on its stomach, dear boy.' To which Mungo Dickson fervently agreed, wishing he could maintain that permanence of shape his military collection enjoyed.

Mungo's next door neighbours were Gabriel and Jacob Braithwaite. Not that they were particularly neighbourly in the sense of the word. They barely nodded 'hello' to each other over the garden fence, or when they passed each other going in and out of their homes on Harbourne Road. Mungo just had the two neighbours as his was the corner house, overlooking the railway, and Gabriel's and Jacob's was the second one in. The house around the corner, separated by a high wall and nearer to St Pauls Road, was owned by a recently-widowed young woman whose name, he thought, was Meadham. He didn't talk with her much, either. The dead husband had been considerably older, old enough to be Mrs Meadham's father, he thought. Mungo shrugged his shoulders at such a notion.

Unmarried he might be, but imagine being married to someone that much older or younger than you? It didn't bear thinking about.

Mungo's private opinion concerning Gabriel Braithwaite, was that he was a queer cove and not one given to personal cleanliness. When he thought of this he shuddered. To Mungo, keeping mind and body clean was of paramount importance. Gabriel, he had noted more than once, often stepped out in grubby clothes when he passed by Mungo's place, on his way to St Paul's Road. Mungo surmised he would be going to Highbury Corner and the shops in Upper Street.

He also suspected Gabriel's mind was as mucky as his clothes. Once, when in his back garden dead-heading the roses, he had spotted Gabriel looking out of his upper window. A pair of binoculars, glued to his eyes, were focused on Amy Clifton and her friend, Jodie something or other. Amy was Gabriel's other next-door-neighbours' daughter, and when she and her friend sunbathed in skimpy bikinis in the garden, Mungo was sure he watched them. He had looked pointedly up at Gabriel and cleared his throat rather noisily, causing the man to retreat quickly behind his grimy curtains.

Mungo only ever invited Gabriel Braithwaite to dinner the once. Never again, not after he ridiculed his soldier family and made rude remarks about how much he ate. 'You're like a giant aubergine,' he said. 'You want to take some of that flab off…a nice fat lettuce sarnie wouldn't do you any harm.'

He also thought Gabriel was 'damaged', though he did not quite know how or why. He knew he and his disabled brother, Jacob, had been somehow related to a person of importance, Norman Hartley-Edwards M.P. who lived and died next door before he, Mungo, came to live there. Beyond that, his knowledge was scant: London was not known for its present-day neighbourliness. There was only one thing in this area of the city that bound people together in friendship, the Arsenal football club. Beyond that one venue, the Emirates Stadium, he supposed people went their separate ways and lived their separate, private lives. Besides, football was not his game; it had to be the oval ball... and Twickers the venue, then the Oval for summer cricket.

Mungo was glad he had his military 'family' of soldiers. At that moment he was holding a Bavarian cavalry officer in his fleshy fingers as he watched from an upper window, to see his 'damaged' neighbour slink past the house on his way to the shops. Once Gabriel was lost to view he forgot him. He was thinking of someone else... someone from his past, from his schooldays.

Mungo Dickson intensely disliked Darwin Harrison-Forbes for a similar reason to the Braithwaite brothers, though he was unaware of that. His hatred would be much older than theirs, going back to his boyhood almost fifty years before. He was practically old enough to be Harrison-Forbes' contemporary. They had attended the same minor public school way back in the late sixties: D.H.F. had won a scholarship to Guyver Manor School. This indicated he was academically bright but also showed, at first, his woeful social inadequacies, which left him at the mercy of some dreadful teasing and mockery from some of the senior pupils.

His name, Mungo recalled, had not been Darwin Harrison hyphenated Forbes. The surname was Fawkes: he remembered that because of the infamous provincial terrorist, of Gunpowder Plot fame, back in 1605. And his first and second names were not Darwin Harrison, more like Darren and Horace.

Mungo paused in his painting of the tiny military figures, carefully wiped his hands on a turpentine rag and dipped the brushes into an oil solution to keep them soft. Darry Horry Fawksie, that's what they used to chant. He could hear it now, those jeering voices of a particularly nasty lower-sixth set who terrorised the younger boys of the junior school. They had it in for Darren Fawkes, though Mungo wasn't sure why: he suspected it was a social-class thing. Plenty of the other boys in school considered them nobs and snobs. These bullies often reduced Fawkes to snivelling tears around the back of the changing rooms in the sports block.

When they left the school, a certain peace reigned throughout, much to most boys' relief. The new head boy was George Anderson, a distant relative of Sir John Anderson, the inventor of the wartime shelter. George Anderson was a real 'brick', admired by all. He was a tall, handsome young man, with clean cut features and dark wavy hair that he kept slightly longer than cadet-officer length: forgiven because of his skill and power on the rugby field and as an amazing bowler during summer cricket. He was kind to the juniors, often mentoring them through their first worrying, and often miserable, term away from home.

Darren Horace Fawkes was, by then, in the lower sixth and had gathered around him his own set. He had also undergone a name change, Darren to Darwin and had dispensed with his second Christian name including it instead into a new double-barrelled surname, Harrison-Forbes. He edited and ran the school magazine, and sold it to almost every member of the school, by cajoling the older boys and bullying the younger ones into buying it. At ten pence a time, with 500 boys in the school, he enjoyed an impressive turnover of about £50 a month, almost as much as a clerk in a moderate organisation earned in those days.

He and George Anderson, however, did not get on. Darwin H-F was crafty though, and avoided confrontation with the popular head boy. Whatever secret carryings on he participated in, he contrived to keep them from Anderson. They were both good at sport, both academically bright, but one was scrupulously fair-minded while the other had an innate cruelty that made him take pleasure in pulling the wings off butterflies, or watching the suffocation of honey bees he had imprisoned in screw top jars: that kind of callousness. This brutality extended and included little boys, Mungo remembered. Harrison-Forbes would imprison them in his bed, where the screwing did not involve the lids of glass jars and the pulling off was replaced by pushing and penetration. Mungo knew what went on. He often heard the little ones crying in the shower next morning. But nobody told on Darwin H-F. It wasn't the 'done thing' to snitch on anyone. Not then. Mungo was two years younger than the lower-sixth-former, but escaped his vile behaviour simply because he was slightly overweight, maybe more than a little overweight, which earned him the nickname, Chubby.

Almost forty-five years on, he thought, Darwin Harrison-Forbes has emerged again. A bit like Dracula being washed up in Whitby two centuries before. Mungo spotted an article about him in yesterday's Telegraph that he had spread on the table prior to his painting his latest acquisition, a set of Bavarian soldiers from the Napoleonic models he had purchased on eBay.

"The Nobel Peace Prize winner, Darwin Harrison-Forbes, is to speak at the Teme Literary Festival", the Telegraph reported. He smoothed out the sheet of newspaper and read through the article, curling his lip as he read and muttering under his breath. 'So, you bastard, you're still around. Still like little boys, do you? Or are you getting too old now? Can't get it up any more?'

Mungo knew nothing of Harrison-Forbes visits next door those years ago. He had not moved in to this house until 2002, the year after Norman Hartley-Evans M.P. had died during Prime Minister's Question Time in Parliament. But he remembered this silver-haired and silver-tongued monster who was staring at him from the newspaper, who had attended Guyver Manor School those years ago.

He walked over to the window, and watched as a goods train trundled along the track, then a passenger train glide by almost noiselessly in the opposite direction. He saw a young man, or the back of his blazer, as he descended the corner basement of number five. Mungo allowed a smile to play about his lips. So the old dear who lived there had a visitor. That was a rarity. He had never seen anyone go there, not for many years, when a young boy used to haunt the place. *Joined the army didn't he? That chappie looks like he might be military... the short hair and upright bearing. Perhaps he's a friend of the little boy who grew up... maybe it's even him?*

Mungo drew away from the window, wiped his hands on a piece of linseed-soaked rag. *Enough painting for now. Time to go downstairs and make some coffee.* Coincidently he had received the Teme Festival program only that morning in the post and had not had time yet to digest it. He began to read through the program again, wondered how he had missed the bit about DHF giving his talk. Mungo was planning to go on the Thursday and Friday of the second week. Desmond Carlisle was giving a talk on his latest book, about Rourke's Drift, and a second on the following day about the military strategy of British and Austrian troops involved in the Napoleonic wars. 'Perhaps,' he mused, 'I could stay on and listen to the monster being questioned by Caius O'Neill, the Festival organiser? 'Should prove interesting.' he spoke out loud, 'but do I really want to come face-to-face with him again?

5 GABRIEL BRAITHWAITE

Gabriel Braithwaite was on a mission, an artistic mission. He needed more paints of the brighter hues: cyan, and cerulean, vermillion, titanium-white, orange-yellow and yellow ochre. Today he was going to begin a portrait in the style of Vincent Van Gogh: one, Patience Escalier, a shepherd from the Camargue. During his 1880's sojourn in the south of France, Van Gogh had painted the old man. Of course, Gabriel doubted he would ever see the original, thinking it would probably be in the United States. But the art book Jacob (his brother) has given him for his birthday this morning informs him the original is actually here in London: in the Tate Gallery. *Maybe Jake and I can go and view it one day.*

Earlier, Gabriel had opened his one and only present in bed, Jacob having given him the wrapped parcel after dinner the previous evening. In it was this large, beautifully illustrated, book containing many Van Gogh portraits that Gabriel had never seen before. He did not usually go in for portrait painting but this one had arrested him as he rubbed his thumb transversally along the golden edges of the leaves, alternately caressing and slowly turning the pages.

The old shepherd's eyes were red-rimmed but still piercing in their intensity, and full of a countryman's wisdom. His gnarled and weathered hands rested on a shepherd's crook, betraying their years spent outdoors, under night-time stars, the glaring sun by day, driving rain and harsh winds that sometimes blew across the Camargue region. Gabriel particularly liked the way Van Gogh had painted the old man's blue smock: how the creases and folds, painted with bold black strokes, illustrated the shepherd's rounded shoulders and slightly hunched back.

Everything about the portrait suggested a man of limited means, a man who led a solitary life, apart from his sheep and, possibly, his dog. Yet, within this solitary lifestyle, Patience Escalier seemed to have had the personal discipline to trim his beard. Gabriel felt a moment's remorse at his own lack of personal discipline. He almost promised himself to smarten up a bit, especially on this his birthday. Only 'almost' though. Smart clothes reminded him of those past evil times and the terrible punishments he would rather forget.

Gabriel would like to have met this old man, talked with him, walked with him in the flat lands of the Camargue. Today it was sufficient to begin a portrait of him. He would need a large canvass, more brushes, and the appropriate paint colours. Find time to visit the Upper Street Gallery and talk with Aubrey and Lally Penhaligon.

He let himself out quietly, not wanting to disturb

his still sleeping brother. Gently he shut the street door that overlooked the fenced-in trees and the Overground Railway beyond, which was lower than the road. A freight train was passing, showing glimpses of itself through the newly budding trees as it click-clacked along the line. Gabriel turned left, almost tiptoeing past Mungo Dickson's house, not wanting to encounter his screwball neighbour who 'played with' toy soldiers. Not today. He was eager to get to the Upper Street Gallery and purchase his art materials and drop off some books at the library. Mungo's weird discourse would throw him, take away some of his keenness, dampen his enthusiasm, on this, his thirty-eighth birthday. He scuttled by the next house round the corner, the one owned by that young widow, Mrs Meadham. There was a window open on the ground floor; meant she must be back from one of her stays away. Three in as many months he reckoned, and wondered where a person went to so often...

He likened the traffic on St Paul's Road, Highbury to the rush of a tube train as it raced through its black tunnel towards the station platform. For the umpteenth time in his life, Gabriel was glad he lived at the back end of Harbourne Road, away from the noise and speed. Once on the main road he kept as far away from the kerb as possible, all but clinging to house railings as the roaring traffic sped by. There were times, like this, when Gabriel felt – and looked – much older than his thirty-eight years. Bit of a wimp really... sometimes.

He had never learned to drive: no need to if you lived in London. Plenty of buses, trains, and taxis too – if you felt flush. He also had no need to work to earn a living; though he enjoyed his three nights a week at The Railway Arms, helping out.

Thanks to a certain Norman Hartley-Bloody-Edwards, both Gabriel and Jacob had been left a comfortable income from a carefully-planned trust fund. A man whose memory Gabriel revered and hated in equal measure. The late, rich, politician had plucked him and Jacob from the austere, grey children's home when they were eight and five years old: brought them here to his house in Harbourne Road. Here, where he fed them sumptuous food; roast beef and Yorkshire puddings, jelly and blancmange, chocolate cake and creamy ice-cream... and groomed them into sharing his bed night after agonising night for year after year.

By day he arranged to have them tutored by a bear of a man, 'Mr Forster, Sir', who caned their bare bottoms if they got a translation wrong, gave an incorrect spelling or a mathematic miscalculation. On certain evenings, they had to shower and dress in best clothes, blazers and grey shorts, white shirts and striped ties, the better to show themselves off to Uncle Norman's dinner guests. All males: all in their dinner jackets, black ties, and crisp, white dress shirts. Except when the meal ended and everyone 'retired' to the drawing room. Then the jackets came off and cognac was served, in large balloon glasses for the men, small sherry glasses for the boys. Jacob often fell asleep by this time and had to be carried upstairs to bed by Uncle Norman's manservant. Lucky Jacob...

Gabriel was passed from guest to guest, from lap to lap, like the children's game, 'Pass the Parcel'.

Each guest peeled off an item of his clothing until he stood in the middle of the room, as naked as the day he was born, shivering like a frightened puppy. On nights like these he was lucky to get to his own bed by two in the morning. The only concession was they were let off lessons for the morning; and in the afternoon Uncle Norman requested that Mr Forster go easy with the cane... though Gabriel remembered how Uncle Norman had enjoyed soothing their bruised and ravaged buttocks with baby oil. Only it didn't really soothe, did it? Not with what followed so often.

Gabriel crossed over St Paul's Road at the traffic lights close to the Alwynne Castle and, hopefully, left his bad memories on the other side. He was so engrossed in his thoughts, with avoiding traffic, and intent on getting to the art gallery he almost collided with Mrs Clifton, his next door neighbour from number three.

'Oh, morning Mr Braithwaite,' she said in her silly little-girl voice. Gabriel's eyes dropped to the ground as he mumbled a reply and rushed on. He had no wish to prolong conversation with her and did not hear her say to herself, 'Funny old bugger' or hear her snigger.

A police car screamed by, followed by another, causing a temporary slowdown to the cars and buses. Gabriel wondered what the drama might be, and quickly dismissed it: nothing to do with him. He passed The Hen and Chickens and turned left at Highbury Corner, then proceeded on to Upper Street. He looked forward to talking with the Penhaligons, Aubrey and Lally, the husband-and-wife owners of Upper Street Gallery. His hands were thrust in the pockets of his old trousers, no wearing of best clothes now, not unless it was strictly necessary, say for a visit to the doctor or something. He clutched five twenty-pound notes, an added birthday present from Jacob. *Blood money, more like it.* Even after all these years, since Norman Hartley-Edwards' untimely death from a heart attack, during PM's Question Time, Jacob still showed his gratitude and a modicum of guilt towards his elder brother, who had taken much more of the carnal abuse than he had been subjected to. He once confessed to Gabriel that, during those years with 'Uncle Norman', he had often pretended to fall asleep at table to escape the ordeal that was forthcoming from the male dinner guests. When Gabriel heard this, he had flown into an indescribable rage and punched Jacob so hard that the teenager fell down, hit his head on the stone hearth and suffered permanent brain damage.

Their substantial inheritance paid for the best treatment, but thereafter Jacob walked with a limp, two sticks, and a calliper on one leg. Gabriel, of course, felt a great remorse at what he had done, though he never admitted it to Jacob. He secretly marvelled that Jacob still considered himself culpable for his older brother's suffering during their young lives, though he made no attempt to alleviate Jacob's mental anguish. Rather, Gabriel played on it, especially as his younger brother had to rely so heavily upon him. He salved much of his conscience by helping Jacob to walk again: walking was difficult for Jacob and he refused 'absolutely' to use the wheelchair.

'Please, bruv, going in that bloody chariot makes

me feel like I'm mentally crippled as well as having these useless pins.'

'Ok... Ok, so we'll practise your walking some more. You know,' Gabriel warned, 'you'll never walk quickly again.'

'Even a snail's pace is better than having to rely on you to wheel me around.'

Gabriel would put up with his young brother's frequent mood swings and tantrums, and the inevitable string of insults and foul-mouthed swear words. In return, when Jacob calmed down, he showed Gabriel nothing but gratitude, saying 'sorry' more times than necessary. All in all, Gabriel felt vindicated from being the cause of Jacob's disablement and even enjoyed the undeserved gratitude that his brother displayed. They still lived together, in 'Uncle Norman's' house. Neither had married, or even enjoyed a romantic relationship with a woman. Their childhood experience prevented either of them having anything resembling a normal amorous relationship. That and Jacob's disability...

As Gabriel passed the Turkish family's newsagents and deli shop, he glanced at the A-board outside. What he read made him want to vomit. 'Harrison-Forbes to speak at Teme Literary Festival.' This was a name from his childhood, when Uncle Norman was alive and gave discreet dinner parties to his favoured few. Darwin Harrison-Forbes, or H-F to his friends, had been one of the favoured few: one of the cruellest, Gabriel remembered. He guessed it was the festival that his friends, the Penhaligons, were going to attend; he wondered if they knew this beast of a person. He shuddered and hurried past the newsagents.

He received a further shocking reminder in the library while returning his books. On a table just beyond the library entrance, the staff had made a pyramid of newly published books: leaning against this was *'One Day – Who knows?'* written by Darwin Harrison-Forbes and displaying his photograph, taken as he held hands with a small African child. Again Gabriel shuddered, quickly relinquished himself of the three books and escaped into the sun-lit street towards the art gallery.

To Gabriel's annoyance, Upper Street Gallery still had its 'closed' notice on the shop door. He glanced at his watch, a Rolex Oyster, 'bequeathed' to him by Uncle Norman. 'In loving memory' the late MP's solicitor had implied. This man had, once or twice, been one of the dinner guests, but hoped the grown-up Gabriel Braithwaite did not recognise him as such. Gabriel did, but chose not to show it. Privately, he regarded the timepiece as a shocking reminder of those slow-moving hours of humiliation and punishment and promised himself to sell it as soon as possible. Somehow, this had never happened and it still adorned his wrist, a grim reminder of his traumatic childhood.

He walked up and down, peered into other shop windows at bizarre fashions and curious 'objets d'art'. One piece, priced at some ridiculous sum, reminded him of a purple-and-white-glass baby comforter, another like a jigsaw-patterned lizard. He wondered at the people's mentality who bought these high-priced objects.

Two shops on, an old bag-lady huddled in the doorway, surrounded by an assortment of Sainsbury's plastic bags. 'Spare your small change, guvnor,' she whined at him.

Gabriel hesitated, let go of his twenty-pound notes to dig deeper into his pockets for any coins. There were none.

'Sorry love, haven't got any.' He made to move off and was shocked when she went to grab his hand.

'You sure? Not even a fifty pee?'

He pulled his hand away. 'I just said no, didn't I?' He looked, with distaste, at her tangled hair, her dirt-rimmed face, filthy clothes and moth-eaten, fingerless mittens.

'I ain't eaten in two days,' the old woman moaned. 'Me belly feels like me throat's cut.'

'Not my problem,' he said, and walked away, back towards Aubrey and Lally's gallery. What a waste of space: shame to keep her alive...

The windows and door of the shop were still shuttered. Gabriel glanced impatiently at his watch, forgot the old tramp-lady. He rocked on his heels and played with the five twenty-pound notes in his pocket, when a voice from behind made him jump in surprise.

'Morning, Gabriel.' It was the mild but well-modulated voice of Aubrey Penhaligon.

'Oh, hullo.'

'You're an early bird.' Lally Penhaligon this time: she'd joined her husband on the shop step. 'But of course, my deah,' (Lally called everyone 'my deah' in her tinkly, musical voice). 'It's your birthday today: many happy returns.'

Gabriel stuttered an embarrassed 'Thank you' as Aubrey unlocked the shop and stretched out his arm, inviting Gabriel inside. The Penhaligons were Gabriel's favourite people, always welcoming and informative when it came to a knowledge of art and painters. They were in their early sixties. He wished they could have been his and Jacob's parents, such a lovely couple: they were old enough...

6 AUBREY and LALLY PENHALIGON

Aubrey Penhaligon, an ex-Franciscan monk, had discarded his robes but retained his God. He exchanged the dark-brown habit for more colourful, finer clothes on his pilgrimage into painting. Today he wore his favourite outfit, purple-corduroy suit worn over a pink shirt and a rainbow-coloured cravat. He never wore ties.

A talented painter of both landscape and portraits, Aubrey was once commissioned to paint the entire cast of the Royal Opera House who had just performed Madam Butterfly or Butterfly as the cognoscenti would say. They were very vibrant portraits. No hint of flesh colour on any part of the canvasses; lots of purple and bold viridian, oranges and yellows. Somebody, an old Cockney-Italian chef that Aubrey knew, had once described them as 'the geezers with the 'alf-and-'alf faces', but they were amazingly well received. He had achieved a moderate fame with his characteristic portraits.

Years before, Aubrey met Lally in Milton Keynes,

within the Cathedral of Trees. She was leaning on a holm oak, head bowed, hands clasped almost as if in prayer; except by then she had abandoned her faith, or maybe the faith had abandoned her? Intrigued with her pose, he opened his sketchbook and drew her, unaware she was recovering from a badly-failed relationship and a partial nervous breakdown. Within a few short months they married and he took her to Ludlow, to his hideaway holiday cottage by the River Teme. The cottage was reputed to be haunted by one of the early owners of Ludlow Castle, the *'de Lacy'* family, but neither Aubrey nor Lally laid claim to have seen him. What would he be doing there anyway? Having a spectral affair with the 'lady of the house'?

Thanks to Aubrey's loving care, Lally recovered from her ghastly relationship and the partial breakdown. She put on a little weight, regained her colourful personality; wore flowing kaftans in exciting hues that she accessorised with beautifully-crafted beaded necklaces. 'My bling, my deah' she would say, her chins wobbling as she laughed. Lally (short for Laureline) Willows was a larger than life personality who called everyone 'my deah'. She now had three chins that wobbled in harmony and a mole on her left jaw. A single hair grew out of this and Lally frequently 'tweezered' it when it grew long enough to irritate.

Her hair, dyed to camouflage a somewhat boring grey, was more cedar wood in colour than auburn, reminiscent of autumn when garden-fencing would be painted to protect it for the winter. It accentuated her vivid green eyes that were framed with long, painted lashes.

Lally possessed a beautifully-modulated,

pleasant voice, slow yet precise; she frequently ended her sentences with a hint of surprise as if she could not quite believe she had said that.

Her flowing kaftans were as colourful as her personality, and always accessorised with her eclectic collection of beads and bangles. 'My bling,' she would declare often and laugh, frequently coiling the ornate jewellery around her sausage-like fingers.

Although once a talented painter, she never painted again after her traumatic relationship. Her final effort hung over the fire place of their Ludlow cottage, a Canada goose standing bizarrely in front of an ormolu-framed mirror, the bird's detail so fine you could almost imagine feathers ruffling at any hint of a breeze, and the ornate whirls and curves of the mirror were almost three-dimensional. Instead, she and Aubrey opened the art gallery in Highbury, London, where they sold a huge variety of art materials. They also organised successful exhibitions for his paintings throughout the land, including the *'kudos'* of designing the internationally famous Teme Literary Festival brochure, which contained all the week's programs and enticing snippets about its participants.

In a few days' time, they would be attending the tête à tête between Caius O'Neill, the organiser, and Darwin Harrison-Forbes, Nobel Prizewinner for his book, *'One Day - Who knows?'* Some called it the literary equivalent of John Lennon's song *'Give Peace a Chance'*. Aubrey, however, disliked Harrison-Forbes with an un-Christian intensity. The dislike was almost twenty years old, when the famous man had once commissioned Aubrey to paint his portrait, and agreed to the artist's fee. He had, however, declared his horror at the finished work, refused to pay and said if he had his way he would put a knife through the canvass. They'd never spoken again. Aubrey kept the painting, hid it away in the cellar of his gallery and let it gather the dust of neglect.

Aubrey, the ex-Franciscan monk, discarding his brown habit but keeping his God. Gabriel knew this because he had once asked, 'Do you still believe in God?'

Aubrey had answered, in his typically mild way. 'Well... yes. I've not found any other to replace Him, or my religion.'

'Right,' said Gabriel, not really knowing what else to say. He, of course, had no religion. His childhood pleas and prayers had been woefully ignored...

'We've a little gift for your birthday,' Lally said to Gabriel. 'Just wait till Aubs puts the lights on, and opens the blinds.' She sashayed her way to the counter at the far end of the shop, her rainbow coloured kaftan flowing gracefully as she passed by shelves of paints and pastel crayons, sheets of coloured tissue paper and various sizes of canvass, before she disappeared into a back room.

When the lights went on, Gabriel admired the many paintings decorating the walls, mostly Aubrey's work. He was very talented, Gabriel thought. He loved the colourful portraits of famous people; knew he wouldn't dare be half as audacious as the ex-monk in his use of 'unfleshy' colours on their faces. He recognised quite a few of them, and marvelled how their personalities were reflected in Aubrey's ingenious use of such bold colours as viridian, and purples, bright reds and golden yellows; wished he could paint half as well.

'Here we are.' Lally re-appeared from the back room, holding a brightly wrapped, oblong parcel. She smiled as she handed it to Gabriel. 'Happy birthday, my deah.' She kissed him lightly on the cheek. Gabriel did not flinch at such an intimate gesture. He trusted both Lally and Aubrey; knew they would not harm him. He liked the smell of her perfume as her face brushed his, and wished he had made a little effort to smarten up on his birthday. Lally, however, seemed not to notice his slightly-scruffy appearance. She chatted on in her usual cheerful and bubbly way. 'Wait till Aubs finishes opening up so we can both watch you, unwrapping your present.' She gave the impression of being as excited as Gabriel felt. He gave her a rare smile, as he caressed the shiny wrapping and bounced on his heels while they waited for Aubrey.

The illuminated shop enhanced all the paintings and the materials on shelves and those displayed in the windows. It was, Gabriel felt, like a wonderland of artistic beauty and talent.

'Thank you for waiting for me,' said Aubrey. 'Come on then, open your parcel.' For a very brief moment Gabriel wished the gallery owner had not used that word, parcel, a reminder of sickening evenings with Uncle Norman's friends. But he dismissed the thought: the Penhaligons knew nothing of his past life, at least he didn't think so, and he was not going to tell them about those times. Ever.

Carefully, he unwrapped the colourful paper and was delighted when a box of the finest tubes of oil paints was revealed. 'This is wonderful,' he stammered. 'Just what I wanted. I came here today,' he continued, 'to buy a large canvass, some large brushes, and oil paints.'

'Well, you won't need the paints now,' Lally beamed, her eyes sparkling behind her purple-rimmed spectacles.

'What are you going to paint?' asked Aubrey. 'Landscape? Still life? Or portrait?'

'A portrait actually. My brother gave me a book on Van Gogh's portraits, and I particularly like the one of *'Patience Escalier'*, the brighter one with the orange background.'

'Excellent. I believe there's one in the Tate.'

'Yes, and there's at least another one in America.'

'That's right,' said Aubrey, adding, 'Have you done portraits before?'

'No, never. Van Gogh's Patience Escalier inspired me.'

'Well then, we'd better see what you need. Do you want a large canvass? I think Van Gogh painted on one sixty-nine by fifty-six centimetres, that's about twenty-seven by twenty-two inches.'

Gabriel watched, bemused, as the Penhaligons put together the materials he needed for the project. He chatted easily with them, laughed when they laughed. Today, he was a happy man. He could not remember ever being this happy, except for the day when Norman Hartley-Edwards had died.

Until he saw the poster, with a photograph of that face from his childhood. His joy turned to misery and anger. Aubrey saw him staring at the poster.

'Someone you know, Gabriel?'

'Er... no, not really. He looks like someone I knew a long time ago.'

'His name is Darwin Harrison-Forbes. He's moderately famous as a writer.'

Gabriel briefly wondered at Aubrey's inclusion of the word moderately. 'Yes, I know the name. How come you have his picture here?'

'He's speaking at the Teme Literary Festival next week. You know Lally and I have been inveigled into attending. I designed the Festival brochure.'

Gabriel cut short his visit, said goodbye and thanked them once again for their generous gift. So much of the pleasure had gone and he wanted nothing more than to return home. He could have no idea that Aubrey disliked Harrison-Forbes as much as he did, but for a different reason of course.

'That was an odd reaction. Wonder what it's all about?' Lally waited to ask the question until Gabriel had left the shop, then closed the door, very purposely, behind him.

Aubrey Penhaligon blinked, pulled a face and looked at his wife. 'I was just thinking the same thing... quite a violent reaction, don't you think?'

Lally nodded. 'Mm. He obviously didn't take kindly to seeing Harrison-Forbes' face on the poster... and yet...'

'He almost denied knowing him, certainly shrugged him off.' Aubrey had finished her sentence. They often did that, so in tune they were with each other.

'I hope it hasn't spoiled his birthday,' said Lally. 'He seemed so enthusiastic about painting the shepherd's portrait.'

'Yes.' There was nothing else for him to add.

Aubrey, portrait painter of the great and the good (and sometimes not so good) wandered back into his thoughts, thoughts that were directed towards Darwin Harrison-Forbes, a man he had good reason to despise.

Now, Gabriel is even less happy. He wonders, *Did I kill her, that old bag lady?* He doesn't think so, he only hit her with the box of tube paints. Her own fault, she shouldn't have called out to him again for his small change.

'You must have some now, mate. Been shopping? Spare a quid or two.'

It was when she reached up and grabbed his sleeve and all but pulled him into her doorway shelter, dislodging his carefully held purchases. He had also banged his head, on a rotting window frame. He lashed out then and watched, with horror, as she fell back against the closed door.

Afterwards, he didn't see any blood, did he? He hurried away from her, scared somebody might have seen him with her. There were a few people about, hurrying to their possible destinations, but not many of them pedestrians. Mostly in cars, on bicycles, or buses they were. Too busy with their own lives, he hoped, to notice him or her, the old crow. But before he had reached the safety of Harbourne Road, he heard the wailing sirens of police cars and an ambulance, all hurtling towards Highbury Corner and possibly Upper Street. He shook himself. *Don't be daft, even if I did hurt her, nobody saw me, all too busy with their own lives. Few were walking.* And he was sure no one had passed by the vacant shop doorway that the old bag-lady had made her home. Besides, he had covered his face, hidden it from view with the canvass, and the old tramp hadn't screamed out or anything.

He dared to look behind him and was relieved to see the police cars and the ambulance turn into Grange Road, by The Alwynne, not going on to Upper Street then. He hurried on, grasping the unwieldy parcels, anxious now to just get home. He didn't see his neighbour until she was almost upon him: briefly wondered how she was coming in his direction again from Harbourne Road. She must have gone out, gone back, and come out again while he was with the Penhaligons in their gallery. He winced, reluctant at having to say 'Hello' again. He didn't even like her, let alone want to spend the time of day with her...

An elderly lady looked out of her first floor window onto St Pauls Road below. Rivulets of age had formed on her face, around her mouth, on the outer edges of her eyes, and on her forehead, as she stared myopically at the traffic, incessant and noisy, that roared by below her. On the opposite side of the road, where the pavement widened out, she watched Gabriel struggle by, his arms filled with large parcels. Of what? She watched his fine hair ruffle in the chilly spring breeze and saw how he gripped his parcels tighter: fearful, she guessed, of them sailing away in the playful and mischievous wind. His name was unknown to her, although she knew where he lived: just around the corner in Harbourne Road. She even knew which number, Number Four, and who had lived there with him and his brother before he died: Norman Hartley-Edwards, M.P. deceased.

Through her half-open window, the old lady heard one of the man's neighbours greeting him. Mr Braithwaite was the name she addressed him by, 'Mister Braithwaite.' And what is your Christian name, she thought. The old lady still used that term, would always do so. Not 'First Name' or 'Given Name', like they do these days: not 'Previously-known or Family Name' for a married woman's maiden-name. The old lady was stuck in her ways, old fashioned, whatever. She supposed 'Surname' was still the word in use, then shrugged and gave a little half-smile. What did it matter, anyway?

With Gabriel Braithwaite forgotten, she turned back to the large-print, historical romance she had been reading previously. As she turned back to her book, and Mr Braithwaite's neighbour had walked by, Gabriel crossed over the road, thankful for a brief lull in the traffic. Consequently, he disappeared from the old lady's view, unless she put her head out of the window. But her interest was gone by then and he proceeded on his way unmolested, not accosted by neighbours or strangers that peered out of upper-floor windows.

The old lady moved slowly and painfully into her kitchen at the back of the house where it overlooked the Overground Railway. She filled the kettle with sufficient water to make two cups of tea, peered out of the window as a train rattled by on its way to Canonbury and beyond. She smiled upon seeing a dear little fox curl up at the end of next-door's garden below, enjoying the sunshine no doubt. She wondered who would reach the lower end of Harbourne Road first: the train. or Mr Braithwaite? Then dismissed the thought: did it really matter?

Kettle boiled and tea made, she shuffled back to her window chair in the front room. The sun shimmered through the large area of glass, warming her arthritic shoulder, and reflecting in her teacup. Perhaps she and Benjy, her little dog, would go for a gentle walk after her drink? A modest stroll to Highbury Fields might be good.

Opposite her, beyond the road and the wider stretch of pavement, from a ground-floor window of the four-storey block of flats, the evil face of an evil man looked out. His name was Reuben Phillips, who had been a one-time friend of Jodie Drummond, who was an ex-school friend of Amy Clifton, whose mother had all but collided with Gabriel Braithwaite on his way home from the Upper Street Gallery.

For five years now, Reuben Philips had kept off the police radar; had never been sniffed at by the anti-terrorist squad or the Special Operations branch of the Met. Why? Because he knew how to walk silently, like a cat: how to watch and observe with the stillness of a hawk. He kept no friends within arm's length, yet accepted the loyalty and obedience of his fringe-society foot-soldiers. And since Jodie Drummond had walked out of his life, he shared it and his bed with no-one except Satan, his five-year-old crossbreed.

Reuben owned no car but had a full driving licence and, in a lock-up a few streets away, a Honda motorbike. His crash helmet, with its full-face visor, was a convenient and legal mask that afforded him a temporary disguise when necessary. He also owned a small piece of equipment that fitted neatly and invisibly under a part-denture which gave his voice a metallic sound, as if he had been treated for throat cancer. He could remove it whenever he wished to resume his natural voice, a softly-spoken vocal sound with no particular or traceable accent. Between his eighteenth and twenty-first birthdays, Reuben had studied at RADA. With his dark, good looks and the many accents and inflections he could emulate, he might have enjoyed a moderately-successful career as an actor. Instead, he had chosen his path away from public fame, selected a road that led, eventually, to a quiet and worrisome notoriety. Reuben learned to kill and maim, to instil fear into the hearts and minds of grown men and women: make them lay protective arms around their vulnerable children and send them away, with their mothers, to places of safety. But there were no places safe enough, or far enough, to prevent the penetration of Reuben Philips and his furtive but hostile band of followers. Nowhere except the grave. That is where many of his targets went, either by their own suicidal hands or helped towards an early death by Reuben's strangling hands, sharpened knives over their exposed windpipes, poisoned arrow heads, or recently his IEDs (Improvised Explosive Devices). Never once did his fingerprints betray or identify him, and neither were his footprints or DNA left behind at the scene of crime. He didn't exist, at least as far as the investigating authorities were concerned, in the dark and secret world of domestic terrorism. The sort of terrorism that instils fear into the scientific minds who employ their brains to discover new medicines and medical treatments for healing the human race: those who use small animals to aid them in their research. These were the targets for Reuben and his followers in their fringe animal-rights organisation.

Reuben worked in IT (Information technology), making and mending computers and their parts for a small electronics firm in the Holloway area of London. He paid his rent and council tax by direct debit, as he did for his utility bills. He neither spoke to his neighbours nor chatted to shop workers. He also discouraged his work colleagues, sat at benches alongside his own, from conversing with him either. A few of them, in the past, had tried to be friendly, had tried to see beyond his sinister stare and the tattoos that covered his skin, but he'd discouraged them from verbal exchanges unless necessary. Now he was left to get on with the task in hand and keep his very private life away from his workplace.

However, Reuben hadn't lost his feelings for Jodie Drummond. The hurt from her disappearance had turned to a smouldering anger when he knew she had gone away from her flat, from Highbury, from him and his intimidating disciples, and well clear of England. She had been the only one to share his bed and his very secret life. She alone could have unmasked him. Somehow, despite the stinging pain of losing her, he knew she wouldn't do that, wouldn't talk to anyone about him. Jodie was too much like himself, someone who wrapped herself up in a cloak of secrecy that the world wasn't permitted to penetrate.

He knew she had been friends with a girl called Amy Clifton over in Harbourne Road; knew the friendship had dwindled after she had joined him and his organisation, and ended altogether when she went abroad to work for Hogarth International. Amy, too, had disappeared, soon after Jodie's departure. He had known, when late at night he walked Satan around the little three-sided road for a final piss or shit, that Number Three, overlooking the cutting of the Overground Railway, was only occupied now by her parents. How did he know she had gone? By listening to conversations in the local pubs where old man Clifton sank the odd pint, or where the queer Braithwaite brothers did the same. Not that Amy's disappearance held any interest for Reuben beyond his habitual intelligence-gathering. He stored away snippets of conversation like other people collected bargains 'discovered' at garage sales or online auction sites, hoping that one day those pieces of 'rare' opaque glass might turn out to be Lalique, or the battered old monkey or panda might be a Steiff.

Reuben stored any useful intelligence on a USB flash drive, then deleted anything remotely incriminating from whatever computer he'd used. USB memory sticks were easy to hide and simple to replace. He knew how to destroy them so they left no trace and would not lead anyone back to himself.

On the morning he had seen Gabriel Braithwaite struggle with his oversized canvass and his other parcels, Reuben had also seen the old lady at the window of the house opposite, in St Pauls Road. He knew she had seen him too, from time to time, but if she had been asked to describe him she would have said, 'I think he's quite tall.'

'How tall, madam?'

'Erm... possibly six feet, maybe a bit more.'

'Go on.'

'He had a cap on, pulled over his eyes. Oh... and

sunglasses. Although I'm sure it wasn't sunny.'

'His clothes? What did he wear?'

'Erm... a dark jacket... and trousers. He slouched, I remember.'

Reuben smiled, a crunched-up rock smile which seemed to show his thoughts were somewhere else. He imagined the questioner would spear his questions at her and she would hesitate, be confused... and inaccurate. He owned a variety of caps, hoodie tops and crash helmets. His jackets ranged from dark, as in black, to shades of grey, navy and brown. His wardrobe held slacks, jeans, shirts and tee shirts, woollen jackets and leathers. He also possessed wigs of various lengths, including shoulder-length that could be tied back in a ponytail. There were few who could accurately describe Reuben Philips. And only one who could describe him intimately. He was certain she would never paint the true portrait of him and he wondered, as he strode along St Pauls Road to get a newspaper, where was she, Jodie, now?

Gabriel was thankful to reach the safety of his own front door, having briefly passed by the doors of numbers Six and Five, let himself in and made for the kitchen, from where the delicious aroma of freshly-made coffee and toast meant Jacob was up and about.

'Happy birthday, Gabe. Been out spending your money already?'

'Yeah, got canvass, brushes and paints. Matter of fact, Aubrey and Lally gave me the paints for a birthday present. They're going to Shropshire next week.'

'Oh, right. Of course. There's that Literary

Festival on, at Teme isn't it?'

'Er, yeah, that's the one.' Gabriel put his purchases on a spare corner of the table and sat down to join his brother for breakfast. 'He picked up a piece of toast and chewed on it while Jacob poured him coffee.

'I understand that Darwin Harrison-Forbes is speaking there.' Jacob tried to sound nonchalant, as if he was talking about a casual friend, but the slight tremor in his voice betrayed his real feelings. Harrison-Forbes had found him to be particularly appealing. Liked very young boys, the monster did.

'How d'you know that?'

'It was on Radio Four this morning; I think the Beeb sponsors it, the Festival.'

'Hmm. Well, bully for them.'

'Tell you what, Gabe, I think we should go there.'

'What? Why?' Gabriel almost spat the words out. 'Why the hell should we do that?'

'Expose him,' his brother said. 'Let the world know what a real bastard he is. After all,' he pointed down to his withered leg, 'if it hadn't been for him and Uncle Norman, I wouldn't have this today.'

Gabriel remained silent, chewed on the inside of his mouth. Jake had a point: animals like Harrison Forbes, and the late MP, should be exposed. He was torn. He so wanted to get on with his portrait of Patience Escalier, so wanted to forget his and Jacob's grim past, but the thought of publicly shaming the writer in front of a large audience, and the BBC, was slightly appealing.

'Let's think about it. He's talking on the final Friday, did you say?'

'Yeah.'

'That's more than a week away yet... leave it for now.' He could spend at least the next few days with paints and brushes, working on this huge canvass, bigger than anything he had attempted before. Besides it would help to heal the scabs of those yesterday injuries that kept breaking open.

At the beginning of the next week, Jacob broached the subject again. 'Shall we go?' He was crunching on his third slice of toast, thickly spread with lime marmalade.

'You'll get fat, eating all that... Go where?' asked Gabriel.

'To that festival: you know, the one near Ludlow. Go and listen to the beast.'

'Why?'

Jacob shrugged, his pale fingers cramming the last piece of toast into his mouth. 'Why not? You could heckle him, maybe? Shame him, in front of the audience?'

Gabriel thought about it for a few seconds. 'If we did go and heckle him, surely security would be present. You know, the men in grey suits, trained to kill?'

Jacob laughed. 'I don't think many people get killed at literary festivals. We might get chucked out... in a genteel way, of course. But if we shouted something like *child molester*, I bet it would unnerve him... bastard. Cause him embarrassment in front of a lot of people. Bet they'll televise his talk, someone of *his* world fame. Then his crimes would go global.'

Gabriel poured more coffee, added a measured half-spoonful of demerara sugar and stirred. He breathed deeply and stared into a distance beyond the room. 'How would we get there?'

'National Express from Victoria coach station. They're running a special service right to the festival site; leaving at eight each morning and returning at six-thirty. Well, leaving the festival, that is, at half past six... for the duration of the festival week.'

'You're remarkably well informed. How d'you find that out?'

'On my laptop,' Jacob answered, 'I googled it. Anyway, d'you want to go?

Gabriel sighed, *Jake's new toy*, breathed deeply again and scratched his head as if he was dislodging an old scab. He was, in a way. 'Let me think about it. When is he on, performing, speaking, whatever you call it?'

'I told you the other day.' Jacob sounded exasperated. 'It's Friday, the penultimate day. I can book the tickets online, and the coach seats.'

'Hm,' Gabriel hesitated. 'Today's only Monday and I still have work to do on Patience Escalier. I really want to finish him soonest.'

'That gives you loads of time,' Jacob cajoled. 'You'll have all day today, Tuesday and Wednesday: maybe Thursday as well. We can get a cab to Victoria first thing Friday and come back the same day if you want. The returning coach will get in about nine or nine-thirty. Or we can stay over for the night. You know who'll be there in their country cottage?'

'Yes, Aubrey and Lally.'

'Maybe they would put us up for the night?'

'Mm, maybe. But I don't know if I could ask them... bit embarrassing. I mean, I know they're very friendly towards us, but it's a bit cheeky to spring ourselves on them, don't you think? Besides, they might have house-guests.'

Jacob struggled up from his chair, limped over to the kitchen sink and began to load the dishwasher beneath it.

'Why are you banging about?' asked his brother.

'Cos you're faffing as usual,' grumbled Jacob. 'You've got their number... ring it. They can only say yes or no. If they can't put us up we can always come back the same night.'

Gabriel stood up, cleared the rest of the breakfast things from the table. There were times, he thought, when Jacob could be quite immature, sulky like a teenager. 'Well, if you really want to go.' He said it reluctantly.

'I do. Come on Gabe,' Jacob pleaded. 'We don't go out much... except to The Railway a couple of nights a week. Big deal.'

Gabriel relented, gave his younger brother a softened gaze. 'Ok, we'll go.' He was pleased to see Jacob's face brighten, but still had doubts as to the wisdom of confronting their old enemy. Wasn't it opening old wounds? Their wounds? Wounds that were never far from the surface, anyway. And what about Harrison-Forbes? What would his reaction be to their tearing open this can of worms? Gabriel remembered that cruel face, the dark, menacing eyes and the way this evil man had flipped his little-boy body over like a playing card... except playing with cards doesn't injure a child's body... or a child's mind.

Gabriel wasn't looking forward to the repercussions, the violent ejection, and the media publicity. And what about his friends, Aubrey and Lally? Surely they would be acutely embarrassed at such a spectacle? He wished he had not agreed to their going. Too late now... Jake was already hobbling towards his little office next door, and to his beloved computer. Gabriel also left the kitchen and climbed the stairs slowly, his appetite for painting Patience Escalier now slightly diminished.

Late Wednesday afternoon, however, Gabriel stood in front of his almost finished canvass. He nodded his head in self-approval. *Not bad, Mr Braithwaite, even if I do say so myself. You have captured Escalier's wisdom. Those eyes! Brilliant: they follow you around the room. No escaping Patience Escalier's stare. Well done.*

He called downstairs to his brother. 'Jake, come and look at this.'

'You finished it?' Jacob began his slow ascent of the stairs. After five agonising minutes he limped into Gabriel's attic studio, stood in the doorway, speechless at first. Then, 'Gabe that is awesome... best painting you've ever done. You could almost think you're looking at the original Van Gogh. Brilliant.'

Gabriel smiled, cradled in his brother's praise. 'Not bad is it... is he looking at you?'

'Sure is, searing into my soul. Is he looking at you too?'

Gabriel nodded, 'Yep, right into my eyes, giving me his wisdom.'

'Mesmerising.' Jacob moved slowly into the room. 'You've caught the colours very well, and the old man's posture. Gabriel Braithwaite,' he said, a huge smile wreathing his face. 'The new Van Gogh.'

'Can't wait to show Aubrey and Lally. Think they'll like it?'

'Of course they will. It's a masterpiece.'

Gabriel grinned. ‘Not quite, but I’m pretty pleased with it.’

‘You can’t take it with you to the Festival, though.’

For a brief moment Gabriel’s day darkened. He had been so absorbed, so lost in painting, he had forgotten they would be going to Teme’s Edge. Still, at least he would hopefully meet up with his two friends and be able to tell them about his ‘Patience Escalier’. Whatever else was going to happen, would happen...

‘I’ll take a photo of it,’ his brother said. ‘Then you can show it to them. Never know,’ he grinned, ‘they might even offer to hang it in their gallery. Fame at last for Gabriel Braithwaite, painter extraordinaire.’

Gabriel smiled too, his anxieties temporarily dispelled. Painter extraordinaire, it had a ring to it.

7 WEDNESDAY EVENING

Matilda was bored: seems like she suffered this tedium a lot lately, even sometimes on her exotic holidays. Back here in chilly, cold UK there was not much to do, except watch boring old telly: same old, same old. Or go to the pub. And yes, she was bloody sick of looking at Freddie's chocolate plastic urn. She leapt out of her chair, dropping the TV control as she did so. 'Bugger! S'pose that'll be broken now.'

She placed it on the small table next to her chair, the one with a large glass of wine on it, her third that evening. She went over to the shelf where the urn sat, squat and smug, among the dust-collecting books that her husband had once read. 'You are definitely going. Now... tonight.'

In her anger and annoyance, she snatched the plastic vessel, forgetting its weight and its smooth, slippery surface. In a split second, the urn had slithered from her hands and fallen onto the woodblock flooring that edged the room. The lid came loose and a cascade of tiny grey/white crystals spilled onto the shiny surface, some reaching to the edge of the cream shag-pile rug that covered the rest of the floor.

Matilda stared in horror, imagined this odious substance coming alive and oozing like flood water into every corner of the room. She ran out into the kitchen, yanked the dustpan and brush from the cupboard under the sink and ran back into the room again. Kneeling down, but careful not to get any of the disgusting powdery stuff (she could not think of it as human remains, it was anything but that) on her clothing, she swept it up and poured it back into the chocolate-coloured container. Standing up and holding the urn more securely this time, she placed it on another side-table. 'You stay there,' she mouthed at it. 'I'm gonna fetch my coat and you and I are going for a short walk.'

She passed through to the hallway and took down her coat from the rack. She could see, through the mottled glass of the front door, that it was dark outside and she felt a moment's relief. It was, after all, staying lighter in the evenings now the clocks had gone forward, but – she glanced at her watch – it was a little after eleven o'clock, well time for darkness now. Surely there would be no-one about? Not down this end of the road? Unless... someone was walking their dog, like that weirdo with his Staffy from over St Pauls Road ... and leaving its poo among the rubbish that blew against the railway fence? She sighed; she had to take that chance. *I can't be doing with you any more, Freddie. You're blighting my life. Bad enough when you were alive. Bit of a control freak then, weren't you? Well you're not controlling my life anymore.*

Matilda let herself out, quietly shutting and

locking the door behind her with her new key. She'd had to change the locks when she returned from Portugal. Silly cow that she was... she had locked herself out. Luckily for her, she'd had her passport still in her bag, along with a card showing her name and address, so was able to prove her identity to the locksmith.

'We have to have positive ID before we change anyone's lock,' he told her. 'In case it's squatters who are trying it on.' It had cost her a few quid, that silly mistake.

She looked right and left but this back end of Harbourne Road, where it overlooked the railway, was in almost total darkness. There was a street light up at the far end and she could see lights from the flats over the other side of the rail tracks, but too far away to give any definite illumination over here. Freddie and his container felt curiously light. No more, she thought, than a new-born baby: not long now, only a few more feet and she could dispense with him over the wire fence. The fence was high, taller than her, but she managed to lift the plastic urn over and above it. She tipped it upside down and watched the white crystals as they blew away in a sudden gust. *Good riddance.*

Gabriel and Jacob Braithwaite were at the other end of the Harbourne Road railway fence, on their way back from The Railway Arms. 'Isn't that the widow lady?'

Jacob peered along the dark street. 'Yeah, I think it is. What on earth is she doing?'

'Dunno, except it looks like she's getting rid of something over the fence. Can't be her husband,' Gabriel added and chuckled. 'He's well dead and gone.'

'What about his ashes?'

'Was he cremated then?'

Jacob shrugged his shoulders. 'Aren't most people nowadays? Cemeteries filling up and all that.'

'Mmn. Hope that isn't his ashes then. That'd be illegal wouldn't it?'

His younger brother laughed. 'Expect it is. But who's going to report her? You? Me?'

They watched as she walked back to her house, observed her disappear around the corner before reaching their own front door and going inside.

Once settled in front of the TV, with a glass of whisky apiece, they talked about it some more.

'I bet that's what she was doing... getting rid of his ashes,' Gabriel took a sip of his whisky. 'I'm gonna go and have a look tomorrow.'

'Thought we were going to Ludlow tomorrow?' Jacob looked anxious. 'I've packed our backpacks in case we do decide to stay.'

Gabriel sighed and tutted. 'What about tickets and the coach fares and everything?'

'All sorted, I told you. I booked it online, all of it.'

Gabriel sighed again. He really didn't want to go, not to the festival and especially not to confront Darwin Harrison-Forbes. Hard to see a way out of it now though, and he regretted ever consenting to go. Too late... Jake had made all the arrangements now. Damn it.

'Wait a minute, it's only Wednesday today, not Thursday. Thought we were going Friday morning.'

Jacob looked bemused and confused. 'So it is.' He glanced at the date on his watch. 'Got the date wrong on here. Yeah... Wednesday.' And he proceeded to change it, but he shook his head. 'No Gabe, I told you, couldn't get seats on the coach for the Friday, only the Thursday. It is Thursday when we go.'

Gabriel wasn't a happy man.

Back in her own home, Matilda grinned at the empty space on the bookshelf. She had tossed the plastic urn into her wheelie bin, then taken a filled bin bag outside and put that on top. The dustmen wouldn't be collecting the garbage till Monday. *Doesn't matter, I'll have another bag by then... hopefully. I should have put it in with the recycling, the plastic and all that.* She giggled at the thought: *A recycled human ashes container? I don't think so.*

She wandered through to the kitchen and poured herself another glass of wine, wondered whether or not it was the Braithwaite brothers she had seen turning into the street while she was at the railway fence. Hoped she was wrong, or at least that they hadn't seen what she was doing. She sipped her wine. Forget them. Even if they got nosey and went to have a look tomorrow they wouldn't see anything. It wasn't as if she had tossed an old mattress over there. That sort of thing had happened before. People from the railway had eventually moved it when the residents of Harbourne Road had complained of the flies, some even seeing rats there. Worse then, she remembered: they had found a body, badly decomposed and half-eaten by foxes, under the mattress. At the time, she and Freddie had questioned how anyone could get a body over the wire fencing. Police, however, later discovered where the fence had been cut with wire cutters. They never did find the murderer, but she remembered reading, somewhere, they thought it might be a ritual killing, as the corpse was that of a young child. She smiled... she had no sympathy, only relieved that it wasn't hers; never did like children, did she? Mike never knew she got rid of their chance of a child, her one and only embryo: told the doctor she had been raped and no way did she want to carry a rapist's child. The doctor had patted her hand and reassured her. Two days later, she was pregnant no more and Mike had known nothing about the whole sordid business. There was no rapist and Mike would never be a father, not through her making him one... and she certainly had never wanted a child with her second, aging husband either.

Well, she thought, there's another body over there now; only it won't be recognisable as a corpse. No remains, apart from a few ground-down crystals. Even they would be reduced, blown all over the place, judging by those high winds out there tonight, and those March winds in April. Funny old world.

She switched the television back on, unwilling yet to retire for the night, and flicked through the channels. Surely there must be one decent film showing? Her mind, however, kept going back to the Braithwaite brothers. She really hoped they hadn't seen her, or what she was doing with Freddie's ashes.

A knock at the front door badly startled her, its resonance echoing through the hallway. Who could it possibly be at this time of night? Eleven thirty... not Jehovah Witnesses that's for sure. She put down her glass of wine, half-finished, and struggled to lift herself out of the chair. It was her fifth glass, the dregs of the bottle. She stumbled through into the hallway and, through the frosted glass of the front door, glimpsed a figure well-lit by the overhead security light outside. Deep down she knew it was stupid to open the door, but Tilda was a curious type. It was a man, she could see that, somehow familiar too. She smiled to herself. Not Freddie, though: he was well gone now, "Over the (fence) and Far Away". Probably blown down the line by now, on his way to the East End. Maybe, out to sea.

She moved towards the door, switched on the hall light, then made sure the security chain was in place before she opened the door. It was Gabriel Braithwaite.

'Yes?' She peered at him through her wine-infested, myopic eyes. He held something out to her through the narrow gap that the safety chain allowed the door to open. He had, she thought, a sinister leer on his face.

'I think this is yours.'

What he held out was a flat cylinder, made of chocolate-coloured plastic. It was wet and had a few grey-coloured crystals clinging, limpet-like, to it. She knew what it was, and the comprehension made her want to vomit over it and onto his hand.

'What do you mean, it's mine?'

'The lid off your urn, or your late husband's more like.' He thrust it into her hand, curled his lips, displaying long and uneven 'tombstone' teeth. They looked a strange shade of yellow in this light and she could smell his beer breath.

Matilda, dumbly, took it from him and he withdrew his hand from the gap, seconds before she shut the door and double-locked it, wishing there was a bolt to draw as well. And reinforced wire over the frosted glass. Maybe she'd organise that... soon.

Neither of them had said goodnight. She stood there with the damp lid in her hand.

'D'you know what, Freddie?' she whispered to the few remaining crystals that clung to the chocolate-coloured plastic. 'You've kept your bloody promise, haven't you? Remember how you said you'd never leave me? Think again, Freddie Meadham.'

She walked through to the kitchen at the back of the house, shuddered as she thought of her odious neighbour. He must have seen her earlier and guessed what she was doing. So bloody what? Wasn't a crime, was it? Too late now for him and his crippled brother to make waves. Freddie must have blown every which way but where by now. Except for this. She looked down at the lid, shuddered and pedalled open the waste bin. She dropped the offending article into it. She would empty the bin tomorrow; she was most definitely not going outside now: not for anyone or anything. Not at this time of night.

She moved over to the sink, ignored the detritus from her evening meal and ran the hot tap over her chilled fingers. The water stung but she felt it to be cleansing, like wiping off dead flesh from... No, don't go there. She counted to thirty, slowly, second by second. She'd learned somewhere, she didn't know where, couldn't remember who told her, that you had to wash your hands under the tap for thirty seconds for them to be considered clean, germ free. After the counting she turned off the tap, dried her hands on a clean tea-towel and hung it back on its hook at the side of the sink unit. She went towards the fridge and plumped for a nightcap. Meant opening another bottle: so what? She'd finished the other one when Mr Nosey-bloody- Braithwaite had knocked at the door.

It was almost three a.m. before Matilda roused herself and made the effort to go up to bed. She knocked the empty glass over and watched it roll across the rug. It could stay there till morning. No point in bending down now, she'd probably fall over. Her mouth, as she ran her tongue over her teeth, felt thick and fuzzy. P'raps she'd swallowed a teddy bear, ha-bloody-ha. Her eyes drooped. Straight to bed, no teeth brushing, no washing off her make-up: Go directly to bed, do not pass GO, do not collect £200. A silly memory from childhood, Monopoly. With or without Daddy?

Matilda couldn't even be bothered to undress, just slipped off her shoes and slid under the duvet, pulled it up to her nose and fell immediately into a deep sleep. Sometime during the hours before dawn she dreamed of swimming pools and handsome, muscular men admiring her scantily-clad body as she sunbathed in a skimpy bikini. Somehow she was joined by the two girls from Harbourne Road, Amy and her friend Jodie Drummond, there by the pool... and the Braithwaite boys swinging brightly coloured lead soldiers that belonged to Mungo Dickson. And Freddie... He was there, frowning, shaking his head. He hit her, slapped her face, rocking her head and causing her excruciating pain, making her groan out loud.

Only it wasn't Freddie, and she was not by the sunlit pool with her neighbours. Oh no, she was in bed, still fully clothed and with a hangover to end all hangovers. She groaned again and vomited into her pillow.

8 JODIE DRUMMOND

When she was seventeen, Jodie Drummond killed her stepfather, Paul Davies. She had hated him ever since the day he snatched the watch from her wrist and trod it under his size eleven boots, grinding it into the back-door step.

'Now see if you tell me lies, you and your bloody clouds. They're CLOUDS: not PEOPLE, not REINDEER, not SLEDGES. Just conden-bloody-sation,' he screamed at her. She was seven and she hadn't told a lie. All she said was, 'Look up there, Paul, you can see Father Christmas on his sleigh.' She was staring at a strangely-shaped passing cloud. By the time her stepfather looked up from his racing paper, the cloud was evaporating and taking on a different shape.

She stared through her tears at the crunched up pieces of glass and metal, at the screwed and bent pink watch face and broken hands. And the torn strap, where Paul had ripped it from her wrist. She could hear him ranting on and on, like a clanging of giant bells ringing in her ears, wishing he would bloody shut up. *Bloody, bloody, bloody: sod, sod,*

sod. Looking up, eventually, at his ugly unshaven face contorted with his anger, she knew she would hate him until he died. Seconds later, her hate turned to fear as the look on his face changed to an ugly and frightening, evil smile. He grabbed her roughly by the arm, making her cry out in pain. 'I'll give you something to cry for, you little bitch.' And he dragged her indoors. She wanted to scream for Mum, guessing that something really bad was about to happen, but she knew Mum was out. Gone shopping to the supermarket, a bus ride away, for their tea.

What happened to the seven-year-old child took moments, well less than half an hour, not even involving token rape. By the time Paul Davies had wrenched up Jodie's dress over her head, and pulled down her knickers and unzipped his jeans to reveal his manhood, Jodie threw up all over him. His penis had quickly shrivelled and he roared his disgust with a backhander to the side of her head. Then he pushed her so hard she fell and hit her head again on the wardrobe.

'Get out of here, you piece of filth. Go and get cleaned up before your mother gets back.' She had crawled away, clutching her knickers and pulling down her dress over her bare buttocks, tears streaming down her face and vomit clinging to the corner of her mouth.

'And don't even think of telling her anything about this. She won't believe you anyway.'

Every night, for the next ten years, Jodie prayed for the day to come when she would get her revenge; hopefully he would die of some disease that gnawed away at his stomach and slowly ate into his entrails.

Or a bone disease that crushed his ribs into splinters and punctured his lungs, causing him to bleed and die screaming in agony. At times, she even began planning his death in grim detail.

The day arrived that heralded her seventeenth birthday. Gone was the scrawny little seven-year-old. Now she was an attractive teenager, with long, dark brown hair framing her well-shaped features on a flawless skin. As she entered the kitchen, she looked at the two of them, Mum and Paul, hunched over the kitchen table: dressing gowns on, uncombed greasy hair and last night's beer bottles still at Paul's feet. There was a vodka bottle on the drainer, two thirds full. Jodie knew it would have been Mum's second bottle last night. They stared up at her from drink-ravaged faces, each attempting a smile.

'Happy Birthday, Jodes.'

She attempted a smile back: one that didn't reach her eyes. 'Thanks,' she said, 'Where's the cornflakes?'

Paul swept a careless hand towards the cupboard. 'Still in there. Help yourself kid.'

She guessed their breakfast had been endless cups of tea and cigarettes; thought they might have made a little more effort on her birthday: nice cooked breakfast maybe? *Fat chance, not with all that muck inside them.*

'Got summink for you, Jodes.' Paul pasted a grin onto his stubbled face, eyes red and bloodshot from last night's drinking. He held out a small, oblong leather box that he pulled from the pocket of his dressing gown.

'Here, take it. Happy birthday.'

She looked from him to Mum and back again, for a moment speechless. Biting back the words, *now that 's a surprise*, she took the box from her stepfather.

'Thanks Paul, Mum.' She stared at it, wondering what it contained. A necklace? A bracelet? Maybe a set of dice, knowing his gambling habits and warped sense of humour.

'Go on then, open it.'

She set down her schoolbag and sat on a third chair at the small, round table. She flipped open the ornate metal clasp and gently levered up the lid. Inside, on a soft, blue felt lining it lay. She stared, shocked, mesmerised. Her mind went back to that day ten years ago, when she vowed through her tears and sadness that she never wanted another watch. Not ever. Never.

'It's a good one,' Paul said. 'Comes from Edwards in Upper Street. They only sell the best.'

Jodie stared at him, at the pathetic creature he had become, remembering the towering bully and would-be rapist that day. *Now look at you, you pathetic, half-baked alkie.*

'Go on, Jodes, put it on.'

She kind of despised her mother as well, and her gravel voice, rough with cigarettes and vodka: like a wire scouring pad. She resisted the urge to throw the watch onto the table. Violently. Powerfully enough to smash it to pieces, like he had smashed hers, the one her real Dad, Tommy Drummond, had given her before he died.

She swallowed the hate, suddenly felt sorry for what they had both become. Still, she struggled to show her gratitude, smiled thinly at them, lips not parting, horizontal, and eyes expressionless. These two were not her loved ones, had never been since that day ten years ago.

'Ok,' she said, balancing the watch over her wrist as she buckled the black leather strap. It was tiny, quite chic, with a white oval face surrounded by silver stainless steel and a ticking second hand.

'D'you like it?' asked Mum.

'It's erm... yeah, it's lovely.' Then 'Thanks you two. Any tea in the pot?'

Paul's hand shook as he passed it over to her. He fingered her hand as she took it from him, giving her a lecherous look. She suppressed a shudder.

In your dreams, perv.

Conversation waned as they slurped their tea and smoked endless cigarettes. Jodie ate her cornflakes, sipped from her mug, and eventually said, 'Cheers' to them both, as she left for school. Another year and she would be gone. On the way to school she texted Amy, her friend from Harbourne Road, and was pleased when her friend texted back 'happy birthday'. As she arranged to meet Amy in the newsagent's she wished she lived there at Amy's instead of with Mum and Paul on this awful housing estate. 'Chocs are on me' she texted. She thought about the watch and her stepfather. God he made her skin crawl! *I'll get you one day, you'll see.*

Jodie slept now with a baseball bat in her bedroom. Just in case. He hadn't yet succeeded, although Paul had tried to enter her room more than once late at night. But she had never forgotten his attempted rape, all those years ago, and she was not going to let it happen again. Mostly she jammed a chair against the door. He usually tried after he and Mum had been drinking heavily downstairs, especially after the rows, the shouting and screaming. And the blows when Mum fell or he knocked her to the floor.

So many times she had wanted to rush downstairs to protect her Mum, but she was constantly scared of him; knew whatever she said or did would be enough for him to slap her as well, maybe worse... Why Mum had put up with him all these years was beyond her. She, too, had tiptoed around him, pretending to be invisible... for ten long years. *Tiptoeing Around Paul Davies... it would make a good title for a story.* She smiled to herself... not a humorous smile.

Lately he seemed to show her a different attention. Creepy, staring, licking his lips. She guessed what he was after. *No way, not in a zillion years will you lay your filthy hands on me again.* She had sometimes seen the bulge rise in his crotch, inside those baggy grey jogging pants, and wanted to vomit, preferably all over him, like she had that day. *Dirty bastard. Anyway only one more year, that's twelve months, fifty-two weeks, 365 days, and I'll be out of it.*

That night, after she had enjoyed a day of birthday treats and good wishes at school, another row began at home between her mother and stepfather: as usual, with a bottle smashing in the sink.

'You cow. You snivelling piece of rotting meat.'

Then her mother's rant.

'You're not much better, Mr High-and-Bloody-Mighty Davies.'

Pot, kettle; kettle, pot, thought Jodie as she

curled up into a ball in bed. *Happy bloody birthday Jodes, my arse.*

More banging and smashing of glass, more shouting and slagging each other off.

'For God's sake, you two,' Jodie whispered from under her duvet. 'Why don't you just kill each other then we can all have some peace.'

It ended as always, with a thump as Mum hit the floor. Him raging, using every foul word he knew, and Paul knew plenty. Then the bumping as he lurched into the hallway towards the stairs, a smell of alcohol pervading the house, downstairs and up. Jodie crept out of bed, clutching the baseball bat in both hands. She hid behind the door breathing in and out as softly as she could. She heard Paul outside her bedroom door, saw the round brass handle, reflected by street light, turn ever so slowly. He sounded unsteady and grunted with effort.

When he had pushed it open far enough, she shoved the door against him, heard him stagger backwards into the small hall landing, so close to the stairs, dangerously close, fatally close. It took her no more than two seconds to get out there, as he reeled in his drunken state, and push him down the stairs. Such a little effort on her part.

His head hit the banister rails several times as he fell. Jodie was sure she heard a crack as his neck broke on impact with the hard tile floor at the foot of the stairs. She went back to bed after that, putting the baseball bat on top of her wardrobe where it always lived. She slept then, a peaceful, nightmare-free sleep, not waking till morning.

The coroner recorded a verdict of accidental death, despite there being no witnesses. Jodie gave her evidence, dressed demurely in her school uniform, no hint of make-up, looking young and very vulnerable. Not that she could help much; she had been asleep and heard nothing. Mum could not add any more; she too had slept, head on arms at the kitchen table. A second bottle of vodka had been opened and was a third of the way down. There were nine empty bottles of strong ale as well, with Paul's saliva on each of them.

Mum gave him a splendid funeral paid for from the insurance money. One of those black-plumed horse and glass-carriage affairs, routed all around the estate and past his favourite pub, The Railway Arms, where his drinking buddies bowed their heads in respect as the carriage went by. Amazing how the traffic slowed down and even stopped, in places along St Pauls Road, for the cortege.

In the black limousine following, Jodie hid her grinning face under a large, black wide-brimmed hat and held tightly to Mum's hand. Her body shuddered with suppressed laughter. Mum squeezed her hand.

'Hush, Jodes, don't cry love... it'll soon be over. Be brave for my sake.'

There were no more live-in stepfathers or uncles... whatever. Mum died six months after Paul, her liver finally refusing to absorb more alcohol. Likewise, her lungs had reached saturation point as far as the toxic nicotine was concerned. Jodie last saw her mother behind the screens that surrounded her hospital bed. An oxygen mask covered much of Ellie Davies' ravaged, sunken face and finally she lost the struggle for one more breath. She died quietly, almost silently, uttering no farewells to her only daughter.

Jodie was still at the High School, studying for her A levels. The teaching staff, in sympathy, gave her extra coaching and encouragement to pass her exams, which she did at eighteen. Three A*'s and a B+. She was on her way...

She moved from the rough estate to Grange Road, Highbury, (not far from Amy's road) where the Housing Association gave her a neat little, one-bedroomed flat in exchange for the three-bedroomed house. It was within walking distance from the job she had secured at Hogarth International, and left behind were the bad memories, in that cluttered, grubby home and the overgrown, ugly estate gardens. Hers was the top flat, fourth storey, overlooking the tree-lined St Pauls Road.

Her first week at the office saw her fending off at least three pairs of groping hands. She bit the fingers of one pair, squeezed the testicles of another and ground her heels into the cheap shoes of the third, splitting the non-leather top and piercing the soft skin between two of his toes. *What was it with men? Couldn't they be in the same room as a female without getting a hard on?* She remembered fending off boys at school with their clumsy fumbling. Yuk!

Sometimes it made her wonder if she might be a lesbian, but the thought of being groped by another girl or a woman filled her with as much disgust. That was it. Jodie decided she was just a loner, apart from her friend Amy, neither seeking nor wanting sex or love. She wasn't a team player either, though she knew there would be times when you had to pretend to be one. It was a way of climbing whichever social ladder suited you. For now, she would just fit in, quietly, on the periphery. Do the job and nothing more.

Some weeks later she met Reuben Philips near the entrance to the block of flats where the wheelie-bins were kept. His pad was on the ground floor. He was tall, over six feet, with close- cropped dark hair that capped a thin but pugnacious face. Reuben kept a dog, a vicious-looking cross-breed, which was against Housing Association rules. But one look into Reuben's demon eyes, surrounded by piercings and his tattooed neck meant you didn't report him.

He persuaded Jodie to attend a secret meeting. An obscure and slightly chilling branch of an animal rights type movement. There she met more tattooed and demon-eyed people, people who planned and targeted their next victim to terrorise; daubing paint on their cars, smashing windscreens, slashing tyres. And breaking up any kiddy toys that might be lying about the garden. They put dog turd, or filled condoms, and phlegm into envelopes and posted them through the victims' letter boxes, sprayed garage doors with 'murderer', 'torturer' and pasted rotten eggs on house windows.

At first, Jodie drank it all in - like the alcoholic her mother had been. And Paul Davies. All except for the tattoos and body piercing. She preferred her body the way nature had fashioned it. Also – as she told Reuben the night he quietly but deliberately divested her of her virginity – it was a way of remaining anonymous, unnoticed in a world she preferred not to socialise in.

She stayed with the group for two more years,

making a pretence of adopting their ideas and ideals. Privately she thought they were a bunch of sadistic yobs with scarcely a brain cell between them. Except for Reuben. He had brains and evil mixed together... and those deep, hate-consumed eyes. Jodie was frightened of him, knew she had to break with him and the group, especially now there was talk of explosives being used. If her firm found out, she would not only be sacked, but probably be investigated by them and the Metropolitan Police.

One morning, after an evening meeting in Reuben's pad, followed by a restless night in her own bed, not his, she was called into the HOD's office at work. Alan Curzon was a mild seeming man, yet with a hidden, dignified strength. Jodie knew a moment of fear. Had her boss, or someone else in the firm, discovered her liaison with Reuben and his dangerous cronies?

'Come in Jodie,' Alan Curzon gave her a reassuring smile, as he stood behind his desk in an 'oldie-worldie' fashion. He pointed to the chair opposite his own.

'Sit down. Please,' he added.

When they were both seated, she gave him a questioning look, and hoped he did not sense her fear.

'Now,' he said, 'you've been with us for a little over two years, is that right?'

She nodded. 'Yes, that's right, Mr Curzon.'

'You enjoy it here?' He swept the room with his arms as if he was embracing the whole organisation of Hogarth International.

'Yeah, I do. Yes.'

He paused, made an Eiffel Tower of his fingers.

'You know we have a branch in Paris?'

'Erm, well... yes. I know there is a branch there, but that's all. I don't know anything about it.'

He smiled, paused again. 'Would you like to visit it, see what it's like? Maybe work there in Paris?'

She hesitated, though her mind didn't. What an ideal way of escaping from Reuben, from the group. She blinked. 'Yes, I would. One thing though, do they all speak French?'

He laughed a warm chuckle. 'Yes, it's their first language, but there are several British staff there and everyone speaks both French and English. I understand that you do too.'

She wondered how he knew, and then remembered her CV. 'I haven't spoken French since I left school, but... It's like riding a bike; you soon pick it up again.'

'Exactly,' he smiled again. He had a nice smile, she thought. He reminded her of her dad, the real one, of what little she could remember of Tommy Drummond.

A week later, she flew into Charles de Gaulle Airport and was met by one of the firm's drivers, who introduced himself as Antoine. 'But please, call me Toni.' (He pronounced it Tonnee). Driving swiftly, he transported her through the city centre, allowing for a brief tourist excursion, before arriving on the outskirts of Paris to what appeared to be a new town with recently built houses. This was close to a modern industrial site and a retail site that boasted hypermarkets, restaurants, children's play areas and night clubs for the adults. She was introduced to Anna Duprès, HOD of

Hogarth Paris, in a brightly lit, spacious office. Anna shook her hand and spoke English with hardly a trace of accent.

'Delighted you could come to Paris.' Though she pronounced it Paree. 'Welcome, Jodie. Now, coffee and, after, the grand tour.'

The coffee was strong and bitter. Just the way she liked it, especially as it was accompanied by small, almond-flavoured biscuits.

After being shown around the grounds and buildings of Hogarth Paris, she and Anna were driven out to see the housing estate; bright houses built of white stone, with neat, flower-filled tubs in small front gardens, and paved backyards, which had built-in barbecues and pergolas, some of which dripped with hanging vines.

'There are three-and two-bedroomed houses for the families,' Anna explained, 'and one-bedroomed starter homes that can be exchanged if children arrive.'

Not for me. I'll stick with the one bedroom, preferably on my own.

Deciding to accept the offer of transferral to Hogarth Paris, Jodie opted for no more Reubens and no more animal-rights groups...

Once again she was on her way...

Three years later, Jodie returned to the UK, disillusioned with her job, her French colleagues and with France as well. She wished she could just escape to some uninhabited island, have only gulls and fish for company: not very practical, she knew, but she was fed up with the human race, sick and tired of clumsy seductions and, generally, discontented with her life. She had changed her looks, had her hair expertly cut quite short, and managed to save a fair amount during her time with Hogarth Paris, thanks to a generous salary with bonuses, cheap housing and several affairs with munificent boyfriends, none of whom particularly 'floated her boat'.

She decided not to return to London. Instead she moved west, to the outskirts of the cathedral city of Hereford. There she paid a year's advance rental on a small, terraced house, in a nondescript though quiet street, but one reasonably close to the college, where she enrolled for an art degree course. Strangely, she had been influenced by a Parisian boyfriend who was a writer of children's stories.

'You know, Jodie,' he had said to her. 'I think you 'ave the artistic talent. Perhaps,' he had missed out the 'h' in perhaps in his very French way. 'Peut-être, you should consider a career in art.' He stroked her naked shoulder as he gave her this advice. They were lying on his bed after a belated lunch and recent love-making. 'Then,' he smiled and kissed her hair, 'You could illustrate my books for me.'

His praise had come after he had earlier watched her sketch a cheeky pigeon that insisted on stealing food from the café floor. She drew the bird on a paper serviette, screwed it up and threw it at the pigeon, causing it to hop and fly away to the adjoining café.

'Now you 'ave ruffled 'is plumes, 'is feathers as you say.' Jean-Pierre laughed as the bird flew away.

Jodie shrugged her shoulders. 'Vermin,' she declared, 'that's what they are. I don't like them near my food.' What she left unsaid was the bird's penetrating eyes reminded her (bizarrely) of

Reuben. She wished she had a small bomb to destroy the Parisian pigeons. No matter, she knew someone who did...

During the year she returned to the UK, Jodie began writing a novel. It was about a wicked stepfather and his impact on his stepchild. She put as much venom into it as possible to heal the mental and physical injuries inflicted upon her and her mother by Paul-Bloody-Davies. And yeah, she had the title, '*Tiptoeing Round Paul Davies*'. Writing night after night, inventing some of the hurt and remembering particular incidents, gave her a feeling of catharsis... but not one of peace.

She casually mentioned about writing the novel to her art tutor.

'Excellent,' he said. 'Maybe you can illustrate your own book. Thought of a title for it yet?'

'Erm... sort of. But clouds and their shapes have some significance to the story line, might make for an interesting cover.' Jodie neglected to mention about the Father Christmas cloud that had been the catalyst for her hate of Paul Davies.

'There you go then,' he said, 'plenty of scope for your artwork.'

She liked his encouragement and by day she enjoyed her art course, painting clouds in their various forms; and a still-life of a smashed and broken timepiece that won her tutor's praise. 'Reminds me of Salvador Dali,' he said.

Most nights she scribbled away in longhand, filling notebook after notebook. She promised to buy herself a laptop very soon, before the notes became too copious and time-consuming to transfer to a word processor. It was when she went to the electronics shop that she bumped into someone she knew from her days in Highbury: Amy Clifton.

They screamed at each other in recognition and Amy hugged and kissed Jodie, much to her embarrassment.

'How come you're here in Hereford?' Jodie asked.

'I work here now, a little Greek restaurant in Dean's Alley. Moved here a couple of years ago. Well a bit more, probably two years and four months now. And you, Jodes?' she added. 'What are you doing here?'

'Buying a laptop at this very minute,' Jodie grinned and this time actually gripped Amy's hands, unwilling to let go of a familiar person. She had made no friends since moving back from France and had severed all friendships over there.

'Ok, I've got nothing to do. Shall I come in with you?'

'Yeah, why not? You got a computer?'

'A netbook. Matter of fact I need a small bag for it. Might as well get it in here... although Asda's are cheaper. Maybe I'll wait till I go food shopping tomorrow.'

'But you'll still come in with me?'

'Course.'

The girls linked arms and wandered around the computer section of the store, reminiscing about Highbury. Jodie asked Amy about her parents.

'Don't ask, Jodes. I had a massive fall out with my old man just after Christmas, a couple of years ago... New Year to be exact. I mean, come on! Don't we all celebrate New Year?'

Jodie laughed. 'You do if you live in London.

Actually, it's not bad out here. I went to a hog roast and fireworks display. Pretty good it was too. We organised it ourselves, us students.'

'Lucky you. I went up to Trafalgar Square with some mates, got hammered, and was sick on the doorstep when I got home. My old man wouldn't let me in the house, would you believe? I had to spend the night on the frigging doorstep, freezing to bloody death.'

'Omigod, poor you! When did he let you in?'

'Not till about seven o'clock in the morning. Plus, it rained and blew into the porch, so I got soaked as well. Upshot was, I packed my things and moved out: went to stay at a mate's flat, on your old estate over at Grange Road. Then I decided to move here, two or three weeks later.'

'Why Hereford?'

'Dunno really... except the Greek guy I worked for in Upper Street told me his son had a restaurant here, Dionysus.'

'The god of wine, innit?'

'Yeah, that's the one. Manalo, the son, is a great guy, nice boss.'

'That's good. So have you been in touch with your folks since? Told them where you are?'

'I've been back to see Mum, but I make sure it's when he's at work. I'm blowed if I'll ever talk to him again, miserable old sod. In any case, it was time I moved out. Couldn't afford to rent in Highbury, but I gotta nice little pad here in Hereford, only walking distance from the restaurant as well.'

They chatted on, discussed some of the dotty neighbours and 'Yes,' Amy said. 'They're all still as dotty, those two weirdo brothers next door to

Mum's, and the mad galloping-major with his toy soldiers.'

Their catch up was interrupted by a young salesman. 'Can I help you guys?'

'Please,' said Jodie. 'I'm looking for a laptop, or even a netbook. Anyway, something small, that I can carry about.'

'What about a tablet?'

She hesitated. 'No, not really, I prefer a laptop, or a netbook.'

'Ok, if you guys come over here, I'll show you the latest ones.'

Half an hour later, Jodie walked out humping a laptop, a small printer, the latest Office program, and a free 6 GB memory stick, against her hip.

'Fancy a bite to eat?' she said to Amy.

'Yeah, why not? Anywhere in particular?'

'There's a nice little place near the city centre. Organic food and organic wine as well.'

Amy giggled. 'I like the sound of organic wine, long as it doesn't have worms crawling out of it or something.'

Jodie grinned. 'Don't think so.'

After they were seated and had placed their order of two chili con carne jacket potatoes, they enjoyed the first sip of chilled local wine.

'Not bad,' said Amy. 'Not as good as Pinot Grigio, but quaffable.'

Jodie grimaced. 'Bit sharp, but drinkable. So it should be at that price. More like London prices.'

'That's what you pay for organics. Think they charge you extra for the earth around the potatoes and God knows what on the grapes.'

Their food arrived and for a few minutes they ate

in silence.

'You heard of a guy called Darwin Harrison-Forbes?'

Amy thought for a moment. 'The name's familiar. What's he do?'

'He's a writer, world famous allegedly,' said Jodie. 'He came to our college not so long back: an arrogant sod.'

'D'you know,' Amy said, 'Now you mention it... him, I'm sure he used to come to the house next door to us. Years ago, I was only a little kid but I'm sure my Dad talked about him to Mum. Sort of thing they don't talk about in front of you when you're a kid.'

'Yeah, like S. E. X.'

Amy laughed. 'That's the one. There used to be some talk about child abuse next door. It was owned by an MP and he had these two nephews. You know, the ones I've just talked about... the Braithwaite brothers? Well they're grown up now, of course. In their late thirties or early forties I should think. Remember the eldest one used to look out of his window when we sunbathed in our bikinis?'

'Oh, that one.'

'Yeah. There's been some talk about it in the papers. Ever since the Jimmy Saville affair a few years back. He's a bit of a creep, the eldest one... Gabriel his name is. Odd name to call a boy... really. His brother's the cripple, walks with sticks and got one of those iron things on his leg.'

'Calliper. Yeah I vaguely remember him, didn't get out much did he?' said Jodie.

'Yeah, that's the one.' Amy nodded. 'Anyway looks like we're talking about the same guy, this *perv*. What was he like, this Harrison-whatever? When he came to your college?'

'As I said, arrogant. We're designing book covers this term and he came to talk to us about the book industry. I've been writing this biography... about Paul Davies. My ex-stepfather, remember him?'

'Yeah, didn't he die, fell down the stairs or summink?'

Jodie grinned and lowered her voice. 'Pushed more like.'

Amy's eye's widened. 'No, really? How come?'

'I did it. He came upstairs one night when he was drunk; tried to get in my bedroom. I shoved the door against him and he fell against the bannister. Only took a little push.'

'You're kidding, Jodes.'

'Am I?'

'You're not kidding.'

Jodie shook her head. 'Nope. I did it and good riddance. He used to beat my mum up... and me sometimes. I hated the ground he walked on. Vowed when I was little I'd get my revenge one day.'

'How d'you get away with it? And how come you never told me before?'

She was spared from explaining to her friend. At that moment, the barmaid came over to clear away their plates. 'Everything all right?'

'Fine,' they said. Jodie added, 'Can we have two more glasses of wine?'

'Sure. Same again?'

'That ok for you, Amy?'

'Erm, no. Think I'll have a Pinot Grigio this time.'

'Large one?' asked the barmaid.

'Why not? Be a shame to refuse.'

'Same for me,' said Jodie. 'I'll have Pinot as well.'

She waited until the barmaid disappeared with their plates, then told her about the time she spent with Reuben and his weird associates before she went to live in France. The barmaid returned with two large glasses of wine, cleared their empty ones and said 'Enjoy' before she bounced off towards the bar again.

Amy waited until she was out of earshot, her eyes bulging. 'My God, Jodes, you've been through the hoop a bit haven't you?'

Jodie smiled, but not one with humour in it. 'You could say that.' She took a gulp of the chilled wine and stared into space. Amy looked at her friend's steel eyes, glanced away again, and joined her in the momentary silence. She sipped her own drink, then after a while she said, 'And what's with this Harrison-Forbes nut? What's he done to upset you?'

'He made me look about this big,' Jodie held up her thumb and forefinger, and pinched them together, 'in front of the whole class.' Her eyes narrowed.

'How come? What did he say?'

'Well, he came over to where I was working, looked at my sketches and said they were interesting; not good or bad, but interesting. Asked me if they had any significance. I told him I was writing a book and was trying to design the cover for it. "Oh yes?" he said, "And what is your book about?" I told him it concerned child abuse. He didn't like that, you could tell.'

'No. Understandable if he was one of the pervs who used to visit them next door. So what else did he say that pissed you off so much?'

'I showed him my manuscript . Well, I couldn't really call it that, just a bunch of handwritten notes I s'pose, all in spiral notebooks. He flicked through them about a hundred miles an hour, too fast to be able to read a single word. "Is this a novel or biography?" he asked me. He had one of those sneering kinds of voices that make you want to punch them. I told him it was based on my life with an evil stepfather. Then he did kind of sneer, and waved his hand at me like he was dismissing me. "Get over it," he said and just walked away, after slapping my notebooks down on top of the artwork I was doing.'

'Ignorant bastard.'

'Yeah, arrogant too. The rest of the group thought it was a laugh. I didn't. I vowed then I'd get him back one day... who knows.' Jodie laughed as she said this. 'That's the name of this book he's just won the Nobel Peace Prize for, *'One Day - Who Knows?'* He'll know soon enough, you can bet.'

Amy took another sip of wine. 'What you gonna do?'

'You really want to know? I've got a wicked idea forming,' she paused. 'Don't know if I ought to tell you though. Might have to shoot you.'

'Yeah right. Shall we have another?' Amy was beginning to slur her words, and Jodie didn't feel that sober herself. She grinned and nodded.

'Why not? Let's get slaughtered.'

Amy stayed the night at Jodie's house. It was nearer than her apartment, plus she was incapable of getting home on her own. Jodie, although imbibing as many drinks as Amy, managed to stay comparatively sober. She got the barmaid to ring them a minicab and piled her new-found friend into it. The barmaid came running out with Jodie's parcels. 'Don't forget these,' she shouted.

'Cheers,' said Jodie, relieved. 'You've saved my life. I only just bought them this morning.' She grabbed the over-sized bags and climbed into the cab with a giggling Amy and a po-faced driver looking on.

'I hope she's not going to be sick,' he warned. 'It'll cost you double if she is.'

She wasn't and Jodie didn't have to pay double. She did, however, have a struggle between her bulky purchases and a very drunken friend. Eventually she dragged Amy through the front door, along the narrow hallway and into the small sitting room at the back of the house. Amy flopped into an armchair and fell asleep immediately. Jodie left her there all night, covered with a spare duvet, and a bowl by her side in case... Her last thought before falling asleep herself, was of the man she had begun to hate, Darwin Harrison-Forbes. Yeah, she wouldn't mind disposing of him with a small explosive, but one that would blow him into tiny fragments. *You wouldn't be so famous then would you?*

9 DARWIN HARRISON-FORBES

Darwin Harrison-Forbes was oh so conscious of having achieved world-wide fame for his book, *'One Day, Who Knows?'* And he would live off the glory of it, possibly, for years to come. The spin-offs, such as attending events like the Teme Literary Festival the week after next, giving motivational talks, and being interviewed on such occasions throughout the world would earn him five-figure sums at each attendance. Plus, travelling to these venues meant no expense was allowed to be spared by those who desired his presence.

It was 5 a.m. and in twelve days and a few hours' time he would be thrilling a capacity audience with his eloquence. Now he luxuriated in the Teme Edge Hotel's only suite that boasted a sumptuous four-poster bed, estimating the monies to be earned as spin offs from this fame. He sneered – of course – and drew the line at decorated mugs and T shirts, but mildly considered leather book markers, signed photographs and TV chat show interviews. He might even be consulted, in times of trouble, by the media, to give his point of view, impart his wisdom, enlighten and comfort the populace. And there would always be more sales of 'One Day', with second, third and possibly fourth reprints. There was also Kindle: it had to be considered. Of course the online books might not include the favourite photo of himself... pity about that.

He turned over and casually stroked the hair of the little boy who slept – exhausted – by his side.

'Come on,' he whispered. 'Louis, or whatever your name is, time to rise and shine and get your little butt out of here.'

The boy curled tighter into the foetal ball he'd assumed after Harrison-Forbes had satisfied himself on him late last night. He muffled into the pillow, 'My name's Lew-iss, not Lou-ee.'

'Whatever, dear boy. Beside the point. What is important now is you move your cute little arse and skedaddle out of Uncle Darwin's suite.'

'You're not my uncle,' came a further muffled protest. Nevertheless, the boy straightened his naked body, slid his legs from under the goose-feather duvet, and touched the carpeted floor with his feet. He brushed a hand over his tear-stained face, rubbed knuckles into his eyes, and stood up.

Harrison-Forbes switched on a bedside lamp to enable the boy to find his folded clothes on a nearby armchair and gradually dress: all the time, the youngster averting his eyes from his tormentor.

'Here,' said the man. 'A reward for your sweet company.' He tossed the boy a fold of twenty-pound notes, possibly ten of them, and smirked when he saw how swiftly the boy picked them up. 'Now go through the back door I showed you last night and walk down the fire escape.'

It was still dark outside, and chilly in the spring

air. The boy shivered; vowed he would never do THAT again. Never, never, never. His name was Lewis Drummond and he was the youngest cousin of Jodie Drummond... the girl who understood about bombs.

He knew, vaguely, of this girl cousin. But she did not know him. Her father had died before properly introducing her to his brother's offspring, and years anyway before little Lewis was born. He was eight, the middle child, between three elder brothers and three younger half-sisters. They lived in a lowlier part of neighbouring Ludlow with their widowed mother and a random selection, from time to time, of her lovers. Lewis, the typical middle child, was a tearaway, a little bastard according to his mum and whichever 'uncle' was in residence at the time of his misdeeds.

'You'll come to no good,' Gran often warned him, when he got chucked out of the house and escaped to hers. Gran was possibly the only person that Lewis ever loved, caring little for his brothers and half-sisters: all wankers. It was Gran who told him all about his dad, and her elder son, Tommy, who'd died. She thought she had a granddaughter belonging to Tommy but she'd never seen her.

'Tom's wife never stayed in touch with me,' she told Lewis.

'Bit like my Mum then?'

'Yes,' she replied and wrinkled a prune face as she said it.

Now he crept along deserted streets as dawn was breaking across an orange-streaked sky. His head hurt from the alcohol the perv had fed him, and his body from the other treatment... He had a vague memory of bathing in a really posh bath, and the lotions and potions bestowed upon him while he soaked away the street grime and drank copious amounts of whatever was in the glass, and that drowned in lemonade. Then came the baby oil and the exploratory fingers. He shut out the rest as his head cleared to what promised to be a bright new day. The folded money snuggled between his fingers pushed deeply into his jeans pocket. Not a reward, he thought, more like blood money, his blood and the perv's cash.

Gran would have a treat today. She deserved it. Always took his side, no matter what. She didn't like 'the uncles', and wasn't that keen on her son's widow, or Lewis's siblings. Apart from little Annie, the baby, who Lewis sometimes pushed round to Gran's in her buggy. Lewis of course, was Gran's favourite, the one who reminded her of both her dead sons as she often told him.

He would have to be careful, about the treat. Mustn't let Gran know just how much money he had, else she would think he had pinched it. He certainly didn't want to tell her how he 'earned' it. No way. He could hide it in Granddad's old shed. Gran never went down there since Granddad died. Frightened of the spiders she said. He would take it out bit by bit, as and when he needed it. And give her more treats.

By this time, he had reached the nearby town of Ludlow. He looked at the church clock. Still only six o'clock. Too early to go round Gran's. She'd have a heart attack if he arrived at this time... What to do? Then he saw a snack van pulling into the market area. Great, he could get a bacon sarnie and a mug of tea. That would warm him. He then remembered he only had twenties. Bugger. He could invent a story; say he was picking up an order for some night workers or something. Yeah, the van man would probably buy that. He stopped in a shop doorway, trying to shelter a bit from the chill morning air, stamping his feet and digging his hands deeper into his jeans pockets. When the man opened the side canopy and Lewis saw steam coming from the hot water urn, he sauntered over, trying to look as casual as he could.

'Morning sonny, you're an early bird. What can I do for you?'

'Erm, can I have two teas to go and two bacon sarnies, please?' *Remember, please and thank you sounds good.*

'Both for you?' The man grinned.

'Nah, one's for me, Dad. He's on the early shift and Mum didn't get up to make him anyfing to take with him.'

'How come you're about then?'

'I sometimes come with my Dad to erm... well... when Mum forgets his snack tin.' *Nosey sod ain't you? Still, just smile and stay cool.* 'Oh, Dad's given me a twenty to pay for this. Says to say sorry, but he an't got any change.' He pointed in a vague direction where he knew there were roadworks.

'Been robbing the bank, has he? The man joked.

'Summink like that.' Lewis grinned back. 'Anyway, is that ok? Can you change it?'

'Sure, sonny. But don't make a habit of it, being my first customer. The market traders'll be here soon; they usually have plenty of loose.'

Ten minutes later Lewis found himself a bench near the castle entrance and sat down to enjoy the sandwiches and hot tea. Both warmed him inside, and the sun beginning to rise and shine thawed his chilled body. He pushed thoughts of the perv to the back of his mind: wondered how he was going to spend his money. First thing, buy Gran a nice bunch of flowers as soon as the stall holder was ready to sell. Maybe get her a little statue or something as well, or a vase.

He finished both sandwiches and most of the two cartons of tea. Now he needed a pee. The toilets weren't open yet. Plan B, as his older brothers would say. He dived behind a tree, close to the castle, and watched the steam rise from his urine. He could do with a poo but that would have to wait till he was at Gran's house. Bog paper and all that. Plus, he wasn't sure how painful it would be after last night... perhaps walking would stop him thinking about it, and wanting to go.

Darwin Harrison-Forbes admired the face that stared back at him in the mirror. He turned from side to side examining each profile: decided both were equally as good. He liked his strong, square jaw, the few but attractive crows' feet feathering from the corners of his steel blue eyes, and the striking effect of a permatan from years of travelling to far flung places. Agreed there was an occasional top up on a sun bed but that was for his eyes only so to speak.

He grinned at his reflection, bared whitened teeth for inspection, licked them as he searched for any signs of aging on the rest of his face, any etched lines that plebs called wrinkles, and was relieved when he saw few.

'You'll do,' the mirror mouthed back. Yet as he

turned away, hands deep inside his dressing gown pockets, he swore he heard his reflection mutter 'Darren Horace Fawkes'.

With a darkening face and lips turning to a scowl, the permatan frowned. It was a name from the past, his past, long ago boyhood when school bullies would chant 'Darry, Horry Fawksie' over and over. Not any more, that name from the past would stay there, buried deep.

'I am Darwin Harrison hyphenated Forbes' he sneered at the mirror. 'Made up, it maybe but only we know that, you and I,' he scowled at his reflection.

He moved away, ignored the truth-seeking looking glass and thought about his entrance onto the Festival stage taking place in less than a fortnight. The street urchin was already forgotten; he had served a purpose. And been showered away.

Later he was meeting Caius O'Neill to go over the program and his needs on the day. A dressing room of some sorts, obviously. With flowers, champagne and a pretty make-up artist. Male or female, he could handle both. Caius - the Festival organiser he imagined, would already be there, hand outstretched, a beaming welcoming smile illuminating his admiration for the great, the internationally famous, Darwin Harrison-Forbes, as he climbed out of a chauffeur-driven hired vehicle.

A discreet knock at the door interrupted these ambitious thoughts, followed by, 'Room service, Mr Harrison-Forbes.'

'One moment.' He glanced again into the ormolu framed mirror, ran a swift hand through his hair, nodded approval to his reflection and gave an abrupt command to 'Come.'

The middle-aged woman who carried in his breakfast tray gave him a polite 'good morning' as she set the tray down on the circular table in the bay window. She was a disappointment. She was the housekeeper.

'Oh morning,' then, 'What's happened to the young lady who brought my breakfast yesterday?'

'She's had to go back to Latvia, sir.' She continued setting out plates and cutlery and the toast rack.

'Hm, funny time to give the staff a vacation, what with the Festival looming.'

'Er...yes,' she agreed. 'A family matter I believe. A bereavement.'

'Huh, trouble with employing these overseas staff. Family before fealty.'

The housekeeper smiled at him but did not offer a comment. She straightened up from her task, smoothed her black uniform dress under its white apron. 'Is there anything else sir?'

He gave a perfunctory glance at the table. 'No that's fine.' He fingered the five pound note in his pocket, decided it should stay where it was. There'd be no caressing this one's bottom or pinching her nipple. A curt 'thank you' dismissed her.

He poured coffee from the silver-plated coffee pot, added a small lump of crystalline brown sugar and barely a teaspoonful of cream. Under a silver plate cover he found scrambled eggs and grilled rashers. Next to this was a matching toast rack, butter dish and silver-rimmed, glass jam dish. He leaned back in the chair, gave a satisfied sigh and proceeded to eat a hearty breakfast.

He was ruminating on a day, some weeks ago

now, when he had visited an art college in Hereford. He had been asked to judge an in-house competition for book cover designs. The young woman that he spoke to regarding her artwork had also shown him a couple of filled spiral notebooks. Told him it was a novel she was writing.

As he remembered this, he washed down several mouthfuls of egg and bacon with an excellent breakfast coffee and occasional sips of freshly squeezed orange juice. He smiled, one that did not reach his eyes, thinking about her effrontery. Cheeky little tart. Had there not been all the other students, and their tutor, he would have sent her away with a flea in her ear. Instead he graciously asked her what her little story was about.

'It's not a little story,' she had hissed at him. 'Seventy-five thousand words long and counting.'

'More like a novella, my dear. What's it about?'

'It's principally based upon child abuse.'

'What, yours?'

'Maybe.'

'Get over it,' he mouthed and turned away, giving his attention to a rather lovely-looking teenage boy who had the gentlest brown eyes. He briefly watched her walk away but hadn't heard what she muttered to herself. The words most certainly didn't flatter him... or guarantee a long life.

Now his thoughts returned to the day, just over a week ahead, when he would walk onto the stage from the wings, a stage that was going to be draped at the sides in pale blue, the colour of peace. The backdrop, Caius told him, was to be of a river, somewhere in the Third World, and, apart from two gold-backed chairs, the only other ornament would be a white dove on a plinth. *Pity it couldn't be a live one, the audience would love it.* As Darwin appeared from the side, the background music of John Lennon's *'Give Peace a Chance'* would be heard.

Darwin suspected that Caius thought it all a bit naff, but not so the audience, he was sure. Darwin had heard the song, of course, he grew up in the Beatles' era. But the torture and want of the poverty-ridden countries that he constantly travelled was their pain, not his. His share of the charities donated was considerably more than that meted out to the unfortunates he met. Didn't he deserve it?

10 THE FESTIVAL VENUE

The Salopian village of Teme's Edge is renowned for its chequered history. One of intrigue for and against the king: of confiscated lands, and these same lands being restored a generation later. Nowadays it is a place of relative tranquillity. Moderately famous some of the time and quietly insignificant for much of the year... except when the rains come. And they tend to come with a vengeance, as if to punish the present incumbents for the evil deeds of the past.

They sweep down from the Welsh hills, swelling the River Teme with broken trees, bloated sheep that refuse to or just cannot swim, and dislodging huge rocks en route. Sometimes they snatch great swathes of riverside homes and gardens, leaving the villagers angry, bereft, cold and wet. They have been known to take one or two hapless people as permanent hostage, dragging their thrashing bodies along with the debris and away from the village they call home. Local folk say they can hear the cries of these drowning souls. Especially on the anniversary of the great flood of 'seventy-six'.

Especially when October looms close in the wake of the last week of September.
The village of Teme's Edge lies close to the eleventh-century market town of Ludlow: its next door neighbour, so to speak. With surrounding rich farmlands that have been producing prime meat, quality cheese, butter and an excellent assortment of fruit and vegetables to be sold in Ludlow's ancient market for hundreds of years.

The River Teme, that for most of the year meanders through both town and village, once provided plentiful trout and salmon, carp and pike for the Castle table, feeding generations of the *de Lacy* and *Mortimer* families and *Richard Plantagenet, Duke of York*. Today it is fished on a more moderate scale, for sport rather than sustenance.

It is the meadow, however – Edge Meadow – that divides and unites both town and village, where centuries ago jousting tournaments and country fairs were held. In between these annual events young boys rode their small ponies and horses, practised knighthood skills, and determined, one day, to join those noble men who served the lords of Ludlow Castle and the King.

Hundreds of years later Edge Meadow has acquired a different fame. It has become the venue for the Teme Literary Festival, attracting the great and the good from a global audience and equally world renowned writers, speakers and entertainers. The tongue has become mightier and more in use than the lance or the sword.

Caius O'Neill and Grant Saunders sat together in the main marquee, arms casually draped around the backs of their chairs. Jason, the head barman, approached them.

'Hi Jase,' said Caius. 'Bring us two coffees, will you mate? Croissants too, if they've arrived.'

'They have too,' the barman answered, his soft Scots brogue, soothing to their ears. 'Would ye like butter or jam, or both?'

Outside could be heard the banging and hammering of more marquees being erected and furnished with staging and temporary flooring.

For twenty years now, Caius O'Neill has organised this formerly rather modest event (once inviting, no doubt, the private and indulgent sneers from the likes of well-established Literary venues and their Festivalgoers). He has honed it, improved its facilities, and encouraged his many workers to make provision for larger, international audiences: he has persuaded businesses, banks and the BBC to become sponsors and local people to declare themselves as Friends of the Festival. He has succeeded.

Almost from its first year he also persuaded his good friend, Grant Saunders, to come on board. Grant, one of the few people Caius was confident could, and would, provide sustenance for the thousands he had predicted would attend the Festival. He knew Grant was capable of catering for the finicky and the robust eaters in equal measure, with a flair that would impress all who ate at his table.

They first met at technical college, where Caius studied business and event management and Grant was rapidly becoming the rising star of the catering study group. After qualifying Caius had – surprisingly – drifted into the world of television, on the accounts side rather than entertainment. Grant had borrowed money from the bank and some from his parents to buy a well-equipped catering van that he took to races, field events and the smaller county fairs; all thanks to his friend for supplying him with future events that might be covered by local television networks. He soon had a fleet of vans, had paid off both the bank and his parents with generous interest, and dispensed mouth-watering savoury chicken, beef, and pork-and-apple baps to large crowds of hungry eaters. He yearned, though, to serve more sophisticated foods, own his own chain of restaurants. He grew tired of these 'little events' as he thought of them. Which is when Caius called him, suggested a meet up in one of Ludlow's favoured hostelries to put a proposal to him, after they settled down with two pints of local ale in a quiet corner of the bar.

Caius talked of a literary festival, one that would attract the cognoscenti from all over the world. 'Given the chance and a bit of luck,' he told Grant, 'we could be looking at a business that will go global. But,' he warned, 'it would have to show itself to be the cream of sophistication, and compare very favourably to the Royal Show. Might even,' he grinned, 'be as famous as the Chelsea Flower Show and Wimbledon.'

'I like it,' said Grant. 'And I take it you're asking me to organise the catering?'

'I am indeed, my friend. I think you're more than capable and more than ready for the challenge. It'll cost you, though,' he added. 'You'll have to provide a field kitchen, as big as any hotel kitchen, and tasteful restaurant and bar areas. We wouldn't want the divas and the luvvies to scratch their little bums on park benching, now would we?'

Grant took the gamble, sold all his vans and bought a double-decker-sized pantechnicon, which he filled with outside-catering equipment: stoves, grills, ovens, bain-marie, refrigeration and pots and pans large enough to bathe in. He chose tasteful furniture for the striped-marquee restaurant areas and bistro-style for the bars. He retrained his staff, promising them rich pickings from fewer events. They had faith in him, as he had faith in Caius O'Neill. And the mutual trust paid off. As Teme Literary Festival grew, so did the wealth and fame of Caius and Grant. They branched out to Spain, France, and Italy, adopting small towns and turning them into book towns and organising literary festivals to promote them. There was talk of America and Africa. Caius was confident he could go universal, while Grant, already a millionaire through Saunders Catering Company, or SCC as his fleet of vehicles informed within their logo of a chef and a hog roast, knew he would go along with his friend.

This year the Festival was celebrating its twenty first anniversary, with a huge program of events, speakers, and authors, all boasting international fame. Among the authors were several who had served in the media covering wars from the Falklands Campaign, Northern Ireland, Bosnia, Iraq, and Afghanistan, to the present day conflicts and the latest terror groups. Many had left the media to become full-time writers, achieving renown with the written word, entertaining millions and now sharing a face-to-face pleasure with audiences of hundreds in the Literary Festival marquees. They were being joined by biographers from the world of entertainment, stage, radio, cinema and television, and fluttering the hearts of ladies of a certain age, many of whom would gladly lose their mature virginities to the aging Lotharios. The male audience drooled likewise over the female personalities, some of whom had aged gracefully, while others had become lacklustre to boringly dull. All was forgiven because fame had kept their flame alive. However, their tottering, alcohol-related performances in the morning streets of Ludlow and Teme's Edge did little to endear them to the local constabulary.

Twelve Days Later

Grant looked quizzically at Caius. 'Seems like you'll have quite a party gathering, before his performance. Didn't think you were that fond of the twat.' He was referring to Darwin Harrison-Forbes on this, the penultimate day of the Festival.

'Sure as hell I'm not. It's more to do with thanking Gerald and Helen, and Aubrey and Lally.' He paused, took another mouthful of coffee. 'I thought a little drop of bubbly before your man's performance will be a sweetener for us: get us all prepared for him. I'm hoping,' he added, 'he won't show up till after lunch so we can have our little private shenanigans without him.'

Grant was pleased his friend was inviting Gerald Seymour, his favourite author, and even more pleased the invitation extended to Helen Blundi, the Shetland author and a distant cousin of Caius.

Grant quite fancied her.

'Anyone else?'

'Erm... I wondered whether Geraldine Canova might like to join us. I know she's booked for DHF's performance.'

'Ah yes, the lovely Geraldine from Aylesbury.' Grant paused. 'Suppose you'll have to include her scatty friend... what's her name?'

'Vivacity, aka Viva. Mad as a bucket of frogs that one. At least,' Caius chuckled, 'she won't drink that much. She's thinner than a twiglet.'

'Yeah, a blade of grass in a rainbow suit. She certainly is a colourful old bird.'

The two of them fell silent, drank their coffees.

Grant said, 'You fancy Geraldine, don't you?'

Caius nodded, grinned. 'Yes, I do. She's grown on me these past few years... since she's been coming to the Festival.'

'How come you've never taken up with her, then?'

His friend sighed. 'Don't know really. Time and distance, I suppose.'

'Oh come on man, Aylesbury's not exactly off the planet. You could be down there in a couple of hours, especially the way you drive that Porsche of yours.'

'Maybe I will, this year.'

11 VIVACITY DICKSON and GERALDINE CANOVA

Vivacity Dickson was a first cousin to Mungo Dickson, their fathers being brothers. There the similarity ended. Her friend, Geraldine, considered that Viva was a glitzy, colourful person, who loved bright, bold colours, the favourite being all shades of purple. These amazing hues suited her tall, slim figure, especially with her (she often implied) prematurely grey hair that she wore in an intricately plaited pony tail, pulled back tightly from her face and tied with an equally colourful array of woven ribbons or disciplined into place with ornate tortoiseshell combs.

Viva liked stretch jeans, knee-length, good leather boots and several layers of blouses, or shirts, and sweaters over the jeans; on top of which she wore some amazing dress jewellery, collected on her travels around the world.

Before taking early retirement from her career as a teacher, in an all girls' grammar school where she taught English Literature and Language, she had also made a comprehensive study on treating the symptoms of anorexia nervosa and bulimia, especially in young people. Her pupils were the pampered daughters of the moderately rich and, some, famous. Which meant that more than a few of these girls were acutely conscious of their figures. Dieting for some was difficult, to the point of being impossible, hence bulimia became an alternative to starvation regimes. Others were happy (or desperate enough) to diet anorexically, to the point of starving themselves, and thus gain the coveted Size Zero in clothes.

Both of these were medically known as conditions rather than contagious diseases. Somehow, though, Viva managed to become 'infected' with anorexia. Not that she broadcast this, preferring instead to imply that her thinness was due to some life-threatening disease. Viva retired and enjoyed the generosity of her fellow teachers, who gave her a glorious send-off and vouchers to spend in a travel agency of her choice. Champagne, her favourite tipple, flowed and there was a well-laden table of party food. Vivacity, of course, ate little or nothing, though she contrived always to have a tiny morsel between delicate fingers when the photos were being taken, and a glass of fizz in her other hand.

The Vivacity of today did not mix overly much with people, enjoying just a few chosen acquaintances, such as Geraldine and some ex-colleagues. Her dolls were her friends, her family (apart from cousin Mungo), and these few well-met acquaintances.

She loved her antique china dolls with their

bright shining eyes: both the boy dolls, the girls, the babies and the grown-ups. Much as cousin Mungo loved his model soldiers. Each of Viva's dolls had a name to suit their personality and their role in her family. Head of her 'house of dolls', and occupying the most important seat (next to Viva's, of course), was Arsenia. Strong and powerful, Arsenia's thick, dark, wavy hair was piled on top of her head and held in place with a real tortoiseshell comb. Her brown, glinting eyes were almost as black as their dark irises.

Arsenia ruled Viva's bizarre household; at times even over-ruling Viva herself when some important decision had to be made. The other dolls, though not quite afraid of Arsenia, certainly held her in awe, and gave her respect. The only female doll who would like to have opposed Arsenia was Neima: a personage who considered herself equal if not faintly superior. Like Arsenia, she had long, dark hair, though not as long as the senior doll's, and not so luxuriant, hers being severely straight. She had slanted, tapered eyes, with a slightly Japanese look to them. They were as narrow as a knife slit and probably twice as cruel. Viva knew Neima resented Arsenia being indulged and dressed in the most extravagant and magnificent clothes. But, if truth were known, Neima would have to confess her own were not so unadorned as to be considered mediocre compared to those of her rival. She had to be occasionally 'chastised' by Mother and reassured that she was equally loved. Viva would shower the cold, china face with loving kisses and soothe the silent doll with 'Silly darling, love you, love you.'

Viva had even named one Mungo, not after her

cousin but after their distant ancestor, Mungo Park, the late eighteenth century Scottish explorer of Africa. Mungo Park's sister had married a Mr Dickson, a seed merchant from London. Viva and Mungo were descended from them. So, she supposed, Mungo Park was a many-times great uncle and William Dickson a many-times great-grandfather. Like her cousin, she thought it a pity it had not been the other way round. She quite liked the idea of being a direct descendant of an explorer; no real kudos in being a descendant of a seed merchant... not really.

Apart from their magnificent dolls' house that stood in a corner of the drawing room, Vivacity's 'family' took up residence on every windowsill, every shelf and every spare armchair and sofa in her huge house. They sat on the seat of her antique cloak stand that lived in the magnificently tiled and panelled hallway, and at the dining table with her during mealtimes. The grown-up dolls drank pretend-tea, or fizz if they were in party mood, out of specially purchased miniature flutes. They ate pretend dainty sandwiches with the crusts cut off, and exquisitely-decorated cakes, that were served on miniature china, and they used tiny silverware of the very best quality. The dolls were Viva's best friends and were treated accordingly – with love and respect. It was they who kept her from dreaded obesity, though she was far from being overweight. Far, far from.

Her parents, she had told Geraldine, recently left her this family home, one of only three in an exclusive leafy avenue on the outskirts of Hereford. She described it, Farley Grange, as very grand, one which included a sizable amount of land that was interspersed with equally huge trees; beech, cedar, silver birch and one or two oaks. To the child, Viva, it had been almost a forest, and one which contained a lawned clearing that was home to a fair-sized golden-carp pond, around which lived her fairy friends, gossamer creatures that only she could see. Beyond this landscape were two meadows that the Dicksons let out to neighbouring horse owners.

Viva had no interest in horses or the equestrian set, never had. Her horse power nowadays being in the form of a huge four by four vehicle. Its number plate bore the registration VD 001. And yes, its colour was purple, her favourite colour.

As soon as she inherited Farley Grange she sold off the meadows to a developer, who was then given permission to build a discreet estate, enclosed as it was by a variety of trees but with direct access to one of the roads that lead, eventually, to Hereford city centre.

Viva knew no one from this new estate, and was quite happy to keep this status quo. Viva had her own 'family' for day to day company, her enormous collection of Victorian dolls, a bit like her cousin Mungo and his companies of soldiers. They were sophisticated and cultured, her dolls, and Viva did like culture. For a very brief moment she thought of her cousin's Highbury neighbours, the Braithwaite brothers. Gabriel, the older one, who she considered, 'damaged', though she did not quite know how or why. The younger one, Jacob, was also 'damaged' but his was a physical disability. He walked in a crooked way with two sticks and a calliper, but, again, she had no knowledge of what was the cause of this disability. She had also learned that a moderately famous MP lived there prior to his death. He was the brothers' uncle, and had left them a considerable fortune as well as the house in Harbourne Road. How lucky, she thought, that those two boys had had such a kindly uncle...

But quickly the memory left her, she saw Mungo so seldom and visited his home in Highbury even less. Today, Wednesday, she was going to the Teme Festival to meet up with Geraldine Canova who she met at last year's events. Geraldine, a fellow school teacher and, like herself, a lover of the written word.

Back in Hereford, Viva packed a medium sized suitcase with various outfits of glitzy and colourful hues. *She does love her colours*. She also spent a full hour in front of her chevalier mirror in the bedroom, completely in the nude, to search for the least indication of fat. Closely witnessing this examination were Arsenia and Neima, her two most respected dolls. They would tell her of any dreaded overweight signs that she might miss. The fact they remained silent assured her there was no extra fat. She ignored small areas of wrinkled flesh: as Mother had always remarked, 'We are given wrinkles to show our lines of strength and character.' Whether that applied to bodily creases did not bother Viva. Her weight remained the same, slightly under what it should be for her height, well maybe more than slightly lower than. No matter, at least she could disguise the thinness with extra layers of clothes, far better than those extra cutaneous layers of skin that cousin Mungo possessed. Ugh. The very thought made her shudder, encouraging her to skip breakfast altogether, even though it would have only consisted of a dry crisp bread and boiled water with a slice of lemon. Viva was certain she saw both Arsenia and Neima nod their approval of this decision. Of course they all lived with her in Farley Grange, all of them, but these two she loved more than the others: she valued and needed their prudent advice so often.

Viva ignored the pangs and pain of hunger, smiled to herself, and got showered and dressed. Her reward for such abstemiousness, the two-day break away with Geraldine.

Geraldine Canova

For the past ten years Geraldine Canova, teacher of English in a Buckinghamshire comprehensive school, has spent the entire week at the festival, attending various speakers and events and enjoying the hospitality at the end of the evening from a friendly couple, the owners of a rather pleasant little B&B within walking distance of the venue. She takes this Easter holiday break every year from the school in Aylesbury, where she tries desperately to install a love of English Literature and Language into so many unwilling young minds.

Years before, her parents would indulge in the final week of Wimbledon fortnight, where they would enjoy centre court seats and strawberries and champagne. Sadly, the tennis entertainment has become too expensive for Geraldine to carry on this tradition on her teacher's salary, especially with the scarcity and exorbitant costs of accommodation, there being very few modestly priced B&B's within walking distance of the All England grounds. Plus, school terms and end of year examinations preclude teachers taking time off to watch tennis. Also, her home town of Aylesbury is too far to consider taking a daily ride into London, so the Wimbledon fortnight is out and the highlight of her year is, most definitely, the Teme Literary Festival.

This year she has arranged to book in the slightly odd, but picturesque, Vivacity Dickson, (who she has met at previous festivals) for the last two days of the events; relieved that Rob and Lily Champion, the owners of the B&B, have been able to manage a room for one more guest.

It was good catching up with Viva when she arrived on Wednesday evening; disappointing though that her friend did not want to join her for dinner.

'I've already eaten, sweetie. Had a meal before I left Hereford. I'll pop upstairs and unpack while you eat,' she added. 'And join you for a coffee afterwards. Unless you fancy a glass of fizz over at the festival?'

'Brilliant idea.' Geraldine recovered from her disappointment, hurried through the early evening supper as Rob and Lily called it, and looked forward to returning to the venue for champers and maybe a chance meeting with Caius O'Neill again.

Thursday Morning

Early, very early, Matilda Meadham had soaked for an hour in a deep bath before getting out and wrapping herself in warm towels and pampering her skin with expensive lotions and potions. The soiled laundry from her bed was spinning around in the washing machine and fresh linen was already clothing her bed. Obviously she had felt disgusted with herself when she awoke... obviously. But she was not going to spend the rest of the day in sackcloth and ashes. No, instead she was going off on a little adventure, to the Teme Literary Festival. Had to be a bit of a laugh, she thought. Matilda had never attended a literary festival before. Got to be a 'first for everything' had become her motto since Freddie's death.

A chance phone call last night from Bob Shackleton (she still could not think of him as stepfather, though she supposed that was what he was), from Teme in Shropshire had prompted this potential outing. He had phoned to ask did she know if Danny and Ralph were away.

'No idea, Bob: haven't heard from either of them... Must be a couple of weeks or more.' It was a lie but she was unaware that Bob knew this.

'How come you're there? Didn't know you were a bookish type?'

She heard his gravelly laughter as he answered. 'I'm not... not really. Just that my firm is doing the security for the guy who runs it. They've given me the charge of the day-to-day running.'

'Oh right.' Matilda examined the phone. 'Any

good, is it?'

'As it happens, yes. There's some big names here from the literary world, and from the music world etc. And tomorrow,' he added, 'there's that guy Darwin Harrison-Forbes speaking, you know, the one who's just written a best seller, 'One Day – Who Knows?'

Matilda said she'd heard of him. 'Sounds interesting. Wouldn't mind seeing some of the performers. Bit late now though, did you say Friday's the last day?'

'Last day but one. Still a few good acts to come on stage... why don't you get yourself up here? I think there's coaches running every day from Victoria. You could always stay over with me and the guys, we've got some large caravans on site, loads of room.'

Matilda looked at herself in the mirror, head on one side as she rubbed a small spot till it reddened with anger and bled. 'Mmn, sounds a good idea, I might well do that.'

She rang off, after promising her stepfather that she'd let him know if she was coming. Why not? What else had she planned for the weekend? Nothing, a big fat O. Plus sleeping in a caravan with half a dozen beefy security men sounded like fun. Now, after her long soak and breakfast of toast and yogurt, she felt better. Yes, maybe she would go...

Matilda heard a taxi pull up just past her house. Her neighbours, Gabriel and Jacob came out of their house carrying small backpacks and climbed into the awaiting cab. She heard the older one say, 'Victoria Coach Station please.' Wondered if they were off to the festival? Could be. Why not? Ok, get your glad rags on girl, you're going as well. Then another drew up, this time paunchy little (ok not so little) Mungo What's-his-name... Dickson came out of his house and climbed into the waiting cab. Again she heard him ask for Victoria Coach Station and watched as he yanked a small weekend case on wheels and a backpack slung over one shoulder into the black cab.

Matilda came away from the window, walked over to the wall-to-wall built in wardrobes and chose an outfit of jeans, white sweater and comfortable loafers. She shoved spare underwear, a change of clothing and – for good measure – a decent evening top into a small case before trundling downstairs. Like the Braithwaite brothers and Mungo Dickson, she called a cab, making sure there were places on the coach by calling the coach station as well. She was lucky, one seat left and a bare half hour before the coach pulled out. Again good fortune was with her, the cabby was prompt and the traffic through to Victoria light. She smiled to herself as she settled back into the freshly polished leather seat. Her hangover was gone and so were the memories of Freddie blowing wild over the railway barrier fence.

Jodie Drummond

For a while Jodie sat with her chin in her fist. She was staring in an absent minded way at the coal tits in her small back garden as they flittered through the blossoming dwarf apple trees, occasionally stopping to peck at the hanging fat balls.

Her thoughts seethed within her, and the glint in her steel blue eyes showed through narrowed slits. How was she going to place the device? Security, she deliberated, was tight, tighter than she had imagined it was going to be.

Amy. She might be able to use Amy as a decoy; to create a disturbance a few feet away. She could take the attention of the polite young men whose muscles bulged under their lightweight blazers. Or Lewis? Yes, she had gone back, but not to the house. She had waited at the bottom of her grandmother's road, knowing he would return to his mother's.

'Why didn't you come in to meet Gran?'

'Don't know, mate. Shy, I suppose. You going back home? Want a lift?'

On the short drive back to his house, she had purchased a pay-as-you-go phone for him, and punched in her mobile number. 'I'll keep in touch. Got something coming up you might want to be part of.'

Now he was part of her small team. What could she get him to do? Would he be capable of putting it in place? It only needed to be under the small stage, invisible to anyone on it, or passing by it. The device was ready to go; neatly parcelled like a boxed perfume bottle. *Avon calling!* she thought, only it didn't smell as good.

She had finished the device off here at home, packed it inside a small, oblong Easter Egg box, 6 x 4 x 4 inches. Jodie smiled with a grim humour: an exploding egg, egg on the face of Darwin Harrison-Forbes, obliterating it forever. Blown egg, blown fingers that hadn't opened the box. It would be hidden from him, under the stage until it exploded... and disintegrated his ugly body which would – unwittingly – be sitting above the Easter Egg surprise.

An hour later, she had picked up Amy from her flat the other side of Hereford and they were on their way. They stopped at a small pub en route, one whose toilets were near the entrance. There they donned wigs, spectacles with tinted plain glass lenses, out of fashion skirts and sweaters, and sensible shoes. They looked at themselves and each other in the otherwise deserted toilet and grinned.

'You look about forty,' said Amy.

'So do you.'

They stuffed their clothes into plain plastic carry bags and went into the bar. Amy ordered two coffees as Jodie found a seat in the window. She pulled out notebooks and pencils from an ample, woven handbag and studiously wrote. She gave the image, she thought, hoping they both did, of two off-duty teachers out for a day at some museum or other. Not that the role-play mattered. Amy collected their coffee from a disinterested, elderly barmaid who couldn't have cared less if the girls had been two-headed monsters from outer space. They drank the lukewarm liquid in two or three gulps, pulling faces at each other.

'Fancy paying four quid to drink that shit,' Amy scowled.

'Don't worry about it. We've got work to get done.'

In the end it had been easy. A few days before, she and Amy, separated by five rows of seats, had watched an earlier performance in the DHF tent (as they now called it). Jodie sat nearer the front, only feet away from the stage. She had examined its assembly; like raised decking, treble the height of the audience chair seats, with gaps in between the railway sleeper sized supports to allow space for electric cables. *Son et Lumiere*. Yeah right. Then BOOM!

She didn't take much notice of the talk given by some aging actor, with his steroid-taking moon face and his hair carefully combed over a balding crown, who seemed to shuffle his words around his mouth before he exhaled them to his audience. The words carried a doubtful humour, one that didn't seem to appeal to them, considering the thin round of applause he got at the end, almost of embarrassment. Jodie guessed his book signing wouldn't be at the end of a lengthy queue of enthusiasts.

According to an arranged plan, she and Amy met half an hour later in a quiet corner of 'The Hook, Line, and Sinker' pub, outside the festival grounds. But not before two staid, bookish types availed themselves of the toilets to change out of their disguises and emerge as themselves in jeans and grey fleeces.

'How many security guards?' she asked Amy once they were settled with chilled glasses filled with Chardonnay.

'Two in the entrance and one each side of the rows.'

'What? Only four altogether?'

Amy nodded, sipped her drink, changed her mind and made it a grateful gulp.

Jodie nodded and deliberated. 'Reckon they'll double that for the DHF arsehole on Friday.'

They sipped in silence, studied at each other and grinned.

'You look a tad different now Jodes.' Amy pulled a tissue from her jacket pocket and wiped away some of the pale make-up on Jodie's face. Jodie managed not to flinch... she would never really like physical contact.

12 FRIDAY

Aubrey Penhaligon was immensely fond of Caius O'Neill. Both he and Lally were. He was almost the son they had never had... That kind of fondness. They were to meet him in the hospitality tent, this morning, before the afternoon event, for champagne cocktails. Also Grant Saunders, another of their favourite young men. Lally said to Aubrey as they walked the meadow, 'You ought to paint the two of them together some time; it'd make an interesting canvass.'

'Yes... you're right, it would. I shall think about it.' And he would... think about it. Aubrey took significant time to consider most things. Life was not for hurrying, as his previous monastic life had taught him. They smiled their way through the first jostling crowds, looking forward to meeting Caius's choice of guests at the reception before the performance of Darwin Harrison-Forbes. Aubrey was also determined to attend that event, to listen to the dialogue between him and Caius, but not with any degree of admiration or respect. Curiosity more he supposed.

'I wonder what Harrison-Forbes performance will be like?' Lally broke into his thoughts.

'Eloquent I suppose. Sincere I doubt.'

'But you still want to go?'

'Why not? Maybe I shall do an unflattering caricature of him while he talks.'

Lally laughed, her special tinkling laugh. 'That's not very Godly, Aubs.'

'Maybe he brings out the devil in me.'

She nodded her head. 'Yes. Maybe he does.' Though she thought this unlikely. She thought her husband the most unlikely satanic character.

They reached the hospitality tent and were warmly greeted by both Caius and Grant, then Gerald Seymour and Helen Blundi, two of their favourite authors. And introduced to Geraldine and Vivacity. Big hugs and kisses all round, followed by bubbling glasses of champagne and bite-sized canapés. Viva sipped at the champagne and pretended a nibble at the smallest canapé, and smiled her cadaverous smile at whoever caught her eye.

Caius O'Neill considered Friday, the penultimate day of the Festival, more important than the last day. That would be taken up with circus-like workshops for the kids, a hog roast towards the evening, then Shane Waddy and the Unstoppables blasting out their music until midnight when the fireworks would begin. Caius smiled, tomorrow would take care of itself. Today was the day. When Darwin Harrison-Forbes would be on the stage with him, answering questions about his Nobel Prize-winning book, 'One Day - Who knows?'

A cold wind swept across the River Teme, sending ripples from bank to bank. It was almost like a threat of returning to winter, stultifying the spring days they had enjoyed all week. Daffodils swayed crazily along the banks and the pennants above the marquee flapped like an angry raft of ducks. Caius checked the overhead heaters of the hospitality tent. All on. Good. The atmosphere inside was cosy, and intimate, with just the eight of them, plus the barman deftly uncorking two bottles of champagne and his assistant squeezing fresh oranges. They watched as he popped the corks and filled their glasses.

'Well, Caius,' said Gerald Seymour, 'Another successful festival.'

'All thanks to you and Helen here.' He raised his glass to them. Flatterer to the end.

'I'll second that,' said Grant, licking his lips as the bubbles burst upon them.

'You certainly pull in the names, cuz,' said Helen Blundi. She had a deep velvet voice with the hint of a Shetland Isles brogue. Her latest book, *'The Blue Rose'* was the third in a trilogy about the northern isles and their historical connection with the ancient Norsemen. It had been a phenomenal success, both here at the festival and in bookshops throughout the UK. Now it was going global, thanks to her transcontinental publisher.

She and Caius were distantly related, either by great grandfathers who had been brothers or their great grandmothers being sisters. Neither could particularly remember. Helen had been more than delighted to speak at the Festival.

'Are you staying to see Harrison-Forbes this

afternoon?'

She shook her head. 'Afraid not my love. I've a meeting with my publisher this afternoon, then flying back to Edinburgh and on to the isles.'

'And you Gerald?'

'Sorry, my old love. Family gathering at the weekend. Must be there.'

Grant studied the body language of both of them. He suspected that neither of them particularly liked Darwin H-F. Not that he was surprised. He considered the man to be a patronising prat; couldn't wait for him to get his show over and leave. Tomorrow's finale should be good and entertaining. Shame about Helen going though. He liked her immensely... wished she lived nearer. His mind was working overtime, at the possibilities between them. She caught him looking at her, gave a slight nod that shook her pale auburn hair, and drew a knowing smile from attractive hazel eyes.

God, what chemistry. Grant tilted his glass towards her and smiled back. Perhaps he ought to take a few days' break once they packed up on Sunday? He imagined tramping the heather and golden sands with Helen by his side. Peat fires and malt whisky at night in some cosy croft. Caius interrupted his thoughts.

'I'll arrange for a chauffeur to take you London, Helen, and I've one who'll take you back to your home, Gerald.' Caius said.

'Oh, there's no need for that, I can catch a train in London.'

'No, no, it's fine. This chappie lives just a couple of miles from you, he'll be only too pleased to ferry you home and spend a few days with his family.'

'Excellent, in that case I shall gratefully accept.' Gerald smiled, his eyes lighting up behind his spectacles.

'Thanks for the signed copy,' Grant held up his book. He was a great fan, had all Gerald Seymour's books right through from *'Harry's Game'* to his latest.

'You're welcome, dear boy.'

They raised their glasses. 'To the festival, long may it continue...'

'Cheers, my deahs.' Lally raised her glass and touched Aubrey's with it. She smiled her engaging smile all round to include the authors and the two other guests of Caius, Geraldine and Vivacity. *What a strange lady, the Vivacity lady. Stick thin and rainbow flamboyant.*

Unaware of Lally's contemplations, Caius admired the artist's wife. She looked splendid, he thought, in her bright yellow kaftan with a bravura hue of sparkling glass beads. Aubrey's purple suit complemented her kaftan and, between them, they were a very bright addition to an otherwise slightly chilly day. The ex-monk's fine hair was ruffled by the breeze they had encountered on their way over the field and he ran his hand through it, attempting to tidy.

'So glad we caught you two before you departed, back to the wilds of Scotland and Devon.' Lally addressed both Gerald and Helen. She enjoyed a squeeze with Caius and Grant while Aubrey hugged Helen and they gratefully accepted canapés from the barman. 'Thank you Jason, most welcome.'

'Are you two are coming this afternoon,?' asked Grant.

'Yes,' said Lally.

Aubrey paused, ruminated. 'Ar... Yes, we are.'

His pausing made Grant aware that at least one other was not a great admirer of the 'big man'. He smiled, a private smile that hid his thoughts. He was enjoying this hour... and the company.

Ossie and Sheila Cutler

Ossie Cutler, is a restless soul who continually paces any room like a caged tiger. He is identifiable by smelling like the old, sometimes musty, furniture he buys at auctions, restores, and sells on again. It is a dank smell, like a basement that has long been disused and kept from the fresh air with its closed and bolted windows and doors. Ossie is tall and mostly bald, shaving both his face and his head fairly regularly.

Sheila, his sixty-year-old wife, is short, plump, and wears her bleached hair in a straggly ponytail. She likes plenty of slap on her face, tells whoever listens that it hides the wrinkles, laughing at her own joke. Ossie and Sheila have no children; it just never happened. Thus they have always been free to travel the country seeking out antiques and antique auctions. They have heard that one of the speakers at the literary festival tomorrow is Antony Johnson, television personality from the Antiques Road Show. The auction they are planning to attend prior to this is a morning one, giving them plenty of time afterwards to travel on to Teme's Edge site from nearby Ludlow. Ossie and Sheila have never been to a literary festival. Reading and collecting books has never been one of their pastimes, but they know Tony Johnson and his expert knowledge of antique furniture. They think it might be a bit of a laugh to see him in his show.

Ossie Cutler is also neither the world's slowest nor the world's most careful driver. Head bent down as he leans across the steering wheel with his right foot pressed firmly on the accelerator, he frightens his wife more than half to death. Ossie's frenetic driving means her hanging onto the strap above the passenger door for dear life, the one she calls 'the Jesus Christ strap'. Ossie's hands often juggle with hand-rolled cigarettes and the steering wheel, while his feet dance between the accelerator and brake pedals as he closes distances between himself and the vehicles in front. She has to shut her eyes when he finds impossible gaps in which to overtake.

'What's the hurry?' she choked when they were on their way. 'We're not late. The auction's not till tomorrow morning.'

'Sorry girl, you know I always drive like this.'

A non-smoker, she almost feels like lighting up one of his thin little roll-ups...or eating it.

Ossie and Sheila are antique dealers from Hardwicke near Hereford. The auction they are attending is one of general effects. Ossie thought it would be a good idea to view the lots and purchase an early catalogue the day before the event.

'Fancy staying the night?' he said.

'Yeah, why not? Where you thinking of?' Sheila imagined a night at somewhere like The Feathers, in a lovely four poster bed.

'Er, well there's a nice little B&B up near the hospital. So Harry the Medals told me. He stayed there a couple of months ago. Came up for a wartime memorabilia auction.'

Sheila swallowed her disappointment. A night out was a night out. Perhaps she could persuade Ossie that they should eat at the Feathers. She imagined you'd get a good steak there.

'Plenty of places to have dinner after we've viewed. Might even treat you to a meal at The Feathers, if you play your cards right,' he laughed. She knew what that meant. Fine, she'd play her cards right, or a whole pack, for dinner at The Feathers.

It is surprising they have never been to a Literary Festival, even though they live so close to 'the town of books', Hay-on-Wye. But discovering that Anthony Johnson, probably one of the country's finest experts on antique furniture and a frequent participant on the Antique's Road Show, is giving a talk there has encouraged them to attend. Tony will be also be selling the latest book he has written about seventeenth century houses and their contents. Being a mate of theirs, they think it might be a laugh to see him perform. Sheila has booked their tickets online and they are tucked in the bottom of her copious handbag that rarely if ever leaves her arm.

The journey to Ludlow from Hardwicke, about thirty-three or four miles, would take the average driver a little short of an hour. Ossie reckons he can do it in half that time. Sheila really wished he wouldn't. She loves Hardwicke, their gorgeous home and the converted barn where they store and renovate the furniture they buy. She also delights in walking through the streets of ancient Ludlow; it is the miles in between that are a nightmare, especially with Ossie's crazy driving. She often regrets not taking lessons and gaining her own driving licence. One way to take away the misery and terror of driving with her husband...

Ossie Cutler was annoyed. He had been outbid again by that snide little sod, number twenty-six bidder. The same one who had outbid him on several items, lots that Ossie was prepared to take or leave. But he really wanted that pair of Georgian mahogany bedside cabinets. He liked the double doors below a single drawer and the shaped apron above the chamfered legs. Nice bit of styling and he reckoned he had potential punters for them, the French's who lived on the way out of Peterchurch. The one satisfaction was that he had pushed the bidding to the limit, making number bloody twenty-six pay through the nose for them.

It was the final lot. Ossie and Sheila prepared to join the queue at the paying office. He'd successfully bid for two nice landscapes, very George Lambert in style; knew he had a definite buyer for those, and a mahogany chest on chest. He pulled out a wad of fifties from his back pocket, winked at Angie, the auctioneer's daughter, behind the glass kiosk and handed over his bidding card.

'Hello Mr Cutler, you ok? Nice to see you here. Oh hello Mrs C, didn't see you there. You ok dear?'

Sheila thanked the powers that be for the comparatively short distance between Ludlow and Teme's Edge, but still cringed as Ossie drove like a maniac down narrow country lanes and even narrower streets. Soon, but not soon enough for her, they reached Edge Meadow. Ossie allowed himself to be guided to a parking place by a little man in an oversized high-viz jacket with a serious face and a jutting arm pointing in a certain must-be-obeyed direction.

Once parked, they followed the crowds, marvelling in the candy-striped marquees, with their flying and fluttering pennants that decorated the meadow right down to the water's edge. Sheila clung onto Ossie's arm. 'Great innit?'

He nodded, smiled at her, remembering last night at the B&B. She still had the oomph, still made him rise to the occasion even if it wasn't as regular as used to be. 'Yeah,' he said. 'Impressive.'

'Time for a quickie before Tony's show?'

'More?' he said. 'Didn't I give you enough this morning and last night?'

'Silly, I meant a quick drink.'

'G and T?'

'Sounds perfect.'

They linked arms and moved towards the beer tent, which was only a few yards away from the marquee where Tony would be giving his talk. It was adjacent to the main marquee, where a large notice outside advertised Darwin Harrison-Forbes and 'One Day, Who Knows?'

'Who d'you reckon he is?' said Ossie.

'Dunno, but he looks a bit of a nob in that photo, don't you think?'

'Yeah, maybe.' Ossie dismissed him and edged his way to the bar.

The noise from the crowd was loud and varied and Sheila was enjoying the festive atmosphere. Later there would be a different noise, not one that was welcome, a lethal sound... but that, unbeknown to either of them, was yet to come. Now she was enjoying the holiday atmosphere. Besides, they were not booked in to see this Darwin whatever his name was; only Antony Johnson, their friend.

'Fancy going to listen to him as well?' asked Ossie. He was in the mood to indulge her, especially after last night's performance. He almost got a hard on thinking about it.

'Dunno. What d'you think?' Sheila screwed up her eyes as she read the advertising poster. Her specs were in the bottom of her bag.

'Up to you, love.' He paused. 'How about... we wait till we've seen Tony's show? If we like it, we can go to this geezer's after.'

'Ok.' Sheila smiled, drained her glass. 'Time for another?'

13 VIVACITY and GERALDINE continued

Geraldine and Viva have so far enjoyed listening to several well-known authors: both have indulged in buying the signed copies of most of them. Geraldine went, however, to a cookery demonstration/workshop without her strange friend. Viva pleaded a headache and said she would go for an Indian head massage instead. Geraldine, who was more comfortably curved than Viva, suspected that anything to do with food was repellent to her friend. She considered the woman's thinness was almost ugly, despite the bright colours, the spectacular jewellery and Viva's singular sparkling personality. Viva, she thought, was most definitely anorexic. But it was not a subject she cared to broach with the older woman. She had tried this on previous meet-ups and been dismissed with an imperious wave of her friend's skeletal hand. 'Just temporarily off my food, sweetie. Ate too much last week on the mini cruise.' *Mini cruise? Really?*

Today, they have booked seats to see Darwin Harrison-Forbes, the Nobel prize-winner, and meet up with Geraldine's other acquaintances from previous years, Aubrey and Lally Pcnhaligon, who, coincidently, had made a visit to her school some years ago, entertaining the students with brilliant art lectures, bright repartee, and a splendid array of colourful dress. Aubrey and Lally who introduced her, a couple of years ago, to Caius O'Neill...

She remembered that day well. The Penhaligons had arranged to meet her at the hospitality marquee. When she arrived they were talking to this rather attractive man who she seemed to recognise.

'Geraldine, how lovely to see you my deah. Come and meet Caius.'

She raised her eyebrows, thinking *Caius? That's an attractive name for such a striking male. And Lally knows him?*

'This is an old friend of ours, Caius O'Neill, he's the organiser of the Festival.'

Of course. I saw his name on the program. They shook hands and she examined his slightly freckled face that was framed with longish grey/brown hair. He smiled, displaying brilliant white teeth. But it was his angular face and square jaw that convinced her; and the Irish lilt to his voice as he said, 'Delighted to meet you, Geraldine. A lovely name,' he added, 'for a charming young lady.'

Geraldine smiled and appreciated his flirtatious compliment. She became even more convinced she knew him from somewhere.

'Thank you for your kind words, sir,' she flirted back. It sounded gauche, but what the heck? When he finally let go her hand she said, 'I know it sounds hackneyed, but I think we've met before. You certainly remind me of someone I knew.' she added. 'You haven't by some chance ever been a schoolteacher have you?'

He laughed. 'No, but my sainted mother was, God rest her soul, her wooden ruler and her size eleven plimsoll!'

Geraldine grinned. 'Thought you looked familiar. I'm sure she was my teacher many moons ago. Delfont Primary School in Middlesex. I still have her signature on my school report, G. G. O'Neill. Never did know what the G's stood for.'

'Grace Gwendoline. I believe she was known as Gee-gee, the flaring horse.'

'How on earth d'you know that?' she said. 'Don't remember you at our school.'

'No, I went to St Anne's in Hounslow.'

'Really? So did my brother, Danny, Danny Duvall.'

'Jaysus, I don't believe it! It was Danny who told me my mammy's nickname. Said his kid sister was in her class.'

'That was me.'

'Small world.' He had a very attractive and penetrating smile.

'And is there a Mr Duvall or whatever your surname is nowadays?'

'Not Duvall anymore, my name's Canova, and no, there isn't a Mr Canova...'

Geraldine was enjoying her reverie: hoped that this year would be the year that Caius prolonged their friendship beyond the Festival week. Of course she appreciated that Aylesbury was a long way from

Ludlow and Teme's Edge. But surely merely a car ride for him? Unfortunately, she did not own one herself, or could even drive, except her bicycle, and you rode a bike, not drove.

Maybe he would ask her to prolong her stay in Ludlow or Teme's Edge? Ask her to stay the night with him? A frisson of excitement ran through her. Oh yes, she would like that, very much...

'For goodness sake, Geraldine. How many miles away are you?'

Viva's voice made her jump. 'Sorry, what were you saying?'

'I was asking if we had time to see Antony Johnson in the Riverside Marquee. He's talking about his book on seventeenth century furniture.'

Geraldine glanced at her watch. It was barely ten-thirty. 'What time's he on?'

'About an hour or so before Harrison-Forbes. I don't suppose he'll speak for more than an hour and I really would like to buy his book. You must know him.' Viva looked at her friend. 'He has antique showrooms near you, in Aston Clinton.'

'Oh, that Antony Johnson. Yes of course I do, his two boys attend my school. Bit of a charmer, him not them. They're a couple of horrors.'

'Yes he is rather gorgeous, isn't he? I'd fancy him myself if he was ten years older.'

Geraldine doubted that. She had never seen Viva take the slightest bit of notice of the opposite sex, not in that way. She considered her friend to be more of a closet lesbian if anything: relieved though, she had never 'come on' to her. 'Yeah, I'm sure we'll have the time. It's still early. I was hoping we'd meet up with Aubrey and Lally this morning.' She neglected to say 'and Caius'.

They wandered through the steadily growing crowds; watched as young parents were being tugged to the various junior workshops and face painting venues, others heading for the catering tents. Geraldine spied several people with glasses of beer and wine. She mentally shrugged her shoulders, supposing, during holiday times, any hour was wine or beer o'clock. Wouldn't mind a bucks fizz herself.

Someone came up behind her, put their large, warm hands over her eyes. She guessed before she heard the voice whose hands they were and glowed. 'Caius,' she said.

'And how, dear lady, did you know it was me?'

'Smelled your aftershave. Musky and masculine they describe it, don't they?'

He took his hands away and turned her round. He planted a kiss on each cheek and a lingering one on her mouth. 'Good to see you, pigeon.'

'You too, big man.' She rather liked his pet name for her. Hoped he didn't use it on anyone else.

'And this lovely lady is...er...'

'Viva, Viva Dickson.'

'Of course.' He gave her one of his winning smiles. 'Good to see you again, lovely lady. Enjoyed much of the program yet?'

They told him the authors they had attended as he took their arms and guided them to the hospitality tent. 'We're just enjoying a glass of fizz with Gerald Seymour and Helen Blundi. Care to join us?'

'Love to,' Geraldine answered for the two of them. 'Who's the "us"?'

'Aubrey and Lally Penhaligon and Grant Saunders, the caterer of this shindig.' He indicated the site with a sweeping movement of his arm.

'Oh it'll be lovely to catch up with Grant again, and Aubrey and Lally of course.'

'We went to Gerald Seymour's performance, and Helen Blundi's. I bought her trilogy,' said Viva. 'Just love her books.'

'And I bought Gerald's,' said Geraldine. She laughed. 'He actually signed it 'To Gerry from Gerry, then his full name in brackets.'

'He's a lovely character,' said Caius and led them into the tent to join the others.

Andrew and Felicity Frith
Two Weeks before the Festival

Andrew Frith was in a dark place, both physically and emotionally. Three in the morning, a graveyard hour, he lay in his bed with his head burrowed under the duvet. It was black, whether his eyes were shut or open; black as black, as soot, as buried under the soil or in a deep, unlit cavern.

He tried to breathe silently, controlled soft, shallow breaths that even his own ears could not hear. He lay perfectly still, on his side facing away from his wife, Fizz. Cocooned in the duvet but not sheltered from his tortured thoughts. He knew they were black too, just contained flashes of insight, of guilt, of 'if only'.

Beside him Fizz slept peacefully in a soft, unburdened sleep. He heard and felt her breathing, and almost enjoyed the gentle rhythm and rise and fall of it. But, if he was honest with himself, the pleasure was tinged with envy. For her blissful ignorance of what he had done. His mind flickered backwards and forwards between the today and the yesterday of his life. He wished he could return to that yesterday, at least go back two years when he and Fizz were still a completely together item; when the shop's book sales were high. Ok, so after twenty-five years of marriage, maybe the sex was more routine than roller-coaster, maybe he got more of a buzz from their successful business than being in bed... until he met Alexia. She was the explosion that shattered his life, his smugness, the monotony of everyday sameness.

One day she had walked into the shop, a vision in a black and white panelled coat and knee length black leather boots. Her shoulder length ash-blonde hair swept casually about her shoulders like a silk scarf as she lighted her eyes upon him. A bird of prey she was and Andrew was mesmerized. He experienced a hunger that he had not felt since his student days when he lost his virginity to a very young Fizz.

What was more of a wonder, he managed to keep the affair from his canny wife. It was easy, he supposed, in some ways; he invented wholesale book and review exhibitions that were a must for him to attend while she kept shop. Yes, he did go to such shows, but for only half the whole day he was away. The rest of the time was spent in Alexia's modest cottage, not a mile away, on a rocky promontory overlooking the river Teme, its pleasant gardens terracing down to the water's edge. Not that he and Alexia spent their precious time together in the garden, more in her bedroom behind closed drapes that shut out the world for a few cherished hours. Andrew enjoyed a love-making that surpassed anything he could have dreamed of, letting his mistress take the lead and steer him into realms of ecstasy and eroticism not found in any books he had read on the subject of sex.

At first Alexia had not encroached too much upon his marriage, though he suspected he might not be her only lover. He did not care: the hours she spared him and he allowed her were sufficient. The memory of them helped him get through the worrying times that were beginning to emerge regarding failing book sales. Was the onslaught of the eBook going to destroy the hard copy? It looked that way, especially the way their takings had diminished in the past year or two. Perhaps, as they frequently suggested to each other, they ought to diversify? Sell stationery (high class of course), maybe art materials as well? They were not as wealthy as they once were and worried that their formerly successful business was going to the wall.

But Andrew and Felicity, from nearby Ludlow, were close friends of Caius O'Neill, and when he told them they would have sole selling rights for all books at the literary festival, it was one of those 'breathe a huge sigh of relief moments'. The sort of boost their failing business sorely needed, one they hoped, that would keep the bank manager happy. Caius was a good man, a good friend; he had kept the promise he had made to them earlier in the year, even charged them a miniscule fee for this privilege, knowing they were going through hard times. What he did not know, neither did Felicity, was that Andrew had been having his affair for almost two years. That, too, was draining their income, and was also draining his self-confidence and his libido, the reason being both women in his life wanted a part of him. The festival concession was a temporary relief from both failing business and Andrew's new problem, one that many a male lover dreaded. Alexia had told him, two days before the beginning of the festival fortnight, 'I'm pregnant.'

'What? Pregnant?' Then, 'You know I'm fifty, not thirty-five like you... are you sure it's mine?'

The vicious slap she had given him told him that that was not the response or the responsibility she expected. He hoped it would not leave a bruise, else how would he explain that to Fizz? How the bloody hell was he to explain anything of this disaster? As he stared at his mistress he tried to picture her as a heavily pregnant mother-to-be. The image was not appealing, neither did he want to think of himself as a father of a love child; he and Fizz had never had children, and never , he thought, missed them in their lives.

'So what are we going to do?' At least he had the decency to say 'We'.

'I don't know, you tell me.'

He sensed tears weren't far away. *Oh, please no, I can't cope with that*. 'Well, do you want it... the baby? How far gone... are you?'

'I've missed two periods.' Alexia sighed. 'And no, I'm not sure I do want it. Single parenthood is not something I relish. I don't suppose you want to divorce your precious wife anyway to give the little bastard a name.'

He resented the way she referred to Fizz. No need for that, not Fizz's fault that he'd been stupid enough to have unprotected sex. 'I thought you were on the pill.' He knew as soon as the words left his mouth they sounded lame and failed to meet her eyes.

Alexis got up, sat down again, rose once more and strode out to her tiny kitchen that overlooked the river. In the distance she could see the pennants flying above the newly erected festival marquees. Her eyes smarted with unshed tears, they were tears of anger, frustration. She felt rather than heard Andrew come up behind her, felt his tentative hand on her shoulder. She brushed it away, turned and faced him. *God, you look pathetic. How did I ever find you attractive?*

'I'm going to have an abortion.'

He swallowed. 'Ok. When?'

'It'll have to be soon, very soon. They won't do it after thirteen weeks.'

'Right.' He chewed on his lip. 'How many weeks...?

'Dunno. Probably six or seven.' She stared at him. 'You know I'll have to go private?'

He winced. *More money to pay out.* 'How much... will that cost?'

'I don't really know, never had an abortion before, never been pregnant either.' She thought about it. 'Probably in the region of a thousand I suppose.'

He shook his head, smiled without humour. 'I doubt I can raise that kind of money, not quickly anyway. We've just forked out for hundreds of books for the festival.'

Her swift reply had a hint of steel in it. 'Well you'd better make sure you sell them PDQ. Junior here,' she patted her flat stomach. 'Can't wait much longer.'

Andrew had never been more pleased and relieved to return to Fizz and their book shop. His mind reeled with Alexis' news and its implications. *Will she try to contact Fizz? Make mischief?* He felt sick to the stomach, had almost pulled up in their small rear yard when he tried to recall what he had told Fizz earlier, what excuse he had given, leaving her to man the shop and catalogue the new books prior to the festival. He can't have said another exhibition? Not at this late stage? Dammit, he was running out of excuses: wished he had never started the affair. Alexis was not a patch on Felicity, nor ever would be. Had he been a religious man - now, he considered, would be a good time to pray. What for? A bloody miracle? Flagellation with sack cloth and ashes might be more appropriate.

He parked the car, switched off the ignition and sat there trying to collect his thoughts, attempting to gather some equilibrium and think what to explain to his wife about his absence. He was surprised to see Fizz come out of the back door and disturbed at the anxious look on her face. *Now what?* He hoped Alexis had not been on the phone to his wife. The thought made him want to be sick.

'Hello love, something wrong?' He had barely climbed out of the car when Fizz rushed at him and flung herself into his arms. 'I think we've had an intruder.' The tears came then and Andrew held her close while she sobbed. He had never seen Fizz like this. He should have been here for her, not messing around with Alexis. If only time could go backwards...

'I fell asleep on the sofa... and something woke

me... a strange noise.'

'Why d'you fall asleep on the sofa?' He shook his head; trite question, didn't deserve an answer.

'I remember looking up at the ceiling and seeing the open door as a shadow. It moved, inwards, toward me. And... there was a figure.' Fizz began to cry again and he held her tight and hushed away the tears and her fear. At the same time, he hoped and prayed none of the new consignment of books for the festival had been taken. He waited a few more minutes until her sobbing stopped, then moved her more gently in his arm so he could see her face.

'Have you checked to see if anything is missing?'

She nodded, sniffed and wiped her nose on her hand. He felt in his trouser pocket for a clean hankie.

'Nothing's gone as far as I can see. Maybe me waking up disturbed him... or her.'

'How did they get in?'

'Don't know... I must have left a door unlocked. Not the shop door though. I shut up early, wasn't feeling too good.'

Andrew felt even more guilt. And shame. This lovely lady who had been by his side forever. He walked her back inside. 'Come on, I'll make you some tea and double check the shop and store room. Go and sit down.' He smiled and kissed her. *What a prize bastard.*

'How did you get on?

'What?'

'At the book thingie?'

'Oh... erm... I didn't get there. Had a puncture and had to change it then go and get it fixed at a garage.'

'Oh poor you.'

How come she hasn't worked out how long it takes to fix a puncture? Not the all-day I've been away?

'I'll go and make that tea, unless you'd prefer something stronger?'

'Mmn, sounds good, maybe a glass of vino would perk me up.'

'How about I open a bottle of fizz?'

'Fizz for Fizz.' She giggled, obviously recovering.

'Right, be back in two shakes.'

He took a look first around the store room, counted boxes and checked shelves before moving into the shop. Satisfied that nothing was amiss or missing he went through to the shop to check it was locked, then proceeded through to the kitchen. He took a bottle of Prosecco from the fridge and pulled two champagne flutes from the shelf. Feeling peckish, he added a small dish of peanuts and cheese snacks, and took them all through on a tray to the lounge, pleased to see Fizz's smile of delight. Alexis went to the back of his mind. Soon, he hoped, she would not occupy anywhere in his thoughts. He'd find the money from somewhere, pay for the abortion and finish with her for good. He was sure the feeling (or lack of any) was mutual. He hoped so.

Two Weeks Later

Now they were enjoying unheard-of sales of books by every author speaking at the Festival. Andrew was relieved. He had borrowed the £1000 from Grant Saunders to pay for Alexis' abortion. But at this rate he would be able to pay the money back fairly quickly.

'You're a bloody fool, Andy,' Grant had told him. 'Fizz is a lovely lady; can't see you doing better.'

'I know, I know,' he replied. 'Believe me I won't be doing anything as stupid again.'

'Pay me back when you can.' And that had ended the rebuke.

Andy had lacked the courage to meet Alexis face to face to hand over the money. Instead he had transferred the money into her account, hoping he would never have to see her again. She did, however, ask for one more meeting.

'I need you to come with me to the clinic.'

'I can't,' he said. 'The Festival will take up all my time for the next two weeks. Unless you can delay it for a fortnight?' he added.

'No bloody chance. Well, if you won't take me I'll have to go and come back by taxi. That'll be another hundred, or thereabouts.'

He paid the extra. Two days later he rang her to see how things had gone, but she put the phone down on him. More relief for him: at least she wasn't going to add to the drama. He began to enjoy the festival and making love to his wife again.

'I'm glad you've come back to me,' she said to him one evening. He was speechless. Had she known all the time? And now forgave him? All he could do was have the strength to look her in the eye, to gaze at her. He was about to say sorry when she put her fingers to his lips, her eyes welling. 'Don't say anything else... let's just go to bed.'

Next morning, he said, 'You know, that's the best

sex I've ever had. Talk about the earth moving!'

Fizz just grinned. 'Plenty more where that came from.'

14 WHEN LEWIS MET JODIE

Twelve days before Viva's catch up with Geraldine and Caius and friends at the festival, Lewis had walked from one end of Ludlow to the other, bypassing both his own street and Gran's. It was still too early to call at his grandmother's and he had no intention of facing the music at home for being out all night. Hopefully he could persuade Gran to say he had spent the night at her place. She'd do that for him, being as she wasn't all that fond of his mum.

The sun was now well above the tree lined horizon and he was feeling warmer, especially after the bacon sarnies and the two teas. He hid behind a tree by the roadside to pee again, badly needing to empty his bowels as well. There was a litter bin nearby with a newspaper sticking out of it. Maybe he could use that? He really was dying to go.

Five minutes later, everything done and dusted, backside wiped on fairly clean newspaper and chucked in the bin, bringing the extra relief that it had not been too painful, despite the monster's invasion of his body last night. Once more he was on the road again, guessing it was now nearer seven o'clock to six, judging by the amount of traffic. He had walked back, as far as the little village where the festival would take place. *Wonder what it will be like? Never been to a literary festival. Boring probably, all those books and words.* Lewis was not very literate, didn't like reading or writing. Didn't like school at all really, but Mum and his brothers made sure he went. Else Mum could get fined or even sent to prison they all reckoned. *Didn't mean he had to do schoolwork though, just be there.*

The site was already filling with workers, erecting more of the huge tents: some men were unravelling large cables that Lewis supposed were electric cables. There were vans of every description, advertising electrics, carpentry, catering, and sound. Luckily for the boy, most of them had logos painted on the side along with their signwriting, so he could identify them. Another crew were putting up colourful pennants on the tent rooftops. Just like olden days, he thought, when they held tournaments here like jousting. He would have liked to do that, ride a fine horse and wear shining armour...

He failed to notice a big, burly man dressed in khaki shirt and trousers with an impressive shield on his shirt pocket, emblazoned with the letters H I. 'What are you doing here, sonny? We're not open yet.'

Lewis was about to give him a cheeky mouthful; thought better of it. 'Sorry mister. I didn't know... I mean... I'm not doing anything wrong, only looking.'

'Off you go then. Time you went home for

breakfast. Been fishing or something?' The man clearly was looking for evidence of this about Lewis's person.

'Erm, no... just taken my Dad his breakfast sarnies from Mum. He forgot them when he went to work.'

'Right.' The security man peered into Lewis's soul. 'Best get home then.'

Lewis gave him what he thought was a friendly, innocent wave and made to move off the site. There, by the entrance was an almost life-sized poster of his tormentor. One of those pictures wherever you stood, the eyes followed you. Lewis felt sick and very frightened... Time to head back again to Ludlow and Gran's.

Jodie Drummond drove skilfully and quickly towards Ludlow. Amy sat beside her. She hoped her friend knew what she was letting herself in for. They had had a heart to heart two nights ago. Jodie told Amy all about her two years with Reuben and his cult followers: how she left when they started planning to make bombs. About her time in France, she said very little, only that the job was well paid and she'd had one or two casual affairs.

'Blimey Jodes, you've been around a bit. More than I've done with my life.'

'Maybe. Anyway,' Jodie paused. 'I'm about to do something now that will definitely put me on the map so to speak. You sure you want to come with me? I can always turn back...?'

'No way! I'm with you. Can't stand the bastard. Always did think he was a creep, leastwise Mum and Dad did. Expect I was too young to know what was going on. I've heard rumours since though.'

'They knew of him in France. There were whispers, but nothing shouted out loud. I just don't like his attitude or his alleged perv ways. He needs to be wasted.'

Amy laughed, turned to her friend. 'You can't blow people up just because you don't like them.'

'I know that. As you say there are rumours. I've heard more than once that he likes little boys, dirty old perv. Didn't you say those two guys who live next door to your folk were once victims of his?'

'That's what my Dad kind of suggested. He knew the MP who lived there; reckoned there were right shenanigans went on there years ago. And the crazy guy who lives the other side of them, the military collector man, called them, the Braithwaite brothers, 'damaged' D'you remember him and his collection of soldiers and things?'

'Vaguely. Chubby guy isn't he? Anyway... Mr D H-F won't damage any more young boys, not after what I've got in store for him.'

Amy gave a nervous glance at the back seat, where Jodie's backpack lay. 'Is it in there? Won't go off accidently will it?'

'No, course not. It's not even assembled yet, just parts that have to be put together.' She stopped in the next layby that was hidden from the road behind a bank of trees, turned off the engine and yanked the hand brake. 'I'll put the backpack in the boot. Best to keep it out of sight anyway, Dunno why I didn't do that in the first place. Now,' she continued when that was done. 'You sure you want to come with me?'

Amy nodded. 'Absolutely. Don't know what my boss will think. I just told them I wasn't feeling well. They weren't best pleased, so I said to take it off my holiday leave. Not that there's much of that... being as I only work the evening shift.' She grinned, like a kid bunking off school for the day.

They drove in silence for a while then Jodie said, 'We'll soon be there. Don't know about you, but I'm starving. Why I decided to leave so early, crack of dawn and all that... Just couldn't sleep I s'pose.'

'Maybe we'll see one of those snack vans in the next layby. Or we can find a café once we get to Ludlow.'

'I think there is one a couple of miles up the road. I've been on this road before, with Reuben and his gang. It's on the other side, but there's not too much traffic yet; shouldn't be too much of a problem,' said Jodie. 'There we are,' and she flicked on the indicator light. They parked up, climbed out of the car and were greeted with the smell of bacon cooking. 'Perfect.' Jodie sounded pleased with herself and Amy wondered how she could act so normal considering what she was planning. She dismissed her anxiety. Breakfast was two minutes away...

By the time Lewis left Teme's Edge and returned to Ludlow, he could hear the church clock chime eight o'clock. He brightened, ok to go and see Gran now. First though, the flowers. He reached the market stalls as the last chime sounded, and went straight to the flower stall. He had separated the twenty pound notes and shared them between the four pockets of his jeans. In each of three pockets he had put sixty pounds and the remaining fourteen pounds (his change from breakfast), he tucked in his right hand pocket. Would fourteen be enough, he wondered, for a nice bunch of flowers? Perhaps he ought to transfer another of the twenty pound notes over? No, he decided, wait and see. The flower seller might get suspicious of a young boy flashing a twenty. He would have to think up another excuse, like he did for the man in the snack van. *My Mum's sent me to buy flowers for my Gran's 70th birthday. Sorry, lady, this is all she had.* Lewis didn't have a clue how old Gran was. Seventy just sounded like an important age.

However, there was no need for lies. The flower seller (he read the word florist on a board in front of the stall) was displaying three prices for her bunches; five pounds, ten pounds, and fifteen pounds. She was wrapping one of the biggest bunches in awesome paper for another customer, and the flowers were a rainbow of colours. When it was his turn to be served, he said, 'Can I have one like that, please?' *Remember, please and thank you are important to grown-ups.*

'Nearly as big as you, isn't it?' The florist beamed at him as she wrapped the bouquet (which is what she called it). He watched, fascinated, as in fingerless mittens her hands deftly turned the coloured foil paper so that the finished wrapping looked like a shining star around the beautiful flowers. 'Is it for someone special?'

'Yeah, it's my Gran's seventieth birthday. Mum sent me to get them.' He decided to pay with a twenty note, then he would have change for a vase he wanted to get on the china stall.

'Oh, in that case, let's add some pretty ribbon.' He stared as she did miracle things scraping along the ribbon edges with her scissors until they hung all curly wurly around the bouquet. Awesome.

'Would you like a little card?'

'Erm... No... thanks. Mum's got a card, from all of us.' *Another lie. Bloody roll on, he was getting good at this.* He paid with the twenty pound note that he had carefully fished out of his left hand pocket. 'Sorry I haven't got the right money; this is all Mum had.' He put the five pounds change in his pocket before taking charge of the biggest bouquet he had ever seen.

'Thank you very much,' he said with a grateful and innocent-looking smile.

'You're welcome, sunshine. You take care now.'

Lewis decided against the vase, did not think he could manage to carry both it and the bouquet. He could barely see over the top of the flowers and stepped off the pavement in one of Ludlow's narrow streets, almost into the path of a motorist. There was a screech of brakes, horrified gasps from several passers-by, and Lewis sprawled on the road, surrounded by broken flower heads that had cushioned his fall. Two young women climbed hastily from the car. 'Oh my God,' said the driver. 'Are you all right?'

He started to cry, but nodded to let her know he was unhurt. Only he wasn't unhurt – the tears were for the terrible night he had endured, the cold morning, and the ruined flowers. The young woman helped him to his feet, tossed the damaged bouquet to one side. 'Come on, we'll get you some more. Did you get them on that market stall back there?'

He nodded again, sniffed, and attempted to dry his tears on his sweatshirt sleeve.

'You sure you're not hurt? Do you want me to call an ambulance?' Jodie had her mobile ready.

He shook his head vigorously: definitely not

that. 'No,' he sniffed. 'I'm ok. The flowers saved me, I just fell over. They were for my Gran,' he added.

'Ok, young man, hop in and we'll go get your Gran another bunch. As big as you like.' She was anxious to get away from the narrow and crowded street. Didn't want any more attention if she could help it. 'By the way, what's your name?'

'Lewis,' he said. 'Lewis Drummond.'

'D'you hear that, Amy?' She turned to her friend who had just climbed back into the car. 'He's got the same surname as me. My name's Jodie,' she informed him. 'Jodie Drummond. Maybe we're related, my Dad came from around here.'

The crowd began to disperse: nothing more to gawp at, drama over.

'What's your Dad's name?' Lewis was interested. And he was feeling better now, safe in the car with these two who were going to get him some more flowers for Gran.

'Was,' Jodie said. 'My Dad died when I was little. I was about your age.' She looked at him through the rear-view mirror. 'His name was Tom Drummond.'

Lewis fell silent. Gran had told him about his Uncle Tommy, and about a girl cousin. 'I think we might be cousins,' he said. 'Gran told me about Uncle Tommy. He died years ago, before my Dad died. I was only a baby when my Dad died so I don't remember him.'

'Where does your Gran, and possibly my Gran, live?' Jodie smiled. 'Is it near here?'

'Yeah, about ten minutes up the road. My Mum and my sisters and brothers live quite close to Gran's as well. I don't like my brothers,' he continued. 'They're all older than me. My sisters are all younger than me.'

'I thought you said your Dad died when you were a baby?'

'He did,' Lewis explained. My sisters have got a different Dad, only he don't live with us. Mum's got a different boyfriend now.'

Jodie smiled, listening to this matter of fact kid. She stopped the car outside a café, close to the market stalls.

'That was lucky, Jodes,' said Amy. 'Wonder how long we can park here? Might be nice to look at some of the other stalls.'

Jodie switched off the engine and peered out at a parking sign. 'It says waiting limited to one hour and no return for three hours.'

'That'll do us. Won't take longer than an hour to browse round the market.'

'Depends what time this young man has to get back.' She turned to him in the back seat. 'You ok for another hour, Lewis? Or d'you wanna just get the flowers and head off to your Gran's?'

'I'm fine,' he said. 'But d'you mind getting the flowers? I'll just sit here in the car for a bit. My knee hurts,' he lied.

'Ok, mate. Amy and I will get them and come back for you, that's if you feel like walking round the other stalls. There's an ice-cream van a bit further up. Fancy an ice-cream after we get the bouquet?'

'Ooh, yes please.' His face lit up, sore knee forgotten. 'But I'll still wait here till you get the flowers if that's all right.'

'Course it is.'

Presently the girls returned with a huge bunch of

flowers, ribbons blowing in the breeze.

'You didn't tell me it was your Gran's birthday.'

Lewis looked up at Jodie, but quickly looked away again. 'It isn't really,' he confessed. 'I had to make up a story cos I only had a twenty-pound note, and I thought the flower lady would wonder where I got it.'

'And where did you get it?' Jodie looked at him keenly, through narrowed eyes. 'She wondered what else this kid had to tell her, suspected there was something not quite right.

Lewis's face crumbled as if he was about to cry again. 'It's a bad story. Promise you won't tell my Gran.'

Jodie had a nasty feeling in the pit of her stomach. She also, for reasons beyond her understanding, had an ugly feeling that Darwin Harrison-Forbes was somehow part of this 'bad story'. Now why would she think that? 'I promise,' she said. 'Tell you what, let's go get those ice-creams and move off from here. We can park up somewhere quieter. That suit you?' She glanced sideways at Amy when she spoke, willing her friend to stay quiet while they got this sorted.

Lewis nodded. A glance in the rear mirror showed Jodie the relief on the little boy's face. She wondered what story he had to tell her and prepared for the worst. But first, the ice-creams...

Five minutes later they were parked in a layby on the hill above Ludlow, the only sound being them licking their ice-creams and a few birds singing in nearby trees. No cars passed by to spoil the peace.

When Lewis had finished his, he wiped his mouth on his sweatshirt sleeve. That sweater is working overtime, thought Jodie. Wonder what tales it has to tell? It seemed finishing his ice-cream was the catalyst for Lewis to tell the story of what happened to him. 'It's bad, what I got to tell you,' he said to both of them. He looked out of the window, at the town below, at the church and the castle, and the little village of Teme's Edge beyond. He could not see the hotel where he had stayed last night. Never wanted to see it again anyway. He stumbled at first, over his words and the sequence of events. But once he started he could not stop until he reached the part where the man had shown him the back stairs of the hotel and had stuffed his pockets with the twenty pound notes.

When he finished, Jodie swallowed, her eyes became slits like stab wounds and she ground her teeth together. 'What was his name, Lewis? Did you know it?'

Lewis paused, sighed deeply. 'I didn't then, but I do now. Saw it on a sign poster at the festival site. Funny name it is,' he said. 'Darwin summink or other. Double barrelled, you know, like two surnames put together.'

'Harrison-Forbes?' asked Jodie. She said the name barely above a whisper.

'Yeah, that's the one. Sort of posh old geezer he was. Cruel though...' he stopped, unable to say anymore. This time he did cry, great sobs of pain and anger and fear. Jodie got out of the driver's seat and went into the back with her new-found cousin. 'Come here, mate. Let it out, let it all out.' She seethed inside as she cuddled him, hardly daring to imagine what this young boy had gone through, not wanting to conjure up explicit scenes anyway. She cradled him, the first time in her life she had ever done such a kindness.

'Bastard,' Amy hissed from the front. 'Dirty, filthy bastard. Needs his cock cut off and shoved down his throat.'

Lewis partly stopped crying hearing this. He almost smiled. Jodie found a tissue in her pocket. 'Wipe your eyes now, Lewis, and blow that snotty nose. Let's go see your Gran.'

'Might be your Gran as well.'

'Yeah, might be.' She got back into the driver's seat. 'It's gone ten now, will she be up and about d'you think?'

'Yeah, Gran gets up early. Cracker dawn she says.' He managed a smile, but quickly wiped it from his face. 'Don't tell Gran what I just told you, will you?'

'Course not. What are you going to tell her... about being out all night?'

'I'll tell her I ran away from Zane, Mum's boyfriend. Horrible he is. Looks like a gorilla with tattoos and earrings. I'll say I stayed late with my mates and then slept in the woods or something. She'll give me an alibi for Mum. She's good, is Gran.'

Jodie followed his instructions and was soon parked outside the house. She saw the curtains twitch and had misgivings about going in. Did she want to meet her grandmother after all these years? Did she want to be involved with this young boy, her cousin, and all his family? She had been a loner for so long, she was not sure about how to deal with this situation, plus she wanted to retain her anonymity for a while.

'Tell you what,' she said to Lewis. 'You go in first, with the flowers you bought. Tell your Gran about staying out and maybe afterwards tell her about us.'

'Why don't you want to come in with me?' he looked anxious and afraid. He did not want to lose his new-found cousin and his rescuer.

Jodie tried to soothe him with a smile. 'Maybe it's better if you tell her slowly about me. Don't want to give her a heart attack do we? Anyway,' she added. 'I need to go get some petrol, then I'll come back. You should have told her everything by then.'

He stared at her, a troubled look on his face. 'You will come back, won't you?'

'Course I will, we will.' She included Amy in the lie.

Jodie watched the boy as he walked up the garden path. When he turned, as she knew he would, she gave him a wave and mouthed 'Back soon', then drove off.

'You're not going back are you?' said Amy.

'Jodie shook her head. 'No.'

'Why not?'

Jodie hesitated before answering. 'Too much involvement.' She concentrated for a moment on her driving. 'Besides – if the lady is my grandmother, she might want me to meet other members of the family, Lewis's mother and his brothers and sisters, whatever. Last thing I want now is too many people getting to know me.' Privately she was beginning to regret the Lewis incident.

Amy sat quietly. She was becoming increasingly aware of a strangeness about Jodie, a remoteness. Was she regretting getting involved with her old school friend and the dangerous plan she had hatched? No, not really. On the other hand...

Jodie drove them to Teme's Edge, and to the meadow where preparations were well under way for the coming festival. There was a smaller, square shaped marquee at the entrance to the site, with a huge board erected in front of it informing the world that this was the booking office, open 10am-4pm daily. It also advised programs were on sale there.

Jodie fished out a ten pound note and gave it to her friend. 'Go and get us a couple of programs, Amy. I'll keep the engine running in case someone wants to move us on.'

'Ok,' Amy climbed out of the car, crossed the narrow road and entered the small marquee. Two minutes later she was back. 'Bloody roll on,' she said.

'What's wrong?'

'A bloody fiver each, that's what's wrong. Can't believe it can you? A fiver for a few sodding sheets of paper pinned together.'

Jodie took a swift glance at the programs, not really a few pinned together sheets, a bit classier than that. She grinned. 'Nice artwork though, see who the designer is?'

'Blimey! Aubrey Penhaligon, him who's got the art gallery in Upper Street. Small world.'

'Anyway,' Jodie said. 'Don't worry about the cost. We need the program to find out when and where Darwin Harrison-arsehole will be giving his performance. I presume there's a map in there of all the venues?'

'I'll have a look,' said Amy. She flicked the pages. 'Yeah, right in the middle of the pamphlet. Wow... looks like there's gonna be at least ten marquees, including a beer tent, a bistro bar, and a restaurant. It's a big affair.'

Jodie did not answer her friend: she concentrated on her driving and left both Teme's Edge and Ludlow behind.

'Where we going now?'

'Back to my place,' Jodie said. 'I've changed my mind about staying up here now. Too early... we could be exposed, invite suspicion if we hang about the site too often. We don't want too many people to recognise us.' She was remembering her time with Reuben and the weirdo cult members; how they moved silently, anonymously, like ghosts.

'Oh,' said Amy. 'What shall I do? D'you think I ought to go back to work for a few days then?'

'Up to you,' replied Jodie. 'I suppose we really ought to be planning what we're going to do after. If you go back to work say, till next Wednesday, and we go back to the festival then, even if we can't get accommodation, I've got a two-man tent. We can pitch up in the woods for a couple of nights.'

'That'd be good. I get paid on Tuesday. We can always do with more money. Every little helps as they say.'

Secretly Jodie was pleased with the thought of being on her own for a few days. She had been a loner for so long that company like Amy grated on her after a while. Besides, she wanted to study the festival site map, and the timing of events, to familiarise herself sufficiently for making her plan to destroy Harrison-Forbes be successful. If she was honest Amy's constant prattle was beginning to graze her nerves, preventing her from concentrating. Perhaps, if she needed to see the site again, she'd go up on her own. Less likely to be noticed that way. There was always disguise... hair dyed, parted differently, clear glass specs, loose clothing that hid your shape... all sorts. Could even cross-dress, be a fella.

Soon they arrived at the roundabout approaching Leominster, turned left and continued on the A49 towards Hereford. A large, dark saloon was tail boarding Jodie, and flashing his lights. 'Impatient sod. What's his problem?'

'Who?' asked Amy.

'The bloke behind me... can't wait five minutes.'

Jodie accelerated, determined the road hog could wait until it was convenient to overtake. When he did pass by, it was not the driver who surprised her, but his passenger, who seemed to be peering angrily out of the rear passenger seat. She smiled to herself. *So, Mr High and Mighty, where are you off to now? Looking for more little boys to abuse? More students to discourage? Enjoy these last few days... cos that's all you have.*

'What was that all about?'

'Not a lot, just some arsehole who wants to rule the bloody road.' Jodie did not tell Amy who was in the car with the driver, but she felt very tempted to follow them. It might be to her advantage to find out Harrison-Forbes' movements. She might even be able to waste him before his oh so important appearance at the literary festival.

Before long they were approaching the outskirts of Hereford. 'D'you want me to drop you somewhere, I mean, where d'you want to be dropped?' asked Jodie.

'Anywhere near the restaurant would be good. Then I can walk round to my pad, leave my bag there and head on into work. Tell them I've made a miraculous recovery,' she added and grinned.

'Ok,' said Jodie. 'I'll give you a ring Tuesday. See if you still want to come with me.'

'Oh I will.' Amy climbed out of the car. 'I'll just get my stuff out of the back.'

15 DARWIN HARRISON-FORBES

Darwin Harrison-Forbes sat back in the comfort of the limousine's plush seats. His arm reposed on a wide arm rest as he drummed his fingers in rhythm to the music his chauffeur was playing on the car radio. Idly he wondered what that young woman was doing on the road. Had she come from Ludlow? Shrewsbury? He thought he half recognised the girl who sat next to her in the passenger seat. But could not be sure. The brief glance he got, though, tantalised him for only seconds. Darwin had an almost photographic memory.

Enjoying the smooth ride and the pleasant music he relaxed again. Then he sat bolt upright. Yes, he did recall the second girl's face, a recollection that gave him some misgivings, seeing the two of them together. What kind of weird coincidence was that? The passenger, he suddenly remembered, was much older than when he last saw her. He thought probably the last time was when he had dined at Norman's place in Highbury, London. Norman Hartley-Edwards MP, the late... and very dead

Norman. He remembered seeing the child entering the house next door, memorable, because the little brat had been screaming her head off at the time. Even the brief look he had had, convinced him it was her. How many girls had such a large brown mole on their right temple?

He guessed they both must live in Hereford, else why were they heading in that direction? Uncomfortable thought. He really did not want to come across them again if he could help it. He had two engagements in Hereford prior to returning to Teme's Edge for the festival; one, surprisingly, with the Special Forces, the other talking with senior pupils at the Cathedral School. He looked forward to both, but hoped to meet some attractive young teenagers at the latter, the younger the better. Both engagements would be finished by Friday morning. Perhaps he might head back to London afterwards? Nothing to do between Friday of this week and Thursday of next week, when he would meet up with Caius and book into the hotel in Teme's Edge. Then next day take the Literary Festival stage, by storm of course. Yes, a couple of days in the capitol might be more pleasant than languishing in some tin pot hotel in the sticks. (Unless there were more Louis' to be had). After all, Hereford being a cathedral city must mean there would be a plethora of younger choristers about. Darwin ran his tongue over his top lip in imaginary pleasure, his lascivious thoughts ran in tandem to his tongue. Nice clean little choir boys, with their delightful castrati voices and manners to match. Yes... perhaps he would stay in the city after all. The hotel was already booked: be a shame to cancel it unnecessarily, and he was sure someone on the staff would be discreet enough to furnish him with equally discreet contacts.

He slept in late after the second engagement, very late. His body, when he turned over upon waking, ached in every muscle and joint. But the pain he suffered between his buttocks was the most excruciating. Could there be a worse pain? He doubted it. Yes, worse when he moved. He felt as if he had been torn apart, ripped in two by a bestial force. It did not occur to him that he had, for years, been inflicting this same punishment upon little boys. Even two days ago, when he managed to procure an eleven-year-old chorister by a singular stroke of good fortune, he gave little thought to the pain his personal pleasure might cause.

The hotel barman had recommended a bar that the military often gathered in. Freddy, the barman, was overtly gay and obviously enjoyed the company of men, not boys. When Darwin had casually questioned him as to the availability of younger boys he said, 'Not my preference, Mr Harrison-Forbes. I prefer my fruit to be ripe, not raw.' His face took on a distinctly frozen expression and Darwin quickly turned his enquiry into a joke. Having nothing better to do the second evening of his stay, he decided to take up the barman's suggestion and visit the bar he recommended. Big mistake. Yes, the military was there, a few. So were several gay couples. Not his scene, despite his previous friendship with the late Norman Hartley-Edwards, who had enjoyed equally gratifying pleasure with mature men or their much younger counterparts. He ordered a large gin and tonic, deciding to make it his one and only in this bar, when he was approached by a guy he recognised from the speech he had given a few hours ago.

'Didn't expect to see you here,' the man said.

'Likewise.' Darwin eyed him in a speculative manner. He sipped his drink.

'Can I buy you another? My name's Garth, by the way.'

Darwin weakened and accepted his offer. 'Thank you, my name...'

'Yes I know... Darwin. Same again?'

'Yes, G&T, ice no lemon, thanks.'

They drank several until Darwin was beginning to feel slightly squiffered. 'Think I might need thum food,' he lisped. 'Fanthy coming back to my hotel?'

'Be delighted to.' Garth gave him a charming smile and a helping hand as they traversed the city on foot back to the hotel. Darwin ordered sandwiches to be served in his suite, along with a bottle of champagne. Why not? It was all on expenses. Garth came free, but not quite. His payment was given in the most brutal sex Darwin had ever experienced.

Lewis Drummond stood in front of Gran's bathroom mirror pulling faces. Gran had suggested he have a bath, get himself cleaned up.

'You look like you've been dragged through a hedge backwards.' It was one of Gran's old fashioned sayings, but she was right, he did look a bit of a mess after being run over by Jodie Drummond, his newfound cousin. Pity she hadn't come back to meet their grandmother; he knew they would really have got on. Something had stopped him mentioning her to Gran. Maybe later when he had had his bath.

16 THE THURSDAY ARRIVAL OF THE COACH PARTY

It was not worth looking out of the coach window for the first hour: crossing London and travelling westwards before heading in a northerly direction merely involved the huge and boring conurbation of suburbia until reaching Berkshire and Oxfordshire. Matilda sat in the centre seat of the back row, the only one vacant by the time she boarded. Her fellow passengers on either side of her ranged from near-hippy to frumpish middle-age. In other words, boring and not worth striking up conversations with. The middle-aged couple spoke in mumbled whispers to each other and the near-hippy couple listened to tinny music through small earplugs. So no conversation either to her or to each other. She couldn't even really appreciate the scenery once it improved, not from her disadvantaged point, squashed between the other four. Of course, there were the backs of another forty-five heads to look at. Must be something interesting to conjure up from them? No...

Mrs Frumpish pulled out a foil-wrapped package from her copious handbag and unfoiled it to reveal wholemeal sandwiches that had a distinct and unpleasant fishy smell to them. *That's all I need.* She passed one to Mr Frumpish that he accepted with a hint of a smile and a 'Thank you, dear' and began to munch on one herself. Matilda wrinkled her nose. *I've smelled better.*

'Would you like one, dear?'

'Pardon?'

'I said, care for a sandwich?'

'Erm, no thank you... but thanks for the offer.' Her previous night's bingeing rose in her throat. *Oh please, not that.*

Matilda closed her eyes pretending sleep, and closed the Frumpishes out of her mind. She was beginning to regret her spontaneous decision to attend the festival. Stupid...

At last! Matilda all but sprang out of her seat then stretched in the aisle to ease away the muscle ache of the three-and-a-half-hour journey. She spotted the Braithwaite brothers in the front seats of the coach and wondered how she had not seen them when she boarded. Then recalled a reserved notice on the first seats. So that was why. Mungo Dickson's head was also visible as she straightened her limbs, with its tonsure ring of baldness on top. *Wonder if the silly idiot is wearing army uniform under his jacket? Or brought along any of his toy soldiers?* Matilda smiled to herself, slightly contemptuous of her weirdo Highbury neighbours, all three of them. Not to worry, she thought, I don't have to mix with them. Best stay near the security men and Bob Shackleton. *Pity he wasn't a few years younger, might be worth a night or two in bed. God sakes Matilda Meadham, he's your stepfather!*

Gabriel and Jacob were the first to alight. Matilda assumed they got preferential treatment because of Jacob's disability. Understandable, she supposed, and watched fascinated as the entry and exit platform was lowered to ground level at the touch of a button. Gabriel stepped off first but Jacob refused his brother's helping hand. She raised her eyebrows, and pressed her lips together. *Huh, independent type*, she thought. It didn't go unnoticed that neither brother acknowledged herself or Mungo Dickson. *They must be aware that both of us are fellow passengers and neighbours.*

After the two got off, the rest of the passengers began to move down the coach. Matilda waited while the first few rows of seats were evacuated, before moving off along the aisle. She saw Mungo Dickson, several rows in front of her, struggle with a small backpack. He too did not turn round to acknowledge her. *You're as odd as the Braithwaites, strange man.*

Mungo had also noted the preferential treatment given to the Braithwaite brothers: last on, first off. As they stood up, Mungo observed the way Gabriel stooped slightly. Carrying the burden of his disabled brother, maybe? He wondered, not for the first time, what had caused the younger brother's physical impairment. *Shame really, good looking young man, a bit of an Adonis.* Mungo knew they were both in their late thirties, but – as Jacob stood up, resting quite heavily on his stick – he thought the younger Braithwaite, with his floppy blonde hair and clean-shaven face, could easily pass for a boy in his early twenties. He wondered why they had come to the festival.

Once they had alighted, with the self-important help of their driver, the rest of the passengers were allowed to exit the coach. Mungo stood up, pocketed the Patrick Mercer book he had been reading and hauled the strap of his overnight bag onto his shoulder.

A few minutes later they were directed from the drop-off point by a little man in a high-viz yellow jacket, holding a square 'lollipop' sign with an arrow pointing on it, who directed them to the first of the marquees. Most of her fellow passengers had collected small cases, others had backpacks or holdalls and several began to wander off towards the marquees. Matilda wandered over to wait by the first marquee, looking around to see if she could spot her stepfather among the crowd. Not that it mattered: it was barely twelve-thirty, time to find a food tent, or at least a bar.

Beyond, she could see the large meadow that was furnished with many striped marquees, their colourful pennants waving a greeting, and crowds of people wandering in and out of the vast tents. There was music playing, loud microphone announcements, children screaming with laughter somewhere or other... and an enticing aroma of food. Matilda's stomach churned. So many hours since she'd eaten her sparse breakfast, and definitely needed to look for that food tent before catching up with Bob. She just had to follow her nose to that delicious smell. The Braithwaites and Mungo Dickson were nowhere to be seen...

'What about the lodgings, Jake?' Are they far from this site?'

Jacob, stopped, leaned on his stick. 'Well, they're here in Teme, so within walking distance, I imagine. We'll ask one of the security men a bit later: they should know.'

'What about these?' Gabriel indicated the two small backpacks he was carrying. 'We gonna lug these around all day?'

Jacob could hear the gloom in his brother's voice. *Oh boy, are we gonna have one of those days?* 'Give them to me, I'll take a turn.'

'Can't we just go and find the B&B first?'

Jacob sighed. It was definitely going to be one of those days.

'Look... shall we just have a little mosey around here first, then go and find the B&B?'

'All right,' Gabriel sighed as he said it. 'Let's go grab a coffee or something.'

'Or something? Like a beer maybe?' Jacob smiled and relaxed when he saw his brother return his smile.

They entered the beer tent and saw Matilda Meadham standing at the bar. Swiftly they moved to the other end, neither wanting to be confronted by her. They saw Mungo Dickson too, who waved them over to where he was standing.

'Hi you two, what'll you have?'

Gabriel smiled, thought their neighbour was being very generous and pleasant, and was determined he would be likewise. 'Oh hi, Mungo. That's very decent of you...wouldn't mind a beer, lager if they have it. What about you, Jake?'

'Same please, Mungo.' He looked around. 'Pretty crowded, aye? Didn't expect so many. Come to think of it,' he added, and grinned. 'Don't suppose I had a clue what to expect. Never been to a literary festival before.'

Mungo succeeded in being served, and nodded his head in the direction of a high table with stools around it. The other two followed him and sat gratefully. All three of them said 'Cheers' and took long gulps before setting their glasses down again.

'So who have you booked to see?'

Jacob answered for the two of them. 'No-one particularly, today. We couldn't get seats just for tomorrow on the coach, hence our coming a day early.'

'Right,' said the older man and took another swallow of his beer. 'I presume you've found accommodation?'

'Yeah,' said Gabriel. 'Here in Teme. We've got friends from Upper Street who have a cottage in Ludlow. Had hoped we might beg a room from them, but they've guests staying till Saturday or Sunday...'

'Not the Penhaligons, by any chance?'

'Er... Yes, as a matter of fact.'

Mungo smiled. 'Actually I'm one of their house guests. And yes, they are full up. Some friends of theirs from Kent have joined them for the festival.'

'Ah...' Gabriel drank his beer. 'They do an exhibition down there don't they? Leeds Castle?'

'Yes, that's right. Ever been down that way?'

'Er... no. Thing is,' Gabriel glanced at his brother's lower torso, 'we don't get out much.'

'Well we got here, didn't we?' Jacob was clearly

annoyed. 'Just because I got this,' he pointed to his calipered leg. 'Doesn't mean we can't go anywhere.'

'No, no. I didn't mean that. But we don't go far... do we?'

Mungo swiftly changed tack. 'Anyone in particular you've come to see?'

'Not today,' Gabriel answered for the two of them. 'As I say we couldn't get a seat on tomorrow's coach up here, so we've had to come a day early. No idea who to see today.'

'Who have you come to see tomorrow?' But Mungo already guessed the answer.

Gabriel finished his drink. 'Same again?'

'Please,' said his next-door neighbour.

'Me too,' said Jacob. He added. 'We've come to see Darwin Harrison-Forbes speak... tomorrow afternoon.'

'Ah, the great DHF: went to school with him.' Then, 'How come you two know him? He's a lot older than you.'

Gabriel looked distinctly uncomfortable, lost for an answer.

'He used to be a friend of our guardian, Norman Hartley-Edwards MP. Uncle Norman died twenty-odd years ago, left us the house as a matter of fact.'

Mungo sensed their discomposure and, knowing DH-F's reputation, guessed the appalling reason for it.

17 BILL and DORIS-FAWKES

Bill and Doris Fawkes had the longest journey on the Friday. Dorrie rose as the sun began to paint its amazing colours into the north eastern sky. Along the banks of the Tees it bounced off choppy water, speckled its reflection onto the cranes that lined the dockside and crept into their bedroom window where the curtains didn't quite meet.

Dorrie sat on the edge of their bed. 'Aye Billie Boy, looks like we got a grand day for travelling down theer.'

Billie Boy turned over in their still warm bed and nuzzled his head into her pillow. He detected a faint apple smell from the shampoo she had applied last night. Dorrie slid her feet into well-worn slippers, shrugged into a winter weight dressing gown and tied it loosely round her thickening waist. Even though it was April they did not get warm spring weather up here on the Tees. Less in their non-centrally heated house.

'D'you knor, ar'm missing her already.'

'Who pet? Our wee Bracken?'

'Aye, ar am that. Still,' she added, 'we couldna

have teeken her with us. Cannot imagine dogs at such a pleece. Hope she'll be orkay in the kennels.'

'Course she will, lass.'

Bill and Doris had an almost traffic free journey down to Teme's Edge: over 250 miles in less than five and a half hours at Bill's steady pace. They left the house after a light breakfast of toast and Doris's home-made jam, washed down with mugs of strong tea, at a little short of six-thirty. Her breakfast was eaten as she prepared some cheese and lettuce sandwiches and a flask of tea for the journey. No way was she going to pay those ridiculous motorway prices. Daylight robbery.

They had followed the sun all the way, reaching Ludlow and Teme's Edge in good time to book into the little B& B and transfer their overnight case to their room, before setting off by foot to the festival site, just a ten-minute walk away.

'That was a bit of a cheek, Billy Boy... Her, making us pay in advance. Did she think we'd run off without paying? Huh.'

Billy Boy glanced at his plump, short wife and smiled. 'I don't suppose she meant bad. I think a lot of places do that nowadays... Sign of the times.'

'Aye well.' Doris left her sentence and gripped hold of her man's arm as they reached the entrance to Edge Meadow. 'Why aye, it's all going on here, pet.' Her eyes roamed round the field of striped marquees and fluttering pennants and the huge crowds.

'There's a beer tent,' said Bill. 'Fancy one before we look for the main tent where me cousin's performing?'

Doris licked her lips, screwed up her nose and

gave him one of her winking smiles that made her look even more like a little mole. 'Aye Billy Boy, sounds like a good idea.'

They joined a group of like-minded souls and patiently queued until it was their turn to be served.

'Sorry to keep you waiting, sir. What can I get you?'

Bill Fawkes felt flattered with the apology. 'No worries, young man. Not your fault we're all thirsty together. I'll have a pint of,' he let his eyes roam along the draught beers. 'Er, aye, a pint of Newcastle will go down a treat. And a half for the missus'll be good.'

The barman swiftly poured the two drinks, placed them on a small non-slip tray, and said 'that's seven pounds fifty, sir.'

Doris heard and widened her eyes to saucer size. 'Ow much? Seven pounds fifty? Daylight robbery.'

Her husband hurriedly paid, gave an embarrassed glance at the barman and indicated a space near the marquee entrance to his wife. They placed the tray on a high, round table, but neglected the stools. They could manage better standing up.

'Might as well be drinking gold dust at that price,' Doris complained.

'It's what you pay at one of these festival things,' he said.

'Could drink all evening in the Working Men's Club for that,' she said.

'Ar knor, lass, but we're here now. Just enjoy the day, there's a pet.'

After they had slaked their thirst he suggested a wander through the site.

'Sounds good to me Billy Boy. Lead on.' Nevertheless, she grabbed his arm for safety and protection against the biggest crowd she'd walked through since Newcastle won 4-1 at home against Blackpool in April 2010.

They meandered in and out of several marquees; not the ones occupied by speakers of course. That was not allowed. But they found café tents, a really posh restaurant tent, another where there were books being sold and some authors signing theirs. Bill wondered, would his cousin sign their book for them? Not as Darren Fawkes of course, he had a far grander name now; and double barrelled, Darwin Harrison-Forbes – really grand...

'Ee look Billy, there's that Helen Blundi. You knor, the one who writes those Scottish Island books.' Doris could not quite manage a stage whisper and several people turned and smiled benignly at her enthusiasm.

'Would you like one?'

'Aye, Ar would that. Haven't got her latest book. But,' she hesitated. 'We could maybe get it cheaper from Amazon.'

He smiled at her. 'look lass, we're here now. Let's not fret about the pennies. Come on, Ar'll treat you to it, and you can get her to sign it.'

Doris beamed. 'That'd be great. Ar've never had a signed copy afore.'

'Come on then, let's join her queue.'

'Don't we have to buy a book first from that bookstall?'

'Course we do, silly me!'

Once Doris had had her booked signed and carefully tucked away in her strong leather bag, they wandered about some more.

'Do you fancy a cuppa and a butty before we go to see the main man?'

‘Aye Billy Boy. You’re pushing the boat out today.’

He squeezed her arm. ‘You’re worth every penny, pet. Come on, we’ll have a cuppa then go over to the main marquee. Will you check you have the tickets on you?’ he added.

‘Course Ar have. Here.’ She plucked them from a side pocket of her bag and waved them at him. ‘Darwin Harrison-Forbes... *“One Day – Who knows”*. Bit of a mouthful, your cousin’s name. Wonder how good he is at speaking?’

Billy Boy looked at his watch. ‘We’ll know in an hour.’

Bob Shackleton, Head of Security

The security was a nightmare: hundreds of people carrying backpacks, festival carrier bags, man bags and copious handbags. Each of these could contain a lethal weapon, knife, gun, even a small explosive. There was no way he could search everyone. Besides – it wasn’t what Caius wanted. ‘It’ll kill the spirit of the festival, Robert,’ he had said when Bob voiced his concern. Better than *being* killed, Bob thought.

He could not justify his suspicions: that was all they were, suspicions, gut instincts. It was vital he watched the crowd, study body language, and tell his men what to look for. What would that be? He smiled without pleasure, more a scowl. *You can’t go by the weight of the bags; books weigh a ton, especially hardbacks. Can’t go by age... height...*

ethnicity of the people. They're all here, a kaleidoscope of humanity.

He just knew there was a someone... Who, he did not know... just someone... there, among the crowds... wanting to do mischief, to commit evil, create carnage. He spoke into his blue tooth, softly, softly. 'All systems alert. Someone, don't know who, someone is carrying. Eyes everywhere needed. Repeat. Eyes everywhere.'

The message went out to thirty men, his team. He wished they were a hundred, three hundred. There must be at least three thousand here today, maybe more: 100:1, high odds. Bob spotted his stepdaughter walking towards the main tent where Darwin Harrison-Forbes would shortly be speaking. In half an hour he thought. A slight smile played about his lips. Couldn't imagine Tilda as an intellectual. He was surprised that she even decided to come yesterday. But it came as no surprise as to her behaviour in one their five caravans last night. Not his, thank God... but he could still hear the muffled sounds and see the occasional juddering of the adjoining caravan. Lucky Steve, he thought. Or was it Travis? He supposed the rest of the occupants were on duty around the site, or at one of the local hostelries. He could not afford to give them all nights free of duties. Too much expensive equipment and items within the site that could 'walk'.

He fell into an uneasy sleep, not quite sure what to think of Tilda making it with one of his men. Granted, she was free and not his responsibility. Still... Sleep overcame his judgement.

Bob placed himself in the wings of the stage – set

up as it was like a theatre – and just out of sight of the audience. He assumed the air of a watchful man and carried the burden of a worried man. If anything life-threatening was going to happen, he reasoned, it was going to be at this performance: any time within the next hour. A glance at his digital watch told him it was 15.45, fifteen minutes before Caius O'Neill and Darwin Harrison-Forbes walked out onto this stage he was guarding. At least fifteen minutes, he thought, before all the audience (who were still filing in) would be seated. Some were shuffling through their programs, others clearing their throats prior to D.H-F's opening words. Some, Bob knew, would suck boiled sweets. He hoped there were no gum chewers. A filthy habit, especially when the gum was discarded on the streets, leaving white pock marks everywhere... disgusting, one of his pet hates.

He watched to see who chose to sit where. The front two or three rows were always taken up by the so-called cognoscenti, their spectacles reflecting the overhead lighting. Backpacks would be placed on the floor between their knees, anoraks kept on or slipped off to join the backpacks. This front row subdivision of the audience always seemed to have a superior air about them, casting disdainful looks towards the rest. Bob shrugged away these opinions. He thought of the word to describe them, prats... This was the 21st century, society being more ironed out, at least here in the western world. Impoverished countries were not in Bob's remit, neither was charity, except for Police Widows and Orphans. D.H-F, he suspected, took more from his so-called charities than he gave or promoted. Not his, Bob Shackleton's, role to judge. He was being handsomely paid to guard the bastard. Not sure now, after what he'd overheard last night, that he wanted to do that. Duty was duty though, an intrinsic importance that was ingrained in him after his years in the police force.

He was surprised to see his stepdaughter's neighbours enter the marquee. Wondered a) why they were here, and b) their determination to sit in the front row, by pulling the 'pity me I'm disabled' stroke. Jacob Braithwaite, that was his name Tilda had informed him last night, leaned heavily on his stick and walked with a curiously twisted gait. Two of the cognoscenti reluctantly (Bob suspected) relinquished their front seats for the brothers, who pinned smiles of thanks to their faces.

The ex-policeman considered the whole episode was contrived, giving him a feeling of suspicion, discomfort, and misgiving. But he dismissed these impressions. *Don't be bloody daft. What kind of mischief can those two get up to? Wave that one walking stick between them?* He also wondered what had prompted them to make the journey up from London to see Darwin Harrison-Forbes in his performance. Did they know him? Maybe they had once been victims? From what Tilda had told him, and calculating them to be at least thirty years younger than D.H-F, it was feasible. He frowned to himself, if not stick waving, what else could these two possibly do? It was worth, he thought, keeping an eye on them... just in case.

His mind was temporarily taken away from such considerations as he spotted two women and a small girl enter the marquee and sit themselves in the very back row. This was empty of any other audience, as were the two in front of it. *Odd... why not get a seat nearer the stage*? Bob thought he recognised the little girl, but not in association with the two females who accompanied her. He struggled to recall where he had seen the girl before. And why. Shook his head. *Don't worry, it'll come to you.* The two women he had no idea about: guessed their ages by what they were wearing to be latish thirties, even early forties. Both wore spectacles and very plain, slightly outdated clothes. Sloppy cardigans over turtle-necked sweaters, with tweed skirts and thick stockings that were wedged into sensible, lace-up shoes. One had a scarf tied under her chin that left only a small oval of her face showing, and a dark, curling fringe that caught in the rim of her spectacles. The other woman wore a beanie type hat pulled down over her forehead, with wisps of auburn coloured hair that were allowed to escape all round. Bob suspected the auburn hair was dyed, but it did not occur to him that it might have been a wig. He kind of smiled to himself, almost imagining them to be children who were dressing up in their grandma's clothes. That thought then gave him a feeling of discomfort, of wariness. Yes... he would definitely watch these two (three), warn the ushers (most of whom were his men) to also keep them under their scrutiny. There was definitely something disturbing about their body language. Was the little girl a willing companion? Were the two women related to her? His thoughts went back to a case he worked on and solved many years ago when he had first joined the CID. It involved a Polish couple, parents of a four-year-old girl who had gone missing. They did not report her disappearance for three days, not until their lodger also disappeared. When Bob and his team had searched the basement flat of the lodger, they discovered a child's swing hanging from hooks in the ceiling, drawers emptied of clothes, a tangled bed, and several child pornography magazines hidden under the mattress.

The lodger was caught in a motel several miles away. With the little girl who was still alive, though badly damaged both physically and psychologically. Bob wondered, hoped, the child's mind would heal. And her body. The day the lodger was convicted and sentenced occurred the same day and in the same court that an old lag was being jailed for repeated burglary.

'Do me a favour, Reggie,' Bob asked him. He told the burglar of the paedophile's offences. 'Look after him, will you mate?'

'Does that mean a reduced sentence for me, governor?'

'Can't promise anything, but we'll see.'

Six weeks later the lodger was found hanged in his cell. The persistent burglar 'found God' and received an early release.

Soon, each row was filled to capacity. An air of expectation saturated the marquee. The universal muttering died down as John Lennon's voice could be heard singing *'All we are saying...'* As the music and lyrics were coming to an end, Bob stepped quietly back into the wings to allow Caius O'Neill lead Darwin Harrison-Forbes onto the stage for a question and answer performance about his award winning book, entitled *'One Day – Who Knows'*. The two of them made ready to sit either side of a small table upon which stood a stuffed white dove, the dove of peace. The audience stood as one to give their thunderous applause... then dropped to silence and their seats as both Caius and D.H-F sat down. Caius faced his guest speaker and Darwin gave a fixed, smirking smile to the back row, unaware who occupied it... He could not, however, miss seeing who was sitting immediately below him in the front row as his gaze travelled back towards the stage. Even after twenty years, possibly, he recognised the Braithwaite brothers. They were staring at him, and not in any kind of sociable way. He shifted slightly in his seat, turned to face Caius and quietly cleared his throat.

His host stood and faced the audience, waited until the last applause and buzzing of conversation died down.

'Ladies and gentlemen,' he said and held up high in his right hand a copy of his guest's book. 'It gives me great pleasure to introduce the author of, *"One Day – Who Knows?"*. Please welcome the world famous Darwin Harrison-Forbes.'

Barely had he finished his introduction than the audience began to applaud again.

Bob chose that moment to disappear from backstage and make his way round to the marquee entrance, speaking quietly into his Bluetooth as he strode. 'All men in main marquee, keep vigilant. Back row priority, repeat, back row priority. I want you close, super-glue close.'

It had suddenly occurred to him that the two sitting with the young girl were not as old as he first supposed. Definitely in disguise and very probably not for fun and frolics. The child was wearing a school blazer (in the holidays?). As he reached the now closed flaps that were the doors to the large tent, he saw the suspicious trio making their way out. The taller woman had her arm across the child's shoulder. Protecting her from what? Bob had a really bad feeling about them now, especially the woman holding the child.

They were walking quickly away from the marquee, almost looked like they were going to run for it. Again he spoke into his Bluetooth. 'Suspects moving away from main tent. Two women, both in hats and spectacles with young girl, about seven or eight. Stop now! Detain!'

He broke into a run and met up with Travis and Steve, still contacting others in his team. The thud of boots meant his men were taking up the chase. Bob dialled 999. He needed back-up. There was something seriously wrong... A few brief words in code and he was assured that he would have the back-up he asked for. 'With you in three,' was the response. It gave him short relief as a loud explosion caused him to stop where he was and to turn around facing back to the main marquee.

The Bomb

As the audience listened, and later would prepare to give Darwin Harrison-Forbes a standing ovation, a bomb exploded under the stage, causing an upward rush of hot air and millions of splintering particles of wood, nails, iron filings and glass, plus whatever else the bomber had packed into this explosive device. The devastating effect impacted upon first the front row, then the second, third and so on. On the stage two glasses and a decanter of water on the small table between two chairs also shattered, and joined the momentum of killing metal, splintering wood and last of all, came the blazing fire. Somewhere amidst this maelstrom were two disintegrated bodies, those of Caius O'Neill and Darwin Harrison-Forbes. They were joined by some of the audience occupying at least four rows. Torn apart limbs were flung everywhere, and the cloy sweet smell burning flesh pervaded the marquee.

For those farther back, and immediately after the explosion, came a numbing, universal deafness; the fire of consuming heat, then a kaleidoscope of bodies flying in all directions in a redness of blood and a cornucopia of coloured clothing that had been reduced to rags. Of Caius and Darwin there was no identifiable sign, just skin, bone, blood, entrails, all shattered into unrecognisable fragments amid a few remains of gold backed chairs that merged in with the other colours of the unfortunate members of the audience who had been sucked in by the blast.

The marquee, partly in flames, flapped like a falling pack of cards, smothering body upon body, and fragment upon fragment that blew in the blast of the wind following the explosion. The marquee's side wings were threatening to take to the air, leaving the dead and the dying further exposed as outside rain began to fall, spattering on the duckboards laid across the field to protect the feet of hundreds of festival goers.

Next came delayed screams and cries: of pain, of terror, shock and blind disbelief as dust and earth combined into a mini tornado to further confuse and panic whoever was left alive inside the marquee. Confusion was the order of the moment; people picking themselves up from the floor, pushing away the wreckage of mangled chairs in their fear to avoid further injury, only to be trampled back down again as others also panicked to flee the scene, to escape from the rapidly spreading flames...

Grant had been lounging at the back of the marquee, everything in his field kitchen prepared for the next wave of diners, the early ones after Darwin's talk that should have ended at five thirty and before a recital by the Ludlow String Quartet due to begin at six-thirty. Grant was protected from the full blast by two hundred and fifty bodies that had been seated in front of him, listening to the great man. But the shock to his body was like being hit by an over-sized sledge hammer. His lips flared with the pain and he groaned out loud, a sound that roared like a Russian bear. But there was no one to hear his agony: not in the marquee, or its tattered and flaming remains. He could not hear himself and would not have heard anybody else's screams of agony. The explosion had damaged his eardrums, taken away all hearing except for a curious and agonising humming sound that affected his nostrils and his throat as well. He gradually managed to push himself up to a crouching position, then to stand up, shaking and dizzy, and nauseous to the stomach. At least, he thought for a brief moment, he still had a stomach to feel sick, more than so many of these poor bastards had.

The electricity had failed, leaving the tent 's

interior mysterious and shadowy. He stared into an internal murkiness. Bizarrely, there was one head visible above its chair back. Half the hair was blown away, leaving a crescent moon of baldness, but no ear on the side of the crescent. Within seconds of Grant sighting this head, it fell to the ground, rolled into what had been the aisle and lay there, sightless and missing half its hair and one ear. This time his nausea did turn to vomit, green slime mixed with a little blood. *Oh Christ, don't tell me... not internal bleeding.* But he had bitten his tongue and that had caused the vomit to be mixed with his blood. His calculating mind worked out the headless body had been sitting in row four. A scrap of remembered conversation heard from a guy upon entering the marquee with two other guys, one with a walking disability who carried a stick. They: apparently knew each other from elsewhere. The head with half its hair missing Grant now remembered was saying something about going to school with Darwin Harrison-Forbes and not wanting to join the other two in the front row. Grant had read his name on an ID disc attached to his backpack. Mungo Dickson. He had smiled when he read the name, knowing there was another Dickson inside, Vivacity Dickson. He had wondered at the time might they be related? She was, he knew, a descendent of some Scottish explorer, not a Dickson but a man called Park, Mungo Park. Mungo Dickson, in that case, could well be related to her. Grant had also spotted a military book peeping out of Mungo Dickson's backpack, a new book, bought possibly, very recently, here at the festival. So he was possibly one of the fraternity who collected antique lead soldiers; 'arranged' battles with them in his attic or on a spare room floor. Bully for him, thought Grant, wish I had time for a hobby. *No you don't. Not toy soldiers anyway...* He felt a moment's sadness for the head, and its separated body. Mungo Dickson, if that is who it was, had lost his last battle.

In the third row from the front, Geraldine Canova, Gerry as Caius now called her had sat next to her friend, Vivacity. What was left of her friend, Grant suspected, was draped lifeless and shapeless over the back of a mostly disintegrated chair. There was something on the ground, next to the charred chair. It appeared to be a long grey plait still tied, but now with tattered, shrivelled ribbons. For a moment the scene reminded Grant of the head of a stuffed doll devoid of its stuffing... But he could see now it was a wig. Viva wore a wig? He badly wanted to laugh but cried instead. A wig. What is it with heads and explosions, he wondered as he sniffed away the tears? He shook his own, still intact head, told himself not to be so fucking stupid. Then wiped his vomit-smeared mouth and struggled to peer through the gloom to see if there was anyone else, or any more remains.

Geraldine was there, also dead and also just pitiful remains, a brightly coloured scarf that she had worn jauntily across her shoulders, now shrivelled and minus most of the body it had adorned. Perhaps that was an arm... perhaps not. He could not bear to look again, and felt a sadness for his friend Caius's loss. Until he realised that there was no Caius. Not anymore. He doubted there would be anything recognisable of his friend to bury. Or that of Darwin Harrison-Forbes. That's if all or most of their body pieces could be found, scattered as they were among the ruins. As for cremation... what for? Grant collapsed on the grass outside the marquee, away from the flames and the carnage. He couldn't stay like this. He must do something... anything. He must rouse himself... get to the food tent.

Fate was kind to one couple who knew Darwin Harrison-Forbes. Bill and Doris Fawkes, DH-F's cousin and his wife, who had driven all the way down from the north-east of England. Bill was too modest to try for front seats for the pair of them, and that humility had saved them. They found two vacant seats at the back of the marquee, next to two young women and a little girl. Doris had smiled at the child and said to her, 'Are you looking forward to it, pet?'

The little girl first glanced at the two women who sat the other side of her before nodding her head. Doris thought it a little strange the way the child's head moved out of sync with her fringe. Maybe a bad haircut. She turned back to her husband.

'Will it be away soon?' and nodded towards the stage.

'Aye, pet. Not long now.' They grinned at each other and squeezed hands. Doris loved her Billy Boy and he was quietly fond of his little wife with her mole-like face.

After the explosion they were temporarily flattened to the ground, speechless as the acrid burning seemed to suck the air out of their lungs. They crawled out of the burning marquee and began to follow Grant, recognising him as the man who had been standing near them at the back of the marquee, and as someone to do with the festival by his chef's whites, only now his jacket was blackened with smoke. The young women and the little girl were nowhere to be seen. The young man, in the soiled chef's jacket, who had stood near to them, was crying, the tears making pale rivulets down his otherwise blemished face. They were unaware that he was a friend of Caius; neither did they know that he considered Bill's cousin a complete and utter twat. Not that it mattered anymore; Darwin Harrison-Forbes was a dead twat. In pieces. Unrecognisable.

What Bob Shackleton saw sickened him to the stomach, the roof in flames, with billowing smoke invading the surrounding marquees. He heard screams, watched as people staggered in all directions, bags banging against their legs or shoulders, eyes bulging in fear. The sun had deserted this festival, to be replaced by rain mixing with black smoke and leaping flames that strained to catch on to neighbouring marquees.

In the not too far away distance he heard the ringing of fire engines and the wailing of ambulances mixed with blaring police sirens. He ran towards the main marquee, or what was left of it. Flaming canvass flew high into the sky, leaving a buckled framework and many injured beneath and beside it. For one swift moment he paused, what if there was a second bomb? But his pause was short-lived; there were many people in there screaming, moaning, whimpering. He had to rescue as many as possible. He was not alone, several of his men had joined him, all heedless of their own safety, or at least more aware of those inside the burning structure.

There were some, many, that could not be saved, or were even recognisable. Mungo Dickson had lost this his last military battle, Gabriel and Jacob Braithwaite had missed their chance of retribution against their childhood tormentor and a subsequent peace. Both were killed, instantly. No time for reprisal against their enemy, Darwin Harrison-Forbes. No opportunity to disgrace him in front of this audience of two hundred and fifty. The blast had happened so soon after everyone was seated.

Matilda Meadham failed in her chance of a literary experience and of a second night with a security guard called Travis Stanner in a caravan. She would be spending weeks in hospital, in the special burns unit, as the skilled medical staff did their best to rebuild her badly burned face. She would not become a serial killer like her mother, Delia, had been. Nor would she marry for a third or fourth time like her mother did.

Had the world been made safe by her horrifying injuries? Or a little safer? But first she had to be airlifted to hospital. Bob made it one of his first priorities, after all, she was his step-daughter. Once he had seen her safely stretchered away he returned to the carnage to do what he could in helping the other victims of the cruel bomb.

Two other survivors of the blast were Andrew and Felicity Frith, the festival booksellers. Their adjoining tent had somehow and miraculously survived the explosion and the fire. It was wobbly but still standing. Books, of course, had toppled, balanced as they were like a tower. So far, they had not gone up in flames. Which was unfortunate for Andrew and Fizz. Under the table were several cardboard boxes containing six hundred books with the title '*One Day-Who knows?*' They were going to be a sell-out, both for their author, Darwin Harrison-Forbes, when he held his book signing after his onstage discussion with Caius O'Neill, and later, another with the two book sellers. It did not take Andrew too long to guess who had been blown up.

Fizz, unlike her husband, was already crying for the dead and the injured. Her body had assumed a frozen statue pose for a few seconds after the bomb went off, so very near to their venue as it was, causing the marquee canvass to blow hysterically like delicate muslin in a gale-strong breeze. Then the books had fallen, and so had she and Andrew. He recovered first, and helped her to her feet again despite the shock and horror. Their arms were thrashing about as they tried to catch books, avoid flying debris, even hold onto other people that were stumbling about in the maelstrom of the devastation.

Other emotions were flashing through Andrew's mind. Not the bomb or who had planted it and where. It had to be DHF who was targeted. Andrew was not concerned how many were injured or dead. He was thinking, counting. How many sales had they lost? How the hell could they sell all these books without their being autographed? How?

Fizz screamed at him. 'The flames are coming

nearer. We've got to save the bloody books.' She was tearing at the loosened flaps of the boxes, trying to move them out of danger. 'Help me, for God's sake, help me.'

He made a split second decision. 'Leave them.' He grabbed her arm as flames began to lick at the tent flaps. She dragged her feet. 'No. No. We must save the books.'

'What bloody for, you stupid bitch? He's dead. He must be. Let's get the hell out.' She guessed who 'he' was.

The flames won over the falling rain. It had been no more than a thunderous April shower which rumbled off like a bad tempered elephant. But it was not replaced by sunshine; that too had disappeared behind toxic smoke fumes which were now billowing upwards. Andrew succeeded in dragging his wife free from the danger and pandemonium. They stumbled towards the river bank, following some of the bewildered and bedraggled crowd.

Fizz still cried for the dead and injured. And her books. Their future. 'We'll be ruined now, for sure.'

'No we won't. Caius 'll have all this insured.'

In the now emptying festival car park, many vehicles remained unclaimed, including an aging Volvo hatchback that was stacked with auction lots from one of the nearby Ludlow auction rooms. Its owners had made a last minute decision to go and listen to a nob with a double barrelled name who would be on after their friend, Tony, had given his talk on seventeenth century furniture. They had even managed to grab seats in the second row.

Ossie was good at persuading people to 'move over, son, for my lady here'. Pity really, it meant that a beautiful converted barn house, with its adjoining barn full of antique objects, somewhere in Hardwicke, Herefordshire would be prey to opportunist burglars. Its owners would be difficult to identify, unless Sheila Cutler's oversized handbag had survived the blast.

Ossie and Sheila Cutler's first and only experience of a literary festival was to prove a fatal one. It was one that caused rescuers dreadful problems with the antique dealers' identifications, both theirs and other fatalities from the two hundred and fifty members of the audience attending Darwin Harrison-Forbes' performance.

Not far from the festival site was a pretty riverside cottage that would be deprived of its post-festival partygoers, and its artist host and hostess, Aubrey and Lally Penhaligon would spend many weeks in hospital being treated for horrific burns. Plus, an art gallery in Upper Street, Highbury and Islington would be left without its owners for the same indeterminate time. Gone would go the rainbow colours of this flamboyant pair. In their place would be cruel signs of damaged facial flesh, pulled taut in some places and painfully creased in others. And he, Aubrey, would he paint again? Would his damaged eyes still have the artistic perspective to see beauty, personality, character in the faces of his famous sitters? What about Lally's benign and cheerful face? What scars might remain? Would she still have to tweezer that mole on her jaw or had the fire burned it down to her jaw bone?

Two of their valued customers of the gallery would not be purchasing paints there again. They were among the unfortunate victims of the bomb blast. Each of them had secured first or second row seats. Aubrey and Lally would never get to see Gabriel's amazing effort of copying Van Gogh's 'Patience Escalier'. Equally, they would not have to order the special paint for their friend, Mungo Dickson, for his restoration of his antique model soldiers. Both these men had borne the deadly effects of a home-made bomb. And Gabriel's brother: all that remained in a recognisable state of Jacob, was his metal calliper. His walking stick was still burning, still showing the odd, pathetic blue flame, but its fire was almost spent, and the hand that held it had little or no flesh left on it.

Bob Shackleton's earlier observation of and concern over two strange women and a child had been swiftly diverted by the explosion and subsequent devastation. These three had slipped away from the scene and found themselves in a temporary deserted place behind the main catering tent. There they transformed themselves by stripping off wigs and spectacles. Next they climbed out of loose-fitting outer clothes. The two women rolled down the legs of tight-fitting Jeggings and straightened skinny T shirt tops. The boy had stripped off a smart school blazer, one purloined from a nearby prep school playing field, where its young owner had been struggling to learn the rules of lacrosse. Likewise, he had discarded a white blouse and striped school tie, and the girlish wig that had given him a temporary change of sex. Under these 'borrowed' garments were revealed a blue T shirt emblazoned with the lettering ‘I am legend’. He, too, had jeans to roll down under a pair of oversized regulation school trousers.

Jodie Drummond gathered together all their discarded clothing and handed out Nike trainers to Amy and Lewis.

‘Give me your shoes and put these on.’ In little more than a minute three young people walked away from the marquee that had hidden them, and separated. Each of them merged in with a bemused crowd who had no idea, really, what to do or where to go. Police with loud speakers, and police with kindly arms directed them to exit gates or, those needing medical attention, to a quickly set up field hospital. These were being manned by volunteers and staff from nearby medical centres.

Grant Saunders had swiftly arranged free sustenance of hot, sweet tea or something stronger for those who just needed to sit or stand still for a while, just to get their bearings, pause for some moments to absorb their shock and fear. He had sat Doris and Bill Fawkes at a table, slightly away from the marquee entrance, in comfortable armchairs.

‘Do you have any injuries that need looking at?’ he asked them.

Both had shaken their heads, numb and dumb, still in shock.

‘He were Billy Boy’s cousin, yer knaw,’ the little woman eventually spoke.

Grant gave her a look that said ‘What?’ Her husband explained.

‘Aye, yer man on the stage, he’s my cousin. Only he changed ‘is name... mine’s Fawkes like his was, only now 'e calls 'isself Forbes, Harrison-Forbes.'

Grant thought he meant Caius for a moment until the other occupier of the stage was named. He noticed how Bill emphasized the 'H' in Harrison and referred to DH-F, his cousin, in the present. A change of names would not bring him back though; from now on Darwin Harrison-Forbes was in the past... and so was Grant's greatest friend, Caius O'Neill. He left these two seated, while he went to organise comfort food and drink for them... and any others who had survived...

The noise of the explosion had died along with the dead, and there followed gradually diminishing screams and moans of those who had not died. The only sound that continued unbidden, once the siren calls and the wailing of ambulances, the police cars and bomb disposal vehicles had ceased, was the rain, falling softly now on the few still-standing tents. A power without any glory, except for its extinguishing the flames on each of the burning marquees. A few flickers of blue came from snaking electric cabling exposed on the ground, but no one was able, or wanted, to appreciate these vivid colours. There were some, a few, who crawled in a daze, not really knowing which direction to take. Others, of course, lay still, some in scattered unidentifiable pieces, some blackened from smoke like scorched bacon.

As the rain continued to fall upon the wreckage and carnage, more sirens could be heard. Those that were conscious listened to their ever-nearer approach and knew more help and rescue was on its way. Some cried, several sobbed out loud, others wept quietly. Many reached out with burned and injured hands towards the sound of safety.

Help came quickly, and efficiently, each rescuer confident of their skills, all knowing what they must do, what must be done, to facilitate an enormous exodus to safety and protection. What they did was done with almost military expertise and competence, and a quiet and determined efficiency. Those that did swear at the pointless, evil carnage did so under their breath, saving any sound they issued as words of comfort and encouragement for the barely alive victims.

Jodie, Amy and Lewis

In nearby woods, above and away from the ruined festival site, two young women and a boy rendezvoused. Jodie pulled out a waterproof package that had been hidden in the undergrowth.

The morning after the festival carnage, a bed and breakfast guesthouse landlady in Teme's Edge banked the monies she had received from those attending the festival. Some, she had discovered, had not slept in their rooms, or come down to breakfast. She wondered why. She had not seen the previous evening's news on television, or listened to it on her kitchen radio. There had been a power cut for over two hours and when the electricity eventually came back on she had to rush to get the evening meal ready for herself and her husband. They ate in the silence of forty years of marriage, save for 'pass the pepper, will you dear?' Both had vaguely heard what sounded like an explosion but shrugged it away as a car backfiring... or a farmer shooting the crows and pigeons, protecting his newly growing crops. She had cleared away after the meal and her husband had wandered through to their private sitting room to watch Corrie. She set the tables around her for breakfast, five tables. She furnished the sideboard with individual packets of breakfast cereal and five bottle of ketchup and the same of brown sauce. The rest of preparation would be done in the morning. Time now to join her husband for Corrie...

Elsewhere, in the far north of England, an aging golden spaniel, lonely in unfamiliar kennels pricked up her ears. She sniffed the air about her, raised her face to a cruel east wind and gave out a mournful howl. The kennel maid looking after her, bent down in front of her cage. 'It's ok pet, your mam and dad will be back soon.' But she was wrong... Mam and Dadda would need hospitalising for at least a few days... if not weeks

18

Alfie and Simon had been driven back to school by their friends, Will's and Richard's father. A bad case of vomit and the squitters, attacking Will and Richie, had cut short their two-night sleepover. Dad and Pops were away on their business trip and wouldn't be back for another two days, and Grandpa and Aunt Matilda were at some literary thingie, so they could not look after them. The boys had been back at the school since late yesterday afternoon, when hastily made up beds, in the otherwise deserted dormitory, were prepared by Mrs Starkey, the headmaster's wife.

The rain had started practically after breakfast, that quiet, polite repast in Headmaster's private quarters, away from the school dining hall.

'Perhaps you gentlemen would like to go for a stroll when you've finished your breakfast?'

'Yes, sir,' Alfie answered for the both of them.

'Except, sir,' Simon inclined his head towards the kitchen/diner window that overlooked the school playing fields. 'It's pouring down.'

'And?' Henry Starkey's voice, slightly sarcastic

and very resolute, had enough meaning in that one word to make the younger boy squirm.

'It's... erm... quite heavy rain.' His voice trailed off and he dared a swift look at his brother. Alfie gave a look back that said *shut up you idiot wimp*. Both boys rose from the table after wiping their mouths on red and white checked napkins and smiling polite thanks to Mrs Starkey.

'We'd best get our waterproofs then,' said Alfie and glared at his brother. When they had left the headmaster's house, they made their way across a tarmacked area into the deserted school building and up a wide staircase to their dormitory. Alfie hissed at his brother, despite there being no-one to overhear them. 'What you say that for, idiot? If we stayed indoors Horrible Henry would only give us some kind of project to work at. Bad enough us having to come back to school early anyway, without having a boring assignment shoved on us.'

'Alfie, it's pissing down.'

'So? Here,' he handed Simon one of two hooded, weatherproof jackets that were hanging on the side of a small pine wardrobe between their two beds. 'We'll dive across the sports field and head for the pine wood. Should be enough shelter under there to keep us dry... and 'misery guts' is bound to let us back in after an hour or two, hopefully.'

They shrugged into the jackets, zipped them up to their necks and laced the hood strings under their chins.

'Right,' said Alfie. 'Let's go for it.'

His long legs took him in front of Simon in two or three strides, Alfie being the older one and built more powerfully. Although they had both, in their time, been physically germinated by both Danny's and Ray's sperms, Alfie was dark, slim and had inherited his natural father, Danny's handsome features. He was taller than Simon, who had Ray's floppy blonde hair and endearing smile. Simon was inclined to be more rounded than Alfie as well as slightly shorter. Like Dad and Pops, Alfie took the role of leadership with Simon a willing follower.

They ran zigzag across the freshly mown field, where a cricket pitch had already been marked out, and last term's rugby posts removed, and were soon reaching the shelter of the small pine wood. It had taken them less than a minute and now they shook the rain off their coats and unlaced the hoods. Pine needles crackled under their feet and the foliage of the tall trees above were like giant mushroom umbrellas.

'Whew! That's better,'

Simon shook his shoulders and laughed at his brother. 'Bit like an escape isn't it?'

Alfie laughed back. 'Yeah, escape from 'orrible 'enry.' He delved into a deep pocket. 'We're in luck.' And he pulled out a bar of chocolate. It was slightly mis-shaped and the wrapper was curled at the corners.

'That'll do nicely sir,' Simon grinned and held his hand out for a few squares. They sat with their backs against one of the larger pines and munched through the slightly discoloured chocolate.

'How long have you had this, Alfie?'

Alfie sniffed, rubbed a fist over his nose. 'Dunno, haven't worn this jacket since Dad bought us our new ones... probably a few weeks anyway. Tastes all right though, doesn't it?'

'Fine.' Simon continued running the melting chocolate around his mouth. Neither boy thought it strange to be eating chocolate so soon after breakfast; a reward for being turned out of house and home.

'Shame about Will and Richie catching the bug, I was looking forward to a couple of days hanging out with them. Still, it was nice of their Dad to drive us up here. We could've come up by train.'

Simon nodded. 'Hope we don't get it, what they've got... wouldn't fancy being sick every five minutes *and* the squitters on top. Yuk!'

'Pity about Grandpa and Aunt Tilda having to be at that festival too, we could've stayed with one of them... It's not that far from here actually.'

'What is?'

'The Literary Festival.' Alfie finished his last square of chocolate, licked his lips and used the back of his hand to wipe his mouth. 'Erm, near Ludlow, place called Teme's Edge. We've been to Ludlow with Dad and Pops, but I don't remember Teme's Edge. Grandpa reckons they used to hold jousting tournaments there back in the fourteenth century.'

'Awesome. Would like to have seen one of them.' Simon finished his last square and cleaned his face on a grubby handkerchief he had found in one of his jacket pockets. He stood up, picked a stout looking branch from the ground and brandished it near Alfie's face. 'Stand fast, Knight Templar. I challenge you to a duel.'

His brother stood up and searched around for another suitable weapon. Soon they were engaged in their mock battle, wielding the small branches like swords with shouts of 'on guard!' and 'surrender, you scoundrel!' until a hefty swing from Simon's stick caused his brother's to break in two.

'Yield, sir knight.'

Alfie collapsed on the ground, 'I surrender, Sir Gwain. Spare me I pray!'

Simon put a foot on his brother's heaving chest. 'I spare you, brother. Rise and go in peace.'

Alfie scrambled up and brushed himself down. He peered out beyond the pine trees.

'I think it's stopping. Shall we go back, Si?'

'Might as well. Maybe we'll be allowed to play on our IPads... It's not a schoolday.'

Later the two boys lay sprawled on a shag pile rug in front of the unlit common room fire, their IPads discarded.

'I'm bored,' said Simon. 'What time is it Alfie?'

'Where's your watch lazy boy?'

'It needs a new battery. I forgot to tell Pops before we came away. Time?'

Alfie examined his own watch. 'Bloody hell! It's nearly twelve-fifty. Mrs Starkey said lunch at one. We'd better get a move on.'

They ran through to the toilets and shower rooms, gave their hands a hasty wash in cold water, only to find there were no towels.

'Bugger,' said Simon. He wiped his not too clean hands down his trousers. 'How come there were towels for us last night for showers, now there aren't any?'

'Cos Mrs Starkey gave us some from her own cupboard. They're back in our dorm.' He too, wiped his hands on his trousers, took a quick glance at his reflection in the mirror above the wash basin and smoothed his hair down with more water. 'That'll do. C'mon Si, let's go.'

'Coming.'

An hour later, after two helpings each of Mrs Starkey's delicious cottage pie topped with twirled and oven-browned mashed potato, and liberal servings of peas and carrots, they found themselves running over the sports field once more. Again it poured with drenching rain, and again they made for the pine tree woods. Three minutes later the heavy rain shower became a dramatic thunder storm, with fearsome flashes of lightning that penetrated the shivering pine umbrella above them. They moved closer to each other. Again the thunder cracked, huge and loud like a massive explosion.

'I reckon it's directly overhead.' Alfie, for once, looked scared.

The ear-splitting noise was followed by another flash of lightning that streaked its way through the pine wood, chasing the thunder clap. The boys' heads shot up as a nearby tree burst into flames, sending sparks raining down on them. They ran, faster than they had ever run before. In fear, in panic, back over the sports field, their feet squelching with every terrified stride they made. They escaped the flaming pine wood, zig-zagging their way through jagged lightning, towards the safety of the red-brick school buildings and the headmaster's house.

Even before they had reached Mrs Starkey's kitchen, they could hear the wail of fire engines.

'Bloody hell, that was quick.' Simon looked back over his shoulder, tracing the approaching sound. 'Sir must've rung them.'

'Well it wasn't me or you, dickhead.'

Simon ignored his brother's sarcasm. He was

used to it, inured to it. 'Coming to watch them?' he went to run back to the field and get as near as possible to the flaming tree.

'Boys... in, now.'

It was a command they could not ignore, wouldn't dare to. Headmaster stood in the kitchen doorway. They moved past him into the warm and dry interior. Outside the sirens grew louder and, as they went towards the window, they could see blue flashing lights. There were two fire engines, hastily but expertly driven over the newly manicured cricket pitches. Alfie and Simon grinned, both guessing sir's reaction to the red monsters' devastating route to put out the fire that had now caught a second tree, and a third.

Simon turned to look at sir's face as he stood behind them at the window, the muscles on his face twitching, a creased frown above serious eyes. In the distance could be heard another roll of thunder like an angry, grumbling elephant as it rolled southward, away from this area of north Shropshire towards a town called Ludlow and a village known as Teme's Edge.

The pine wood's fire was soon extinguished and the sun shone again, even visible through the thin spiral of smoke that slithered its way through disappearing grey clouds... Headmaster thanked the fire crew, and shrugged his shoulders at the curt apology he received for the red monsters churning up his cricket pitches. 'Tea gentlemen?'

The fire chief nodded his thanks, exhorting his men to wipe their feet before entering Mrs Starkey's kitchen. She added generous slices of freshly baked fruit cake to the mugs of tea and smiled at the men's appreciation. There were only a few stray crumbs left for the two boys to enjoy. She saw their deflated faces. No matter she would bake another in time for their tea. The headmaster's wife was a kindly person, motherly, despite never having children of her own. Five hundred boys at any term in the school was sufficient to slake her childless thirst.

A buzzing tone told the fire chief he had a message on his pager. His face, a picture of grim seriousness, after he had taken the message. 'I'm afraid we have to go,' he said and gestured with his head at the crews. Mugs were carefully but swiftly placed on the table, mouths wiped clean of crumbs.

'Big explosion and fire,' he mouthed. 'All crews within thirty miles needed. That means us as well.' They were two miles inside the thirty-mile boundary, and twenty-eight miles from a catastrophe bigger than the small Shropshire town and adjoining village had ever known.

Jodie

The first hint of sunlight behind the trees looked, Jodie thought as she opened her eyes, just like a forest fire. Bright orange seeped through the blackened trees. But it was motionless and tranquil, not flickering like flames, no pungent smoke seeping in through the open window, nor the crackling of twigs and searing leaves. It was interrupted every now and then by birdsong pure and sweet. A few minutes later, the orange glow had disappeared from behind the trees as the sun rose above their top branches. Now they wore the green of pending summer and the sky above them was bright white and yellow under the blinding orb.

Jodie fidgeted in bed, screwing and unscrewing her toes, bending and unbending her knees, clenching and unclenching fingers, as if she was doing horizontal exercises. Her thoughts were active as well. Amy had to go, she was too much of a panicking liability. But how? When?

Jodie had googled all the main dailies, every day for the past few days. There was little or nothing being reported now about the bombing at the Teme Literary Festival. Not a week later. Oh yes, the first few days had been a media feast, both in the newspapers and on television. All sorts of conjectures. Was it a terrorist bombing? Had Isil come to Shropshire? Or had it been personally directed towards Darwin Harrison-Forbes? If so why? What had he, the great man done? Then nothing... so why the news clampdown, blanket reporting? Is it what they called D Notice?

Should she drive back to Teme, to Ludlow? See what was going on? *Don't be bloody daft. Last thing you must do is go back. It's what they expect you to do. Stay here, keep a low profile... What about Lewis? A bit young maybe... to trust at keeping his mouth shut. Or was he? Tougher than Amy...Jodie was sure of that.* Hard little bugger.

Amy had gone to ground. Three visits to the little Greek restaurant where she worked, different times, different days, different dress and disguise, told Jodie she was not there anymore. Neither was she at her flat. Or answering her mobile. Where was she?

Jodie's college work was suffering. 'This is crap,'

her tutor said. 'You can do better than this, Jodie.' Her laptop lay untouched. No biography, no words of fiction, no catharsis for the hatred within her. WHERE WAS BLOODY AMY? *Where are you, my friend?*

Only one thing for it, she must go back to London, to Highbury, to Harbourne Road. She was betting Amy may be with her family... forget the row with her old man, he'd take her back, her mum would insist upon it, especially if she was showing distress. *Keep your mouth shut Amy; no blabbing to the parents, no hysterics... Wonder if Reuben is still around?* All these thoughts kaleidoscoped through her mind...

Once the decision was made, Jodie packed a small bag and left her Hereford home, locking the door securely behind her. 'I'll be back,' she whispered. Only she heard that promise. It was early morning. She walked quickly to the station, looking neither right nor left. She did not need any cheery good mornings from on-their-way workers or fellow travellers. Jodie was back in her own thoughts, her own decision making.

Ten minutes after leaving her small, terraced house, she reached the station. Another ten minutes later she boarded the train for Paddington. She was speeding away from the city unaware that her front door would shortly be forced open by armed men in black uniforms. Their faces were masked, their bodies clothed in protective bullet proof clothing. They were armed and desperately seeking Jodie Drummond, she who was suspected of causing the fatal explosion at Teme Literary Festival...

Harbourne Road, Highbury

Amy Clifton had got her father all wrong. He was not the miserable old git as she had described him. The people she worked alongside in the Hereford restaurant, thought he sounded 'off the planet'. To Jodie, who had known him when they were giggling teenagers, he was... 'well, a bit of a dinosaur', she said.

Tony Clifton had worked for Islington Council in Upper Street for years. Not in an important job, not a physical one either. Just a desk job, complete with telephone and computer facilities and access to those in the outside world who chose to communicate to the council via his head-height screened desk.

He had been secretly proud, those years ago, when he had mastered the computer, became computer-literate as they termed it. Senior in years to most of his contemporaries, he might be, but not senior in rank. Promotion had eluded his staid attitude, his inability to move fast enough with the times. He was, like the younger staff around him, the first port of call at the end of the telephone. He took the calls of the general public and smoothly passed them on to the relevant department, to the true advisers of the council. This was done with a quiet voice and a 'just one moment, sir or madam, while I put you through.' A quick apology for any delay and soothing music, while the person on the other end of the line waited to be connected to the one who could deal with their complaint or question or problem. Tony Clifton had no such skills.

At home he was head of a family of three, himself, Pam, his wife of twenty-six years, and Amy. Amy, his one and only child: Amy, the pretty little girl who had grown up and moved away from them. And no, he had not turned her out because of that New Year's Eve fiasco. Yes, he had made her stay on the doorstep for a few hours, drunk as she was, and vomiting everywhere. He had no intention of making her homeless. Her decision, if she didn't like the house rules. It was only fair, he thought, to impose certain restrictions and standards at home. Wasn't it?

So she left. Just like that. No forwarding address, not a word to her mother. Pam had cried, told him he was a bully. How could she say that? He had never once laid a hand on Amy. Wouldn't have dared. You couldn't anyway, nowadays. Against the law to slap your own child. But he never had. Eventually a letter had come, the envelope was addressed, he recognised, in Amy's handwriting, to be delivered to Mrs Pam Clifton. Pam gave him the letter to read after she had digested it.

'What do you make of that then? Hereford?'

Almost into Wales, he thought. Couldn't have gone much farther. Not exactly an obscure city though, Hereford. Didn't they have a chained library in their cathedral? And the Mappa Mundi? Tony had never been there. Not his idea of a holiday, traipsing around a city, rich in culture or not. He preferred the West Country, Devon and Cornwall, touring in a hired car.

He wished they had had a son; someone to take, once a week, to the beautiful game. Home or away.

Amy had never had an interest in football. Neither had Pam. A son called Anthony, named after himself, would have. A son who called him Dad or Pops, as they walked to the stadium, club shirts and scarves on. Maybe a face paint Arsenal logo for Anthony when he was little...

Instead they had just the one, a daughter. She wasn't even a Daddy's girl. And if he was honest not a Mummy's girl either. Amy had been gone a little over two years. Now she was back. Quiet, withdrawn, tiptoeing around them and herself, trying to be the good child. Was she pregnant, he wondered? He asked Pam when they were in bed the first night Amy had come home, pale, slightly grubby as if she had been sleeping rough; permanently rubbing her arms to stop an itch that wasn't there.

Pam had whispered (in their own home!), 'I don't think so. I'll find out tomorrow maybe. Let her have a good sleep tonight. She's exhausted, poor lamb.'

They had turned over, away from each other. Pam fell asleep almost immediately, quietly and gently snoring. Her child was home again. Tony lay on his side, could see the blink of streetlight through a chink in the curtains. He heard the odd train slide past by the bedroom window, over the small road and lower down in the cutting. It was barely audible on its new track. He wondered who rode trains at this time of night, or early morning?

He heard Amy get up and go to the bathroom. Heard her say to herself through their part-open door. 'Oh God, what have I done?'

He wondered, apprehensive, troubled. What had she done? Was she being sick? Was she pregnant. Somehow he wished she was. Pregnancy, a baby grandchild, he could cope with and knew Pam would love it, the idea of being a grandmother. Deep down he had a sick feeling that Amy was not pregnant; that whatever her problem was, it was more serious than a surprise pregnancy. He had read, only days ago, about a terrible explosion at a literary festival, when many people had died or been seriously injured. At a place near the town of Ludlow.

It wasn't that far from Hereford was it? He turned over, heard the toilet being flushed, a tap being run, that was splashing cleansing water over his daughter's hands. What have you done Amy? He stared into the dark, heard her go back to bed, heard her quietly sobbing into her pillow. Amy... Amy, Amy.

Jodie changed in the confined toilet in between two carriages. This time she was changing sex, in a manner of speaking, as well as clothes and appearance. Her hair, already cut short, she hid under a grey beanie hat. She wore tinted lensed glasses, a grey hooded fleece jacket, jeans and trainers. It took a little more effort with the movement of the train to fix a three-day growth in place with special make-up artist glue. But when it was done she examined her face in the tiny mirror, nodded her satisfaction and stuffed her exchanged clothes in her backpack. She was tempted to throw them out of the window but could hear someone rattling the door.

An elderly lady waited outside the small toilet.

'Thank you, young man,' she said, and mumbled something like 'about time too.'

Jodie didn't bother to reply; she moved swiftly through to the next carriage before she sat down, in case anyone remembered a young woman going into the toilet and a guy coming out.

Fifteen minutes later the train pulled into Paddington Station. She made her way to the underground and sorted a route through to Highbury and Islington. If Amy was holed up with her folks in Harbourne Road, Jodie wondered, will she recognise me dressed like this? Half an hour later she emerged from Highbury station into brilliant sunshine, causing her to blink, even behind the tinted lenses, and re-focus till her eyes had adjusted. She crossed by the pedestrian lights and walked towards St Pauls Road, her backpack slung over one shoulder.

Two seconds later she stopped, rooted to the spot. She stared, then tried to look away. You didn't eyeball in London. Not done. But she couldn't help herself. Three years or more since she'd seen him. He had not changed and her breath caught in her throat as he trapped her in his returning stare. She could tell he knew. Immediately. How?

'Hiya, Jodie, or is it Joe Dee?' he smiled his cold, calculating smile. 'How're you doing?'

She hesitated, looked down at her feet then into his face, her head on one side as she squinted into the afternoon sun.

'Reuben... yeah, I'm fine. You?'

He paused, continued to stare at her, half smiling. Then. 'Come here, give us a hug.'

She moved towards him and allowed his arms to swathe her. They stepped into the shelter of a nearby charity shop, kicked aside the filled-with-clothes bin bags and kissed.

'Long time no see Jodes.' He held her at arm's length and quietly laughed. 'What's with the facial hair? You on steroids or something?'

She grinned. 'No, course not... it's make-up... how come you recognised me?'

'Easy,' he said. 'You were my woman for two years... until you went away.'

She was suddenly conscious of their public place, and her in her male disguise. 'Must think we're a couple of gays,' she said.

'So? Not unusual is it?'

'Suppose not.'

'Anyway, Jodie, or Joe Dee, where were you heading?' He steered her towards St Pauls Road, away from Highbury Corner. She knew he was expecting her to go back to his place. 'Erm, actually I was going to Harbourne Road, to see if Amy's there.'

'And why would you do that. Why d'you need to see Amy? What you been up to young lady boy?'

She cleared her throat, conscious of Reuben's powerful grip as he manoeuvred her towards his flat. She knew what he was doing when they crossed the road over towards the Alwynne Castle. 'What d'you mean?'

'I read the papers and listen to the news. Been anywhere near Ludlow lately? Little place called Teme?'

She pulled him to a stop. 'Why d'you say that?' She was stalling and they both knew it.

He smiled but not with his eyes. They had a force in them that made her feel scared, not for the first time, of Reuben. He had that power.

'Not many people using explosive/incendiary

devices like the one used there.' He paused and coaxed her along again. They were near to his block of flats now and she knew she would not get to Amy's road any time soon. 'Not at literary festivals anyway.' He dropped his voice to a whisper. 'Someone there you didn't like?'

They were in his ground floor flat before she even attempted to answer. Then there was no chance. He pulled her even closer and heeled the front door shut. 'Come here woman.' Then as he rubbed his cheek against her face, 'Oh fuck, Jodes, let's get rid of the beard.'

She unlaced herself from him and ran into the bathroom. It was grubby and cluttered with his things, but she found a flannel and filled the washbasin with hot water, dipped the facecloth in it and began to scrub away the disguise. It came off easily with hot water but left her skin looking red and slightly blotchy. She shrugged. So what? Towelling her face dry she vacated the bathroom. She could hear him banging about in the kitchen and the thud of the fridge door as he shut it. He was pouring something into two glasses filled with ice, something amber in colour. She hoped it wasn't scotch, she didn't like scotch.

He turned to face her and grinned as he handed her one of the glasses. 'That's better, you look more like my old Jodes now. Bit red in the face maybe...'

She took the glass, sniffed at it. 'Mmn... calvados, very nice.'

'Expect you drank plenty of that when you were in gay Paree.'

'How did you know...?'

'I get to know everything Jodes. Like you moving back to the UK, but not to London. Where did you go? Shropshire was it?'

'She shook her head. 'No, Hereford. Been to art school there for the last year or so.' She did not mention Amy being there in Hereford, or the Teme's Edge fiasco. Didn't need to, Reuben seemed to know all about it, or had made a lucky guess.

'Where's Satan?'

'Gone to canine heaven... or hell. The pigs had him put down after he bit one of them.'

'Oh.' What else was there to say? She knew how much he had loved that dog. Vicious brute though...

They took their drinks through to the bedroom. It was just as cluttered as the bathroom and kitchen.

'Lost your maid have you?'

'Not really, just got lazy recently. The sheets are clean,' he pointed his glass towards the bed. 'And nobody else has slept there, except me.' He emphasized the 'me'. He put his glass down on the bedside table that was ringed with coffee stains, and pulled her towards him. 'Come here woman. It's been a long time.'

She thought he sounded like some old-fashioned cowboy from a long-ago Hollywood film. She gritted her teeth. Did she really want this? Too late now, really. There was only one way out and that would not be reachable until she did what he wanted. She drained her glass to give her resolution, placed it next to his and let him pull her down onto the bed...

It was not gentle sex, not brutal either, somewhere in between. Intense, urgent (on his part), forceful and deeply penetrating. Curiously, she kind of enjoyed it. After it was over and he was spent he moved off her, breathing heavily.

'Bloody hell, I'd almost forgotten how good you are.' He felt for a packet of cigarettes on the bedside table and his Zippo, shook two out, lit them, and handed her one, brushing her breast with the back of his hand as he did so. She didn't smoke anymore, but did not bother to tell him, just accepted it. She needn't inhale. She looked up at the ceiling, at the single light bulb with no shade to decorate it: glanced at the posters on Reuben's walls. Gothic. Nothing had changed since she was last in this room. Except one thing. 'You didn't wear anything.'

'No, you're right, I didn't. Assumed you'd be on the pill.'

'Why would you assume that?' There was annoyance in her voice. She wasn't scared of him anymore.

He shrugged his naked shoulders, naked except for the ornate serpent tattoo that wound round both arms, over his back and up one side of his neck. 'Why not? Just thought most of you females did nowadays. Why?' he asked. 'Think you might get pregnant?'

She took another drag, inhaled this time and blew out the smoke through her nostrils. Careful, Jodie, you'll get hooked again. She hadn't smoked since Paris, over a year now.

'I hope not.'

'Not even if it was mine?'

'I've never wanted a kid, don't want one now... that good enough for you?'

He knew she was challenging him. What to? A verbal duel? He grinned at her as he told her a deliberate lie. 'No problem there. I had the snip last year.'

Later he said to her, 'Don't go Jodes. Stay here with me tonight. I'll get a take away.'

'I just want to go and see Amy, see if she's come back home.'

'Might be dangerous,' he cautioned. 'If she's run back to Mummy and Daddy, she might have kissed and told. Might have even told the pigs.'

She turned to him, skin on skin. 'D'you reckon?'

'Yeah I do. She's not like you Jodes.' He grinned and stroked her bare shoulder. 'No one's like you.'

He prevented further discussion with another deep throat kiss, and pulled her close to his nakedness. She could feel his hardness again, closed her eyes and succumbed. This time it would be duty mixed with a measure of fear. Reuben led and others followed. Now he was quietly forcing her to do what he wanted and she could only comply. This time it would not be pleasurable... she hoped it would not last too long.

Tomorrow... tomorrow she would go and see if Amy was there.

19

Reuben saw them first. Through the grimy-curtained window. Saw their dark, half-crouching shadows and the guns they held close. He shook her still-sleeping body.

'Jodes. Wake up.'

Even half-asleep she recognised the whispered urgency.

'What?'

'Outside, pigs with guns. Must be you they're after.'

She sat up, fear already swathing her face, enlarging her eyes. 'Christ, why?'

'Maybe Amy opened her mouth... was she part of your oppo?'

She nodded, pulled a face. 'Knew I shouldn't have trusted her.' She rushed towards the chair where her clothes were, swiftly pulled them on, hopping on one leg as she tugged her jeans over her hips.

'What shall I do?'

Reuben was halfway to the small kitchen with their two glasses and boxes from their takeaway supper. 'Go through to the hallway, I'll be there in a sec.'

She complied, tied her trainer laces as she crept through to the hallway. Reuben was there almost immediately. He dragged up a small, threadbare rug and revealed a square, cut into the floorboards. With a knife from the kitchen, he prised up one side of the square, which lifted the other three to show a dark recess below.

'Squeeze into there,' he said. 'Quick as you can.' His voice was calm but Jodie sensed the urgency behind the cool. The small but adequate enclosure was lined with some kind of soft material, like a blanket. There was enough room for her to sit, almost upright, before he powered the lid onto her.

'You'll be ok, there's air vents. Just don't make any noise and don't bloody panic. You're not locked in,' he added. 'I'll just put the rug back.'

She heard the loud banging at Reuben's front door, and a muffled sound, something like 'police, open up.' She counted probably ten or more seconds before he opened the door to them: heard the rattle and knew he had left the safety chain on. Time to compose himself she supposed.

A thud and the sound of severing metal told her the police had forced the door and broken the safety chain.

'Whoa, whoa. What the fuck...'

Heavy feet thundered on the floor above her. She prayed the secret cover was strong enough to withstand their size-twelve boots, that it would not splinter and betray her hideout.

'Where the hell do you think...' Reuben was obviously following them into the interior of his flat, and not in a good humoured way either.

'Where is she?' Whoever spoke asked the question loud enough for her to hear.

'Where is who?'

'Your whore, Jodie Drummond.'

'Hold on, what the fuck are you talking about? Jodie? I haven't seen her ... must be three years. She's in France far as I know.' There was much banging and moving of furniture. 'You got a search warrant?'

There was a moment's silence. She guessed a nod and a piece of paper shown. 'Well she's not here, so get out.'

More stamping of heavy feet, through each room until they reached the hallway again. She heard the wrench as they opened the door, the slam followed by silence, apart from Reuben calling them all the largest sized bastards this side of hell. A long two minutes later and she heard the rustle as he removed the rug and again prised open the secret cover. She blinked as light flooded in. He grinned. 'You ok?'

She wriggled her way out of the cramped space, nodded. 'Yeah, I'm fine.' And 'Thanks for that.'

He helped pull her out and held her when she was on her feet again. 'We gotta find you somewhere safe, Jodes. They're obviously looking all over for you. Don't suppose Hereford's safe anymore either.'

'What shall I do?' The fear was there in her voice.

'Don't worry,' he soothed. 'I'll think of something, somewhere you can go.'

'What about one of the others?'

He knew she was referring to one of his protest

group. ‘Mmm. Maybe. Erm.’ He led her through to the kitchen where she smelled the remains of last night’s Chinese. ‘Let’s have a cuppa, and I’ll think on it.’

‘I’ll make it.’ She needed something to do, glanced through the small back window, grateful for the grimy curtains screening them from anyone in the back yard of the flats. She found two clean mugs, teabags still in their box and a carton of long-life milk in the fridge. Reuben was already filling the kettle and switched it on as she dropped teabags into the mugs. Her hands shook as she completed the simple task. ‘Gotta have been Amy, hasn’t it?’

‘What about your little cousin, the boy you told me about?’

She sighed, breathed deeply. ‘I don’t know. Could’ve been him. Maybe he bragged about it at school or something. Whoever it was, they’ve put me in deep shit.’

The kettle boiled and he poured. She dribbled in the milk and spooned out the teabags, dropping them into an already filled waste bin. His phone rang, and he signed for her to take the mugs through to the front room.

‘Yeah?’ he followed her, explaining to someone, then giving monosyllabic answers to whoever was on the other end of the phone. ‘Thanks Jase, I owe you.’ He rang off, swilled the hot tea down with a wince and went through to the bedroom. He emerged in his leathers and held a set out for her. ‘Right, put these on, and this.’ This being a full-faced helmet.

‘Where we going?’ She began to pull on the leather jacket and trousers.

‘Don’t matter where we going, as long as we get

you out of here. Don't worry,' he did his best to dispel her fear. 'You'll be safe where I'm taking you. Just till things die down a bit… just till I can think of something else.'

He held her hand. 'Come on. Out this way. They left the flat and went out the back way, through the communal yard where washing blew on several lines. They wound their way through sheets and towels and legs of jeans, avoiding dustbins and kids' bikes. She couldn't speak, not with the visor down, just allowed herself to be pulled along by him.

'In here, quick.' A few streets on they had reached a lock-up garage and Reuben swiftly undid a large padlock and tugged at the paint-peeled wooden doors. Inside was his motor bike, reflecting the sun as it filtered inside. He didn't bother to wheel the bike out, instead he switched on the ignition and motioned for her to get on the pillion seat. He got on himself and revved the engine to a massive roar. As if from nowhere, a young lad appeared, waited for them to clear the doors and shut them after they had roared down the street. She clung onto Reuben's waist as the speed seemed to pull her off. It had been getting on for three years since she had ridden pillion, three years to forget the fear and the thrill.

They reached Upper Street and Reuben took them through side streets she had never seen or could not remember. All she knew was he was taking her to a place of safety. She had faith in him, trusted him, knew he was her security.

Shame about the crazy car driver who cut in front of them, causing them to swerve and hit a bollard. The next few moments were a nightmare…

of the bike throwing her off into the traffic, of car horns and screeching breaks, and an agonising impact into inflexible metal. Jodie was briefly aware of being lifted again into the air and coming down once more, landing on something that was unforgiving and solid. It was then everything went black and silent.

20

As Jodie awoke, she was conscious of everything around her being white: curtains, walls, a vague partition, half-screening her from what she did not know. Even the bed covering was white and a woman standing over her was dressed in a white tunic with blue trousers. Had she died and gone to some kind of weirdo heaven? A strange man, white-coated with a stethoscope snaked around his neck told her it was hospital not heaven.

'You're awake then?' It was an unnecessary question as her eyes were open and making a nomadic journey around the room. Apart from his question, everywhere was silent: she guessed she was in a side ward, the only occupant. She nodded her head to his question and wished immediately she hadn't. A searing pain speared through the back of her head and down through her neck.

'Be careful,' the nurse warned. 'You've had an almighty bang on your head.'

Stethoscope moved towards her, unwound his snake apparatus and listened to her chest. 'Can you breathe in for me Jodie?'

She wondered how he knew her name and felt uneasy that he did. She complied and drew in a cautious breath. It hurt, like the nodding of her head had done, this time on her rib cage. He saw her wince.

'Ribs hurt?'

She whispered 'Yes.'

'Mmn.' That was all he said as he folded up his stethoscope and wound it around his neck again. He turned to the nurse and gave medical instructions that Jodie did not understand but guessed one of them was for some kind of pain killer. She bloody hoped so. The rest of the jargon was beyond her comprehension...

'I'm afraid young lady,' the doctor spoke to her again. His face was cloaked in an expression she could not interpret. 'The police are outside this room and we are obliged to let them in here to question you as soon as you wake. Which obviously you are now.' He paused. 'If you're not up to it yet, I can tell them you are not fully awake... What d'you want me to do?'

'Can you give me a bit longer?'

He nodded. 'Half an hour? An hour?'

'Please, an hour would be good, I think I could go back to sleep... How long have I been here? And where is here?'

'Ten days, and it's the Whittington Hospital, Archway.'

'Reuben? We were riding together.'

There was a slight pause. 'He's fighting for his life. Multiple injuries I'm afraid.'

'Can I see him? Will he live?'

'No to the first question, he's in intensive care, and I don't know at this moment to the second. He is very badly injured, the bike blew up and he was under it. The police are with him too.'

She lay back on the pillows. Her head hurt, her chest hurt more; she hoped they would not be long before they gave her a shot of something... or some strong pills. Actually pills would be better, as an idea was forming in her mind. Through half shut eyes she carefully took in the geography of the room, bed, bedside table, over there beyond the bed, a washbasin and towel dispenser. Next to it a straight backed chair with... her clothes.

'What do I do if I need the bathroom?'

The nurse inclined her head sideways. 'There's a lavatory through that door, en suite sort of thing, lucky girl.'

'Thanks.'

'Don't know if you're ready yet to go on your own. Wait till I get you some pain killers and we'll give it a go if you like.'

Jodie smiled her thanks and turned her head away as if she wanted some sleep.

'Perhaps later.' Both the nurse and the doctor left her, but she glimpsed the dark uniforms outside as they went through the door. That close were they? The pigs? She looked around the room, turned carefully to examine the window behind her and winced with the pain. She breathed in and out in a gentle rhythm until she had absorbed the pain, then dragged herself to an upright position and carefully slid her feet out of the bed and onto the floor. The effort made her feel sick and dizzy.

She made it to the window, calculated she must be on the first or second floor, with a drop of no more than fifteen feet to a small roof garden. At least, that was what it looked like. There were benches and small trees in tubs, and French doors leading back into the building. All only a floor below her. It looked promising. However, she was in no fit position to attempt such a feat, but the alternative was to be chained up to the pigs sitting out there by her bedroom door. Perhaps she could persuade the nurse to keep them out for several hours? *Pigs might fly. Joke.* She struggled back to bed, lay on it exhausted. Within seconds the nurse returned pushing a small trolley.

'Here you go, m'dear, co-codomol, full strength, that ought to knock you out for a while.' She filled a glass with water and handed Jodie two tablets on a small plastic dish. 'I'll tell them out there,' she said. 'That you won't be in any condition to see them till at least this evening.'

'What time is it now?'

'Not quite twelve noon. The tablets should help you to sleep for at least four hours, but...' she pointed an arm towards the closed door. 'they can wait; you don't look a bad girl to me.'

Jodie put on her most innocent expression and tinted it with gratitude. 'Thank you. I really could do with another sleep.'

'Tell you what I'll do. I shall say to them that the doctor said you're not fit to speak for another day. How's that?'

'Brilliant. You're an angel.'

'I'll pop in again at supper time, see if you want anything to eat. Do you want anything now?'

'Oh no thanks, food's the last thing I want. Water's just fine.'

'Ok, dear. Just take these tablets for me and I'll leave you in peace.'

Jodie swallowed the water obediently, making

sure the pills were firmly placed under her tongue and resting against her teeth. She needed them for later, not for now and not for sleep. Another hour's rest would be good for her body, and give her time to work out a plan of escape. She would have to leave Reuben. Pity. But if he was as injured as they implied, she couldn't take him with her; he'd be too much of a liability, too much of everything. Besides, she had been tracked to his place. If he hadn't persuaded her to go there, she would not be here now. Wouldn't have been injured after crashing on his bike.

No use saying if only, she told herself. Just get on with it, it being the now of time. And that is what it was, time, time now to take one tablet, crushed. Then wait for it to kick in. She hoped kicking in time was soon.

A long and painful ten minutes later she had discarded the hospital garment and dressed in her own clothes. They were torn, but not as much as the leathers Reuben had made her wear. The zip-up suit was in shreds. She left it.

Which window to use? This one in the room or see what promise the bathroom one had? She first peered out and down to the little roof garden, and relieved to see it was carpeted with astro turf. If she hang-dropped she would only have a few feet to land on the false grass. Another bonus, her room was at the back of the hospital, less chance of being seen from the road.

She limped into the bathroom to weigh up the prospects of its window access. She struggled up onto the lavatory seat. Good. The window was sideways opening and she had a perfect view of outside and below. When would these damned tablets kick in? Soon...?

She saw one of thc stout wooden benches almost directly below this window. Good, that meant she could hang drop and – with luck – her feet would reach the back rest. Another blessing, the sky had clouded over and was threatening rain. Suggested there'd be no-one wanting to sit out there...

Time to take another tablet. She hoped it would work quickly, give her enough freedom from pain to do all she had to do to gain her freedom. Back to the room; swallow the pill. Five more minutes on the bed and pray the analgesic worked. She glanced at the door and a huge grin spread across her face. 'I don't believe it,' she hissed through clenched teeth. 'They've left the fucking key in the lock.'

With her feet still bare, she limped towards the door, hardly a breath escaping her lips. Slowly, very slowly, she turned the key and gently withdrew it. No sense in leaving it for them to jostle onto a piece of paper shoved under the door. Let them wait until a spare key could be found...

Back to the bathroom. She half-filled a tooth mug, swilled water around her mouth, drank a little and spat out the rest. She felt in her pockets, fretted to find no cash, but identified a piece of plastic as her debit card. At least she could get some cash from an ATM.

The noise of rain pattering against the window gave her a good feeling. It would take pedestrians out of the equation, *and* any patients wanting to sit in the roof garden.

'*Here goes J D.*' She struggled onto the lavatory seat, prised open the window, and – with agony – levered herself onto a narrow window sill. The effort brought on waves of nausea and the last thing she wanted was to sick up the painkillers. They were such an important and large part of her successful escape. Best to pause for a while, but not for too long. She did not want to be seen, not sitting up here or hang dropping down there.

Ten minutes later she was leaning against the garden seat, breathing in and out through her mouth, absorbing the pain of her supreme effort. She took a swift look at the French doors, prayed they were not locked or anyone was near them, near enough to question why she was out there in the rain.

The gods were on her side. The doors opened at her touch and not a soul occupied the corridor. Another bonus, the garden and its entrance were not directly attached to a specific ward, just a passageway that led to several. Well she had no intention of visiting anyone. Not even Reuben. *Sorry mate, you're on your own.*

Next decision, stairs or lift to ground floor? Had to be the lift. Just pray, she thought, that none of the staff seeing to me are in it. Or the pigs changing shift.

Again the gods were good to her. An old couple were the only occupants when she pressed the 'down' button. They looked sad. Maybe one or the other has just been diagnosed with a terminal illness. She gave a mental shrug. Not her business... or problem. 'Doors open' a tinny announcement and she stepped out in front of the old couple who were still clinging to each other. A short, not quite so painful walk took her to the hospital entrance. Yeah, the tablets were kicking in. Pity she hadn't been able to secure more of them. Jodie was one of many leaving or entering, an anonymous face in the London crowd.

A little further on she found an ATM and withdrew a hundred pounds. It would be enough to buy an Oyster travel card and more than enough to pay for a taxi from here to Upper Street. Why go back? Why not? They think I'm in hospital being guarded by armed twats. I need, she thought, to find Amy...

21

Before hailing a taxi, she slid into a public toilet; found a cubicle where she could examine her body. Most of her stomach and chest were bruised, but fading to yellow-bruised. She was lucky, no breaks and very few stitches, those mostly over her left elbow. Outside, she heard another door bang and two minutes later, the flush of a toilet. Best to wait a couple of minutes. She examined her left wrist, no watch. Must have been smashed when she came off the bike. Not to worry, she could pick up a cheapo somewhere. A short burst of hand dryer, then silence, told her she was possibly sole occupant again. She unbolted the cubicle door. No-one there. Her face in the mirror was scarcely recognisable. Pale, some bruising, and the look of someone who hadn't eaten in a while. Easy to remedy that, plenty of eating places between here and Harbourne Road. She needed some clothes too, charity shop style. What did they call them? Pre-loved? Pre-owned? Used, worn and discarded? Whatever...

Leaving the charity shop in Holloway Road, a

new Jodie Drummond walked out in a matching jacket and long skirt, a crocheted cloche hat, pulled well down over her face and ears, dark glasses and comfortable shoes, the sort you could wear in a gym. Time to get a taxi if she didn't want to faint off with the returning pain. Except right next to the charity shop was a pharmacy. She thanked those gods again, the ones that were on her side.

'Can I have some strong pain killers please?' The Asian guy behind the counter gave her a mixed look of suspicion and sympathy.

'I'm just out of hospital.' She managed a pained look. (Not a problem). 'I forgot to pick up some in their dispensary.'

'Where is the pain?'

'All over. But worse round my ribs. I came off my bike, straight into a van.'

The pharmacist tutted in sympathy. 'They really don't care for us cyclists do they?'

She didn't tell him it was a motor bike, gently shook her head in agreement. 'Do you think I could take two straightaway?'

'Of course. I presume you have not consumed any alcohol, and you have eaten?'

She managed a grin. 'No alcohol, and yeah, I had a meal earlier.' It was the closest she could say, not really sure what the time was. The pharmacist disappeared out the back and returned with a glass of water and two tablets in a miniature dish.

'Here, have these two on the house. Keep your packet for when you get home.'

She drank up, paid up, and thanked him, anxious now to be gone. Not to home though. Where was that now anyway? Not Hereford, or Reuben's. She really needed to meet up with Amy...

She got the taxi to drop her off at the Alwynne Castle. There were police everywhere, including, she could see, outside Reuben's flat, and at both turnings into Harbourne Road. Don't panic, she told herself and pushed at the pub door. Inside, it was fairly deserted, a few old boys cuddling halves, probably wishing they were pints and last forever. Plus, a couple of old dears with exaggerated makeup sipping glasses of Guinness. Jodie did not gain their attention and was relieved.

'Hi sweetie,' said the camp barman. 'What's your pleasure?'

Not you that's for sure. 'Er, can I have a cappuccino?'

He grinned at her and simpered, 'Heavy night last night?'

She managed a grin back. 'Summink like that.'

'Find yourself a seat, I'll bring it over to you.'

'Thanks.' She smiled her gratitude.

'No probs.'

She listened to the schlurk of milk being frothed. A milky coffee was as good as something to eat. Perhaps... Maybe sister boy would bring a biscuit with it. Her stomach churned, laden with painkillers and no food. He did, and the bill. '£2.95 when you're ready. No hurries.' Sympathy for the hangover she didn't have.

She sat in the bay window, dark glasses glued to her face, hoping Amy might go by. There were plenty who did, but annoyingly, no Amy. Her coffee grew cold while she stared out of the window. That was fine by her, easier to drink. She ate the biscotto served with it, wished there were two. Perhaps she could order a snack? The pub clock showed a little after twelve noon.

A hand on her shoulder made her jump and swear. 'For Fucksakes!'

'What you doing here Jodes?' It was Amy. And why she had not seen her pass by the window.

'How d'you know I was here?'

'Didn't. Just spotted you as I came through the door.' Amy examined her friend. 'You ok? Look like you been through the wars.'

'Accident... motorbike... Reuben's.' There was no need to waste words with Amy. She was quick to pick up.

'Where is he?'

'In the Whittington, fighting for his life so they told me. It was his bike... and some nutter's car.'

Amy frowned, bit her lower lip. 'D'you wanna drink?'

'What you having?'

Amy shrugged. 'Glass of white I s'pose. Want the same?'

Jodie shook her head, wished she hadn't. It still hurt.

'Best not, I'm on painkillers, strong ones. Had a head injury.'

'Want another coffee then?'

'Yeah, cheers.' She fished in her pocket for a note.

'S'ok, I'll get them.'

'I haven't paid for this one yet.' She handed Amy a fiver and the bill. 'Take it over for me?'

'Sure.'

Two minutes later, Amy was back, carrying a large white wine and another coffee, this time with two biscotti and a cheery wink from sister boy.

Bless... She gave Jodie the change from her fiver for the first coffee and sat down beside her friend.

'They must have missed me by now, there's police everywhere.' Jodie spoke in a low voice, trying desperately not to look all around her. *Avoid acting suspicious. Don't attract unnecessary attention.* She ate the two biscotti; knew her pangs of hunger had diminished.

Amy glanced out of the window. Not that she could see as far as her road from here.

'How come they haven't taken you in Ames? Haven't the police been round to yours?'

'Course they have. And my old man lied for me, would you believe? He told them I'd been back two months, not one. At least, it was when they arrived.'

'So what did they say? What did they ask you?'

'Oh... you know, this and that. Asked me if I knew you and I said yes I did. Told 'em we used to go to school together. Then they asked me if I'd seen you recently, so I kind of told the truth.'

'What d'you mean? You kind of told them the truth?' Jodie managed a smile.

Amy lifted her shoulders. 'Well I said we bumped into each other about six months ago in Hereford City centre... went for a few drinks, then... nothing.'

'And did they believe you?'

'Dunno, kind of, I s'pose, cos when they asked had I seen you in the last six weeks, Dad butted in and told them I'd been back for two months or more.'

'Did they ask you what you were doing in Hereford?'

'Jeez Jodes, this is like the bloody Spanish inquisition! Yes, and I told them I worked part-time in a Greek restaurant down Dean's Alley. Then I said I got homesick and moved back here. Dad put his arm round me and said I was Daddy's little girl who missed her Dad and Mum. Can you believe my old man doing that?'

Jodie smiled again and shook her head. It still hurt but not as much.

'Then he asked them why all the questions, and they said something about they were trying to trace you, and if you got in touch we should contact the police immediately. One of them gave Dad his card with his mobile on it.'

The reflected sun warmed Jodie's back as they sat in the window. She relaxed into its heat, but with mixed feelings of relief after what Amy had told her. Now she needed somewhere to hide out, grimly aware that her chances were slim.

'Strange really,' she said. 'When you consider it's been all over the news, papers, telly, and the radio. And they mentioned a couple of times they were looking for two women and a small girl, that's what they said. Never named any of us though... Gotta be a miracle.'

They fell silent, drank their drinks. 'They raided Reuben's flat, obviously looking for me.' Jodie managed another grin. 'He hid me under the floorboards in his hallway. Right under their size twelve boots.'

'Blimey Jodes.' Amy was speechless.

'He was planning to take me to a safe house, one of his mates... Sod's law, we crashed. Ended up in the Whittington with the pigs outside my door.' She grinned again. 'Only the nurse wouldn't let them in, said I needed more time for recovery. That's how I was able to get away. Hang dropped onto a little roof garden...' She fell silent. 'What am I gonna do Ames?'

Amy looked at her friend, sighed and bit her lip again.

'I've got an idea,' she said. 'My Dad has spare keys for the Braithwaite's house. And Mungo Dickson's. They won't be needing them anymore... How about I get the keys for the Braithwaite's house? Maybe you can doss down there for a couple of days, or even a bit longer? I can always bring you food and stuff?'

Jodie chewed over this. 'Mmn, might work. But what about the police at the top of your road?'

'Might have been to my place again, but my Dad will say he hasn't seen you in years. Which is correct.'

'Might work... you go back now, see if they're still around. Then come back for me. If I'm not sitting here,' she nodded her head. 'I'll be over there in the loos.'

'Ok,' Amy leaned over and kissed Jodie. 'See you in a bit. I'll go buy a magazine, make it look like why I came out.' And she was gone.

Jodie's bladder was full, and she was hot wearing the cloche hat. She didn't want to remove it out here though. She took a slow and painful limp to the toilets but she got there before she was desperate. One of the old dears was in there, applying more garish red lipstick to her wrinkled mouth, then pursing her lips together, massaging the fresh coating in place before licking off the surplus from her dentures. She peered at Jodie through the mirror.

'Been in the wars dear?'

'Sprained my ankle playing tennis.'

'Poor you,' she chuckled. 'Still, as my old Mum used to say – you get more old drinkers than you do old sportsmen.' She cackled at her own joke. Jodie managed a thin smile and excused herself into a cubicle. She sat down on the lavatory seat, removed the cloche hat and massaged her sweat-damp head.

Amy, she calculated, had been gone for half an hour. What the hell was she doing? Not turning me in, surely? Would she? Could she? Nah, she's too much involved herself. Jodie worried herself into not worrying. She moved back into the bar and sat down again. Not in the window seat, that had been taken by four geeks. Loud mouthed, public school accents, raucous Hooray Henry laughter. What were they doing around here? Slumming? She found herself a stool at the bar. Sister boy sidled over.

'Just listen to them.'

'Can't help it can they? S'pose they think we're all deaf.'

'Can I get you anything sweetie?'

She thought about it. Tablets or wine. The wine won.

'Glass of Pinot please.'

'Large or small?'

'Oh go on, make it a large one.'

'Lion for a day or a lamb for life aye?'

'Yeah, something like that.' She managed a smile, wished Amy would come back: a double wish, the Hooray Henry's would drop dead or lose their balls or something.

Amy returned just as Jodie took her first sip of the chilled wine. She was nursing an ear-to-ear grin.

'Sorted,' she said, and held up a key ring with two keys dangling from it. 'Dad won't even miss it. I found some similar ones in a drawer, hung them up in their place. They look just like these.'

'What about the police?' Jodie whispered.

'All gone. *And* the ones outside Reuben's. You can move in as soon as you like.'

Jodie felt the relief wash over her. Safe, at least, for a few days. She would have time to think about what to do next, make a plan. 'Here,' she turned to Amy. 'Help us drink this up. Let's get going.'

Amy obliged. 'We'll have a rummage round their gaff, see what you need and I can shop for you while you settle in.'

Two minutes later they escaped the noisy geeks, blew a kiss to sister boy at the other end of the bar, and made their way to Harbourne Road.

No-one bothered to say goodbye, not the old boys or the old dears with their painted faces, or the bay window boomers. Only one person watched them cross the road from her upper flat window in St Pauls Road, the elderly tenant who watched everyone and everything; who walked her dog around Harbourne Road and into the little park that adjoined the railway fence. The same fence that was opposite Mungo Dickson's house and that of the Braithwaite brothers.

Despite Jodie's disguise, the old lady knew who she was. She had a gift of recognition, how to identify the shape of a head, the way different people walked, and their facial expressions. She could also lip-read, a gift that came naturally to her like other people's photographic memories.

'Why are you back here, young woman? And with Amy?' she asked herself, and prepared to find a coat and her little dog's lead. She must find out what these two were up to...

She was too late to follow them but saw, a few minutes later, where Amy emerged from and whose house it was. 'Hmm,' she said to herself. 'Now why did they go into the Braithwaite's house? And how did they get in there?' She gave a gentle tug on her small dog's lead. 'Come on Coco, let's go walkies.' And she turned back towards the small park that adjoined the railway fence, a plastic bag clutched in her hand in case Coco wanted to 'go'.

Jodie watched the old girl from behind the downstairs curtains. Was she a danger, or not? Worrying... She'd talk to Amy about it when she got back from the corner shop with the supplies.

'Sorry I'm late,' Amy panted when she finally did return. 'There was an old lady mooching about with her rat bag of a dog. Didn't want her see me come in here.'

She dumped two plastic bags on the kitchen table. 'Bought you bread, ham and cheese, some fruit juice, and a beef tomato. Funny name for a tomato innit?' She laughed at her own silly remark. Jodie didn't.

'I've seen that old girl before,' she said. 'I'm sure she lives on St Pauls Road, almost opposite Reuben's. She watched you leave here,' she added.

'She didn't see you did she?'

Jodie shook her head. It still hurt, but not as much. 'Don't think so. She wasn't around when we got here... Did you bring any wine?'

'Oh fuck! Sorry Jodes, I forgot. Anyway don't

worry,' her face illuminated. 'I'm sure I saw some in their cupboard up there. She opened the double door units above them. 'There you go, one of each, red, white and rosé.' She reached them on tip toes. 'I'll stick these two in the fridge to chill. They won't take long.'

'Better put one in the freezer, it'll cool quicker.'

'Ok. Anyway, best go now, Mum'll be home from work soon, she only works part time now.'

'Sure Ames... and thanks. I think I'll have a few minutes shut-eye, I feel knackered.'

'Don't forget the wine in the freezer, else you'll have Pinot ice lolly.'

And she was gone. Relief. Jodie needed the silence as much for rest as thinking out her next move. Grateful though, for a few day's respite from physical effort, time to get her body healed... away from the police.

She had already made a recce of the house, peered into cupboards... and rooms. She knew where the telly was. And a computer. She hoped it didn't have a password, and was in luck... straight in. Same for email... and Facebook. It would be easy to contact Reuben's group followers and very necessary. She needed a passport, extra cash, *and* some euros. His guys would do anything for him, and her... she was still considered his woman. Where to go, though? And how? Boat or plane?

She fell asleep thinking about her immediate future, slept without dreaming. When she awoke, it was dark and for a few moments, she wondered where the hell she was and why she had such a painful body. Then remembered. Her throat and mouth were dryer than dust and badly needed water. Not alcohol. Oh bloody hell... alcohol... wine in the freezer. She moved through to the kitchen as fast as her body would allow. A mobile rang. Where? Whose? Oh yes, Amy had acquired one for her. She fished it out of her pocket and recognised Amy's number.

'Hi.'

'I guessed you'd be awake by now.'

'What time is it?' She yawned and stretched. Wished she hadn't, yawning was not good for her injuries.

'Eight o'clock, just. Mum and Dad have gone out so I'll pop round.'

Jodie was standing by the door when Amy knocked. She opened it enough for her friend to slip through.

'No lights on then?'

'No, just this torch.'

'Yeah, good thinking. Ok. I suppose though,' she added, 'if all the curtains are drawn, you can maybe use one of the table lamps.'

'I'm all right with this.' She held up the torch.'

'Did you remember the wine in the freezer?'

Jodie laughed. 'No, I fell asleep as soon as you went. It's ok though, I pulled it out just now. Not frozen, not iced up anyway.'

'Good, shall we have a glass then?'

'Sure, Ames. I want some water first though; my mouth feels like a vacuum dust bag.'

'I'll get it for you, sit over there.' She indicated an upright chair by a side table. 'White or red. Or rosé?'

'White for me thanks. What you having?'

'I'll have the same. Be back in a tick.' And she disappeared into the kitchen. Jodie heard her bang into something and swear. She smiled to herself.

She shouted into the dark, 'I'll bring the torch through, maybe we can find some candles.'

Amy stayed for the best part of two hours while they discussed where Jodie could go to avoid arrest. She told Jodie about her parents belonging to some vacation club thingie in Madeira.

Jodie screwed up her face. 'Madeira? That's where all the wrinklies holiday isn't it?'

'Not nowadays. They cater for everyone... from cradle to grave apparently. Leastwise that's what Mum and Dad say. In fact,' she continued. 'Mum reckons it's a very mixed bag – as she puts it – nowadays.' She gave a cunning smile. 'I could book us a week or two there. They wouldn't even have to know; I've got all the details.'

'How come?'

'I've booked it before for them. Anyway, it's flexible like. Anyone in the family can use it, the membership. And any time of the year.'

'Sounds impressive. What d'you have to do then?'

'Book an apartment at one of their hotels, then book the flights. All we pay for is maid service and our food, self-cater or eat out. There's loads of facilities, pools, gym club, bars, restaurants. You don't even have to leave the hotel if you don't want to, except Funchal's a great place to visit.'

'How come you know all this?'

'Been there with Mum and Dad a coupla times.'

'I need a passport,' said Jodie. 'Shouldn't be a problem though, I can get one off Reuben's mate, Shane. He's an ace forger.'

'Brilliant. How soon can he get you one?'

'Dunno. Two or three days probably.' She

hesitated. 'How about if I go as a fella? Plenty of guys' clothes here, and Shane can come here to take a photo.'

Amy laughed. 'You don't look much like a guy Jodes.'

Jodie stared at her. 'What about the magic of make-up? I almost fooled Reuben when we bumped into each other.'

'Ok, so ring him, this Shane. Let's go for it. Can't see the police looking for you there... not Madeira. Can you?'

'No way.'

Amy left her again, and Jodie rang Reuben's friend. When he picked up she said, 'Shane, it's Jodie.'

'Fucksakes! Where are you?'

'Not far from you.'

'The pigs are everywhere looking for you. By the way Reub's pegged it. Had a massive brain haemorrhage, last night, so I hear.'

Jodie felt a momentary sadness. Not for the man she no longer loved, but the fact he had died because he was trying to take her to a place of safety.

Shane broke into her silence. 'You all right?'

'Yeah. I need a favour though.'

'What kind?'

'Passport.'

'No worries. Where are you?'

'D'you know Harbourne Road? It's a kind of cul-de-sac off St Pauls Road, almost opposite Reuben's pad.'

'I know it. What number?'

'Four.'

'I'll be with you in half an hour.'

He neglected to ask her why she was there, and she did not offer to explain. That's how they were in Reuben's group...

She went upstairs to root through the brothers' belongings, see if there was anything suitable to wear for the passport photo, for a temporary 'sex change'. The older brother's wardrobe was minimal, to say the least. And grubby. Her screwed up nose insinuated the stale, sweaty smell that came from his clothes. She could have almost gagged. Jacob's clothing was more hopeful. Sweaters, jeans, casual shirts. She tried on some of each; the fit was great. Yeah, she could live in some of these for a while. At least until she got to Madeira. Bound to be plenty of shops there she could use.

Dressed in a pair of his jeans, a T shirt and a V-necked sweater, her hair cut even shorter, Jodie walked carefully downstairs, still conscious of her not yet healed body. At the same time, she felt a twinge of guilt for Jacob's and Gabriel's death at the festival site. How could she have known they were going to be there? And on that fateful day? Also Mungo Dickson... and mad Matilda Meadham, how come she was there? Three innocents that perished because of what she did and one, she has since learned, being badly burned. A wince of regret flickered on her face. Maybe that was why she and Reuben had crashed? Karma? She shrugged. Load of shit. *Don't go down that road, J.D...*

Her stomach heaved a massive lurch at the sight of the figure downstairs in the front doorway. A massive lurch because the figure in its silhouette form was *inside* the door, not outside waiting to be let in. Surely not one of the brothers? Didn't they both die in the explosion? That is what the papers had said. It could not be one of them.

'Shane?'

'Jaydee?'

'How did you...' She stopped in mid-sentence. This was Shane. Typical. He was capable, like Reuben, of anything. What challenge was a lock or two? In his right hand he dangled a bunch of what she presumed were skeleton keys. That's how.

'You all right?' A normal Shane greeting, not an enquiry after her health.

'Sort of. My ribs still hurt, and my shoulder.' She kind of grinned. 'But I'll live I guess.'

'Reuben's dead.'

'I know, you told me earlier.' She leaned against the bannister newel post.

'I went to see him, you know... He pegged it just as I got there. They wouldn't let me see him. Like a load of headless chickens, they were... running around and squawking.' He almost had a grin on his unshaven face.

Jodie was unsure if she wanted to cry. She knew Reuben had been very badly injured, but she hadn't expected him to die. Shane showed no grief. His best buddy. But that was Shane. Hard as a block of ebony and cold as Arctic ice.

'Let's get this photo taken.' Reuben was already dismissed from his mind. His eyes went from head to toe, Jodie's head to toe, and back again as he mentally undressed her.

'Where d'you want me?' She wished she hadn't said it quite like that. Wrong choice of words. She caught the lecherous look on his face.

'Still quite light out. I'll take you at the back of the house.'

She wished Amy was here... desperately.

Half an hour later, she felt around for the unfamiliar clothes that Shane had quietly but effectively stripped from her body. She wondered how long it would be before the love bite he took from her neck would show, and disappear. A mirror in the front room, where he had dragged her after the photo shoot, indicated it was already turning an angry red. She shuddered. Hating him and it. She badly wanted to shower away his cold-blooded and latently cruel sex. You couldn't call it love-making. No way.

'I'll get the passport to you by tomorrow morning. Name of John Drake, same initials see. No charge.' He gave her another lecherous smile.

No way, she thought, you've just had more than enough payment, and wondered if, hoped even, the unprotected sex did not mean anything sinister or dangerous was going to happen to her.

22

Jodie discovered she was pregnant three weeks later, and five days after she and Amy arrived in Madeira, and two hours after they were into a jeep trip around the island. She barely had time to climb out and reach the edge of the track before she threw up all over a red hibiscus bush, much to the disgust of her five fellow passengers, the Madeiran driver, and his English courier.

A fit but elderly lady commented, 'Didn't know men got morning sickness.'

'Maybe HE,' said her husband, emphasising the gender, 'is getting rid of last night's alcohol indulgence.'

'Trust me, John,' she replied. 'SHE is no HE and that sickness is not through drink. After four pregnancies,' she added. 'I should know the difference. I suffered all through the nine months... each time... if you remember.'

If Jodie heard their conversation, and the subsequent remarks by the other passengers, she neither cared nor wanted to defend herself. She just wanted the vomiting to cease, the retching to stop. And that foul, acidic taste, that made her want to gag more, disappear.

Amy climbed down and came to her side. 'You OK?'

'No, course I'm bloody not.' At that moment in time, she neither felt, nor looked like a guy, despite the male clothes disguise. She took a deep breath and swiped her hand across her mouth, felt in a pocket for a tissue.

'Here,' said Amy and handed her a small packet of travel wipes.

The driver had switched off the ignition and climbed out of his seat. 'Are you OK, sir?'

'She's not a sir,' shouted the elderly lady. 'She's very much a female... and probably one with child. And when she's ready,' she added. 'Perhaps we can continue this journey that is costing us seventy-five euros apiece.'

Her husband, sank further into his seat and looked distinctly uncomfortable; the other passengers glared at her and Amy muttered, 'She's all heart, that old bag.'

'I'll be all right in a moment,' she tried a smile for the driver, but only succeeded in a pathetically horizontal stretch of her mouth. She straightened up, breathed in again and was aware of what should have been a pleasant, fragrance from the roadside flowers and plants, but her stomach interpreted the perfume very differently. She gagged again, this time missing the plants and finding Amy's sandals instead. Amy jumped back as if she'd been burned. In a way, she had. The vomit was definitely acid when it left Jodie's mouth.

'Thanks for that,' she hissed, and almost threw up herself as she wiped the offending liquid from the leather straps and her bare feet.

After an embarrassing ten minutes or so, both girls climbed back inside the jeep. The driver started up and grumbled his way to their next destination, The Nun's Valley. Any other time, Jodie would have leapt out of the jeep and climbed to the viewing edge to look over the valley at all the tiny houses below. She would probably even have ooh'd and aah'd with her fellow tourists at the amazing vista before and below them. But not today. Today, all she wanted was to get back to the hotel, to their studio apartment and crash out on one of the twin beds or relax on the balcony that overlooked the brilliant azure pool below.

It was one of those desperate afternoons that dragged by at the pace of the other passengers, those who listened raptly to Derry the courier's (short for Londonderry, darlings), fascinating discourse on the histories of each site they visited. Meanwhile the sun beat down on them and, if there was any AC in the jeep, Jodie had not felt the benefits. Her T shirt was soaked and stuck to her back, her cut-off jeans, ragged at the edges, felt two sizes too small, and her feet – in trainers – were swollen up to her ankles. The day was one more to add to the pain and misery of the past month. She wished she was dead.

'Thank God we're back.' Both girls watched as the jeep drove away with its remaining passengers being taken on to their respective hotels. Amy gave a header towards the departing vehicle as it signalled and turned right away from Funchal.

'Yeah, and thank the sun, moon, and stars none of them are staying here, especially the old bag recognising you as female.'

They nodded at the little man behind the reception desk. He smiled and asked did they enjoy the day? Amy answered for both of them. 'It was… er… amazing.' And added, 'obrigado,' as if he had been responsible for arranging everything. Jodie couldn't wait to reach the lifts at the far end of the wide, carpeted corridor and get back to their apartment.

'I think I'm gonna throw up again.'

'No you won't. Take deep breaths like that old bag said.'

Amy was right. They reached the sixth floor studio flat and slotted their card to unlock the door before Jodie started retching again. Fortunately, the bathroom was first room inside the door.

There was nothing more to bring up; her stomach hurt, and her ribs. Maybe, even if she was pregnant, she would lose the baby with this violent retching?

Amy stood in the doorway. 'You OK, hun?'

Jodie lifted her head from the toilet bowl. 'Not really… I just want to go home.'

But where was home? Where was safe for her? She knew this stay on the island couldn't last forever, not even three more days. Their flight was booked for Monday and today was Saturday. She felt the lowest, the most desperate she had ever felt in her life. So low, death would have been a welcome change. Permanent though. No going or coming back. She levered herself up from the floor as the nausea began to disappear.

'I'm going for a swim, Jodes.' Amy was sitting on the end of her bed slipping on her bikini. 'D'you mind? Or d'you want to come?'

Jodie shook her head. 'No, you go ahead hun. I'm going out on the balcony, I'll watch you from up here.'

Amy slipped on the skimpy two-piece and wrapped a towelling robe around herself. 'See ya.' And she was gone.

A few minutes later Jodie watched her friend lazily swimming up and down the brilliant azure pool below. Palms waved around it, people stretched out on loungers or rubbed each other with sun-blocker. Some read books, others iPads. Young parents dangled their offspring in the clear water. Only she sat alone twenty or thirty feet above them. *I feel like bloody Juliet, only I don't need a Romeo, thank you.*

She wondered, if she was really pregnant, then, whose baby was it, Reuben's or Shane's? Not much of a choice, she ruefully told herself. Whichever... this unborn child was not gonna have the finest of starts in life. For the first time in years she thought about her mother, kind of wanted a hug from her. Didn't remember many of them after Paul-Bloody-Davies came into their lives. She remembered a child's wrist watch with its pink leather strap; the last gift from her father, Tommy Drummonds. And the way Paul had crunched it under his boot...

Jodie began to cry. Another first, or almost. When was the last time she had known tears? Not since the watch incident? But she sobbed then, like a small child. Sorry for herself and yes, sorry for what she had done on that fateful day in Teme's Edge only six weeks ago. All for revenge on one man, and one she had met just the once. OK, so he was a bad bastard, an evil inhuman being, not one who deserved to live after the damage he had done to others. But was it her place to take his life? Not only his, but all those innocents that were blown up with him? And this child, if she was carrying fragile human life, would be the product of an equally evil man, be it Reuben or Shane. One who would grow up to be judged by others for its bad blood. Maybe one who would share their evil in its life?

Yes, Jodie wept, cried away her shame, her guilt, and – unknowingly – these tears flowed on her last day of freedom...

23

Jodie, with the sickness apparently over, felt well enough to join Amy for dinner.

'Not in that buffet restaurant though, too many bodies. Can we go to The Fonseca?'

'Sure.' Amy's eyes brightened. 'I know it's more expensive but some guys down by the pool were saying it's really good.'

Jodie noted the way Amy's face lit up at the mention of the guys she met and felt envious. How long did she have to keep up this pretence of being a man? She would look really stupid if she threw up at the table. A bit late now, to think of that...

'Right, the Fonseca it is then. What's the dress code in there?'

'Erm, smart-casual I think.' Amy grinned. 'You got a tie Jodes?'

'Course I haven't.' she hesitated. 'I'll just wear a V neck and jeans. It'll have to do.'

The menu, though limited, was excellent and tempting. Amy chose the espada, the scabbard fish, and Jodie the fillet steak. They both passed on the starter.

'Bet the desserts are fab,' said Amy. 'I'm gonna leave room for one – just seen that table over there served some. To die for.' She licked her lips and made 'yummy' noises.

'And to drink, senhorita?'

'Ooh, a white wine I think, with fish. How about you Jo?'

'I'll pass on the wine. A sparkling water for me please.'

Amy looked at her in shock. 'No wine?'

'Maybe when the food arrives. See how I feel then.'

She sipped slowly at her sparkling water. At least it was staying down. Maybe she'd just had a bug of some kind?

They glanced around the room at the rich furnishings, huge pots of exotic plants in corners and magnificent chandeliers shimmering from the high ceiling that reflected on the dark marble floor.

'Like a palace isn't it?' whispered Amy.

'Dunno, never been in a palace.'

'Oh, you know what I mean. What you'd expect a palace to be like... Wonder who lived here before it became a hotel?'

The food arrived, hidden under silver domes with ornate gold handles, which the waiter lifted with the flourish of a magician.

'Aqui está'

'I s'pose that's like voila.' Amy whispered. 'Looks amazing doesn't it Jodes?'

'Sure does.' Jodie remembered she hadn't eaten since breakfast. She could almost hear her stomach growl. Be good, she pleaded with it.

'More wine, senhorita?' to Amy. 'Water... for

you?' It was obvious he was having a problem with Jodie's gender.

'No, I think I'll have some red wine now. Shame to enjoy this steak with anything less. Just a glass thanks,' she added, afraid to risk more. They, all three, exchanged obrigado's.

'Such a mouthful every time, don't you think Jodes?'

'Yeah, I do, but the way they say it, sounds more like "brigado". Still... much easier to say thanks...'

'I know... but you know what they say, when in Rome and all that.'

They tucked in to their food.'

'Out of this world,' drooled Amy. 'How's yours?'

'Brilliant... so's the wine.'

They were there in the apartment, guns at the ready, as the girls stumbled, giggling into the small, inner hallway. As soon as she saw them, Jodie turned, ready to run back out into the corridor and down to the lift. Stupid idea anyway, with all that drink inside her. They had left the restaurant and gone over to the pool bar to drink the rest of the evening away with Amy's new-found friends.

As she opened the door, Jodie was confronted by two more armed police, each coming from the opposite end of the corridor.

'In,' one said as the other pointed with his gun. She staggered back into the apartment to see Amy being cuffed, hands behind her back, a mixture of fear and misery on her face. Jodie felt her own arms being dragged behind her and the cold steel of cuffs on her wrists.

'Woss going on?' she lisped. 'What the fuck you doing?'

A man in civvies she had not noticed before came forward. He spoke in a quiet but firm voice. 'In co-operation with the British Police we are arresting you for obtaining and travelling on a false passport, and for the murders of more than one person.'

'What? What you on about?' Jodie attempted bluff, but suspected it was not going to get her or Amy anywhere.

'What about *her*? Why are you arresting her? She's done nothing wrong.' Realising then that her words were incriminating herself. But she saw the swift look of gratitude on Amy's face. *Don't worry, hun, I won't involve you.* She hoped telepathy would work between them.

Events moved quickly. In not much more than seconds they were out of the apartment and going down in the lift, accompanied by two male and two female officers, and the one in plain clothes, all grim faced and uncommunicative. They were marched through reception with few, if any, late night guests to witness their departure. Even the reception desk appeared unmanned, although a door was open to a small inner office and the light was on.

'What about our things? Our luggage?'

'They are being taken care of and will be brought to the station.'

Both girls stumbled down the outer steps, but were prevented from falling by two officers apiece that were holding them upright. They were pushed into the back of a small, dark van, about the size of a mini-bus, and with blacked-out windows. There were bench seats on either side, divided up into single cubicles. Amy was guided to the furthest one on the left and Jodie to the nearest one on the right. Once seated, a bar, waist high, secured them in place. Neither girl could see the other.

'Bit like a fairground ride,' shouted Jodie. She was not rewarded with a reply and imagined a frightened, miserable Amy who was unable to dredge up any humour.

The police accompanying them, took seats, no bars, and stared in front of them without speaking.

The vehicle moved off, leaving the hotel driveway, moving over to the far side of the road before turning left towards Funchal. They could see flashing blue lights reflected on the van's interior. Jodie supposed it was a police car leading them. There was another following that she could see through her rear window, also flashing blue lights.

'What time is it... please?' she asked the female officer opposite her.

'Twenty-three thirty.'

'Obrigada,' she remembered the 'a' at the end when addressing a female. 'O' for a man. She wondered, was it the same for kids? 'O' and 'A'?

After ten minutes or so they were driven under an arched entrance into a large, enclosed concourse. Lights blazed and more armed police were present. Both girls were carefully helped out of the van and taken inside to a reception area. Amy whispered to Jodie, 'Look – there's our suitcases.'

'Wonderful... at least we can change our knickers. Think I've peed mine.'

The remark brought a swift smirk to Amy's face. 'Think I've done worse in mine.'

Their laughter and humour stopped at the sight

of the ugliest man on earth. He was tall, taller than any of the uniformed police who had handled them so far. And almost as broad. He had thick, dark hair that brushed his white shirt collar, a broad sweep of forehead with overhanging eyebrows, and deeply pock-marked flesh on a scowling face. There was an angry, jagged scar that ran from his right eye to under his chin and halfway down his neck. It reminded Jodie of Halloween teeth on a pumpkin.

'A Neanderthal gorilla,' she hissed through the side of her mouth.

'Good evening senhoritas.' His greeting came out as a low, forty cigarettes-a-day growl, slightly menacing and not accompanied by a smile.

'You,' he stared at Jodie. 'Go in there.' And pointed to a small room with its door open and revealing a plain table with four upright metal chairs.

'Take her to the cells.' He gave the second instruction to the two officers still holding onto Amy. She screamed. 'Jodie. Help me.' Her cry echoed down the corridor as she was quickly led away.

Jodie felt sick, knowing there was nothing she could do to help her friend. She was led into the small room with its bare walls and hard floor surface. There was a mirror on one wall, two-way she guessed. And some kind of recording equipment on the table. Her mouth was dry and she ran her tongue around it trying to dredge up some saliva. Yes, she did feel sick, not mental anguish sick, but nauseous. She remembered the disastrous trip around the island, only this morning, and her throwing up every five minutes. *Oh God, not again. Please not now.* Her silent plea was wilfully ignored. She hadn't even sat down when up it came, all the delicious food she'd had for dinner, the red wine, and the late evening Pina Coladas. All over the floor, the table, herself, and over the uniform of the female officer who was separating herself from the handcuffs that bound them together.

The foul language and verbal reaction was universal from both her accompanying officers and the gorilla who was about to interview her. They all sprang back like they were burned by acid. Any other time Jodie would have viewed the scene with a grim delight. But she was too busy trying to survive the nauseous onslaught. She missed the ensuing drama as she slid to the floor in a dead faint...

She came to lying on a hard, rubber mattress, with bright lights blazing above her that reflected onto white-tiled walls. Someone was wiping her face with a warm, damp cloth that smelled faintly of lavender. She tried to sit up, but was held down with firm but not unkind hands.

'Stay still, senhorita, just for a short time, while I clean you.' It was the female officer from earlier, now changed into a fresh uniform. On a chair beside her were clothes Jodie recognised as her own. Or Jacob Braithwaite's. At least they were folded and presumably clean.

'We will get you out of your soiled clothes now, if you feel able to.'

Jodie nodded. This time she was allowed to sit up and put her feet to the floor. It felt cool, not uncomfortable. With the officer's help she stood up and began to remove the vomit-covered clothes, ready to put on clean ones.

'Do you want to wipe yourself anywhere?'

A shower would be welcome but she couldn't see the evidence of one. 'Erm, yes, er...'

The officer gave a slight smile. 'There is a basin over there, perhaps?'

Jodie stood up in the nude. She felt no embarrassment as she moved over to the basin affixed to the opposite wall. There was a small bar of green soap, a white face cloth and a small, striped towel. The officer turned away and bagged up Jodie's soiled clothes while she attempted a strip wash. She lowered her head to the tap, filled her mouth with cold water and rinsed around her teeth and gums, spitting away the acid taste.

'You are with child? Pregnant?'

Jodie shrugged. 'I don't know for sure. If I am, it's only three or four weeks...'

The woman gave a sympathetic smile. 'My sister, every time she get pregnant, she know in ten days. Sick all the time, all the nine months.'

'Oh great, something to look forward to... not.' She walked back to the chair and began to dress in the clean clothes. 'Thank you for doing this for me,' she said. 'Obrigada.'

The police officer stripped off the blue rubber gloves she was wearing.

'Is it back to the interview room?' asked Jodie.

'No, not tonight. I will take you to a cell and you will be interviewed tomorrow morning. It is very late, past one in the morning.'

'Will I be near my friend?'

'Er, no. But you will see her some time tomorrow.' She walked to the door, tapped on it and waited for it to be unlocked from the outside.

Another female officer stood there, not with a friendly face. Jodie thought it best to keep quiet and let them babble away in Portuguese. Seems like she'd caused enough disturbance for one night... They led her down some stairs, along a corridor where there were several steel doors with a small shutter on each one. Where the officers could eyeball the prisoners she supposed.

The po-faced one unlocked the door of a cell halfway along. She flicked her head, a signal for Jodie to go in. Both of them followed her, the nice one pointing to a narrow bed that had a folded blanket on it and a pillow. Opposite the bed was a toilet and a wash basin. A metal chair stood under a barred window through which faint lights showed. On the ceiling was a single bulb dangling from a covered wire, too high, even on a chair, for anyone to reach... unless they were seven feet tall.

'Home from home,' said Jodie. The humour was lost upon her Madeiran guards. Or ignored. They left her without speaking and clanged the door to before locking it. She lay on the bed, wondering what was going to happen next. Next being tomorrow. She wondered how Amy was faring, wished the bloody overhead light would go out. As if in answer to her wish, it dimmed but was not completely extinguished. Better than nothing she supposed and suddenly felt tired, not just tired, bloody well knackered. She almost fell asleep on the hard mattress, under the single blanket, until she was conscious that the washbasin tap dripped. She counted to fourteen between drips. Not exactly torture by water she supposed, then fell asleep.

Somewhere in her semi-consciousness she could

hear bells ringing. Not church bells. These were more strident, almost high pitched. Jodie flattened her hands over her ears.

'Now what?'

The shutter opened and she could see a pair of eyes and the upper half of a nose. The shutter closed and a key turned in the lock. The young female officer who had looked after her last night entered, carrying a tin tray with a tin mug and plate on it.

'Bom dia. Here is breakfast.'

Jodie sat up, knuckled the sleep from her eyes. 'Oh yeah, bom dia. What time is it... please?' No need to be rude to her, she seemed a decent type.

The policewoman set the tray down on a small table she unfolded from the wall beside the chair. Jodie hadn't noticed it last night. She could smell strong coffee and saw the bread roll and slices of cheese and ham. No cutlery and no butter. *Oh well, not exactly Reid's Hotel.*

'It is 7am. When you have finished, bang on the persiana... the shutter, and I will take you to the interview room.'

Jodie muttered 'obrigada' and saw the coffee was black. Fine by her, she didn't fancy milk anyway. Wouldn't have minded a spoonful of demerara though. She spotted a sachet half hidden under the tin plate. Oh, good. She could smell the bread roll and the ham and tucked into it. A gulp of the coffee almost scalded her mouth. *Unbelievable! Hot coffee in a police cell.* Another two mouthfuls of food and something nasty began to happen in her stomach... like a volcano about to erupt. The whole mixture fought its way back into her throat. *Oh no, not again.* But the nausea won. She knelt down by the lavatory bowl and experienced the stale smell of urine, which sent more waves of nausea into her nostrils.

A lifetime later, or what felt like it, she stood up and staggered over to the wash basin to rinse her face and mouth under the cooling tap. She had searched everywhere for a press button or handle to flush the toilet but failed. Might as well bang on the shutter.

A different officer entered; not a smiling one.

'Please,' said Jodie. 'How do I flush the toilet?'

The woman screwed up her face at the smell of vomit.

'Like so,' she said, and pushed a hidden button under the window frame.

'You sick?'

Jodie nodded, miserable and weakened.

'Nothing left in here?' she pointed to her own stomach.

'No... not in mine either.'

A lifting of the woman's shoulders and outstretched hands implied 'bad luck, hard cheese, tough.'

Yeah, all of those, thought Jodie. *No dinner left inside me, no breakfast, I'll be wasting away.* She remembered some old lady, could not remember who or where, once saying 'You lose weight to gain weight.' Terrific...

'Come.'

Jodie walked by the policewoman's side, along the corridor, where raucous sounds of other inmates assailed their ears. Then up a flight of stairs, back to the reception area and the interview room. She wondered where Amy was, how she was coping. Nothing she could do about it anyway.

The room, when she and the officer entered, was already occupied. A uniformed male and Gorilla. He pointed a fat, hairy finger to the chair opposite his own.

'Sit.'

Yeah and good morning to you too, Neanderthal. It was in her head, not in her mouth. Gorilla didn't look the type to antagonise. He had those eyes, she thought, that could pry into the windows of a man's soul.

'No sick today aye?' He said, even broke into a lopsided smile.

'Done it already.'

'So,' he said. 'You are not John Drake,' he held up the false passport. 'Not in that condition. Maybe Jodie Drummond?'

She said nothing.

'Men do not have babies.'

'No, and pigs can't fly.' The insult was not lost on him. *Steady, Jodie, you're making an enemy.*

Someone knocked and entered, whispered in Gorilla's ear. He nodded, stood up and followed the younger officer outside. The two left in the room with her ignored her and talked to each other. She did not have enough knowledge of Portuguese, hardly any in fact, to understand what they were saying, so sat with her own thoughts jumbling about her head. What next? Home, back to the UK? Then what? Prison she supposed. For how long? Gotta be at least fifteen years. That would make her forty when she was released. What about this thing growing inside her? She calculated 'it' would be fourteen and more. A teenager. Older than little Lewis. She wondered what was happening with him. Had he been arrested?

Gorilla re-entered the room but did not sit down.

'I have spoken to the British Police. You and your friend are to be sent back immediately. You will each be accompanied by one of our officers and handed over to your own police at Heathrow. Goodbye Senhorita and obrigada.'

Obrigada? What's he thanking me for? Being sick all over him last night? Any time mate, feel free...'

Two hours later, she and Amy, both handcuffed, were driven to Funchal airport, accompanied by two uniformed male officers.

'No flirting, Jodes,' Amy managed a grin, to her friend's relief.

'As if.'

'No talking,' said one of the policemen.

'Why not? We're not doing any harm.'

'I think you have already done much harm. So, no talking.'

They were first to board, the last six seats at the rear of the plane. Both Jodie and Amy were given the window seats either side of the aisle, with an officer apiece handcuffed to them. The aisle seats were left vacant and the officers plonked small hand luggage and paperwork on them. Jodie leaned around her policeman and turned to her friend across the aisle. 'You ok?'

Amy looked miserable and did not answer, merely shook her head.

'No talking I said.'

'Why not?' Jodie asked her guard.

'Because I already say not.'

It was tempting to give him a mouthful of abuse, but Jodie considered the four hours in the air.

Suppose she wanted the lavatory or worse, wanted to be sick again? Best comply, behave, whatever. At least she had a window seat and could watch the land and sea disappear and reappear the other end when they reached England. She could study the shape of cloud formations... like she used to when she was a kid. She remembered the Father Christmas sledge that Paul Davies could not see... when he smashed her precious watch. A lifetime ago.

In the end she did none of these things. Instead, she slept for most of the flight, only waking when the pilot announced the approach to London Heathrow Airport.

24

The two girls and their escorts were the first to disembark from the rear of the plane. Jodie, heavy and bemused from sleep, stumbled as she moved onto the covered stairway that was connected from the plane to the airport building. She was held upright, still handcuffed to her Portuguese police officer who prevented her from falling. The sudden jolt to her arm brought on another wave of nausea.

'I'm sorry,' was all she managed to say as warning before she expelled a gush of yellow liquid on the metal walkway. The policeman moved swiftly sideways to avoid being splashed by the vomit. He had no spare uniform and would return to the plane when he had handed over his prisoner, while it was being prepared for its return flight to Funchal. He muttered something guttural that Jodie could not interpret, but it didn't sound sympathetic or friendly.

'I'm sorry,' she said again. 'Can't help it.' The foul tasting liquid had gone up her nose and burned like acid. She felt weak, helpless and hapless. Yeah, all those things. A swift, unconnected thought told her she did not feel sorry for Reuben or what had happened to him. It was her who was left to be accountable for this child. She was grimly aware that it was his, not Shane's baby she was carrying. Why or how she was certain of this was not clear... but she knew.

The walk seemed endless. She could hear Amy saying something not far behind her. Was she talking to her or to the man she was handcuffed to? It didn't matter. Jodie would have liked to turn around, look at Amy, but was being half-dragged forward by her own officer. What a nightmare... the whole thing. Treated like animals, that was what it amounted to. Like cattle being hauled to the slaughter by pigs.

When they finally reached the airport building Jodie saw half a dozen armed police, British police, waiting to greet them. The bile rose in her throat again and quickly she put her free hand up to her mouth in a vain attempt to prevent it gushing out everywhere again. Too late... it filtered through her fingers, onto her T shirt and down her jeans. Wave after wave of the foul liquid erupted from her mouth. Where the fuck did it all come from?

Her escort yanked Jodie towards the British police. Jodie fell at their feet. She vaguely heard Amy cry out, 'Jodeeee!' as she faded into unconsciousness.

Days passed, days and nights of confusion. Sunlight hours of sickness and faintness... of courtrooms and prison cells... Of stern handling by police and prison officers, and gentler treatment by medical staff. Doctors or nurses, Jodie was not quite sure.

She never saw Amy again, or anyone else she knew. Except for the old guy from Hogarth International, Bob Shackleton. Yeah, of course, he was the chief of security, COS. She dimly remembered her days with that firm, a lifetime ago.

Gradually, over the weeks of her trial, she noticed a slight swelling of her belly. The sickness subsided and the fainting was replaced by a permanent feeling of lethargy. She had no interest in the proceedings that were leading up to her incarceration. All the witnesses, her solicitor, her barrister, the prosecution, judge and jury, were merely a sea of faces in a jumbled scenario. Perhaps her mind was going. Yeah... perhaps.

Day after day she was led up from below ground-level cells to a glass-screened cage inside the courtroom. She saw people in the gallery above her but recognised no-one, wouldn't have cared if she did. Time was like in a dream, not even a nightmare, just a dream of courtroom days and prison nights.

On the last day of the trial, in a hushed atmosphere, the elderly judge – in his grey curled wig and sombre robes – droned on in his summing up until he reached the fateful number.

'Twenty-five years, with no consideration of remission.'

Twenty-five years? Double her age? She would be an old lady by the time she was freed. For one last time her knees gave way as she fainted behind the glass screen.

The journey from courtroom to the women's prison, Foston Hall in Derbyshire, was a blur. She swayed in her narrow seat to the movement of the vehicle.

It was then she felt a different movement, one inside her. The life within her gave a little kick on the inside of her womb. Like a protest. *Yeah, you too, sweetie. But you're only imprisoned for nine months.* Jodie wept, not for remorse or self-regret. She wept for her unborn child. What did the future hold for him or her?

The months passed slowly but she settled into prison routine. One of the first things she did was to make sure she gained a reputation for being a loner. She was informed by one of the screws that Myra Hindley had once been an inmate in her cell. Big deal. At least she, Jodie, wasn't a child murderer, not like that evil cow had been. But occupying Hindley's cell gave her, she felt, a kind of status, a keep-out-of-my-way status. It worked. Whatever her fellow inmates had been told about her, they only tried the once to be friendly. Until she pierced them with steely eyes and 'fuck off I don't want you anywhere near me.'

She ate her meals away from them, chose the furthest plot in the garden away from anyone else. There she was trained to grow vegetables and fruit for the prison kitchens. She was also given special dispensation to rest when the tiredness overcame her, and – after a short nap – she would wander into the library and read up books on horticulture or stay in her cell resting on the hard bed.

She also eventually learned that Amy had been given a two year suspended sentence for aiding and abetting her escape from the UK, and had been given 300 hours of Community Service. Big deal... at least she was not found to be implicated in the bombing.

As far as Jodie knew, Lewis had never been interviewed and arrested. She hoped he went to live with his grandmother, the old woman would sort him out... and protect him from all those 'uncles' and his elder brothers. At least she'd done him the favour of wasting Darwin Harrison-Forbes. That pig would never harm little boys again.

25

Jodie screamed, 'I can't bloody do this.'

'Well, you've bloody got to now.' There was no sympathy in the prison warder's voice and none in her flushed face either as she winced, not for the first time, at Jodie's grip on her hand.

'I know it's not the best place in the world, in a bloody cell, to give birth. Your fault, Drummond: shouldn't be so eager to get rid of the little darling.'

Jodie screamed again, her knees bent almost double.

'Come on Drummond, one more push and it'll be out. Pant then push.'

Jodie panted in and out until she summoned up the guts and determination for one more push. Her head was wet with sweat, and her cheeks flushed with the effort of giving this unexpected and premature birth to a baby she had neither anticipated or wanted. She strained until the veins in her temple bulged ugly and purple. She gritted her teeth and pushed...

A single wail, not from her lips, suddenly permeated the small bare room. Jodie felt the sensation of a wet something slithering between her thighs and the relief that this thing was no longer tearing her inside apart. A second warder caught the new-born in a towel and examined the tiny creature.

'It's a girl, a wee baby girl.'

Jodie lay back in her single bed, exhausted, emotionless. *A girl, poor little crow.* She felt another pain. Now what? One of them said, 'What about the umbilical cord? Shouldn't we cut it?'

'Bugger that,' said the older woman. 'Wouldn't know where to start.' She paused. 'Best call one of the nurses in the sick bay.'

'Hold on a minute,' said her fellow officer. 'The afterbirth's coming.' And to Jodie, 'You'll have to push again, love. It won't be long then it really will all be over.'

She wanted to cry at the warder's sudden kindness, the word of endearment. But she needed to push again. Not half the pain of the baby, and over very quickly. She did not bother to see what the two women were doing with all the blood and gore stuff. She had done her bit, given birth, not in hospital, but here in the prison, in her cell, because little Miss Drummond/Philips had chosen to come four weeks early.

'The ambulance should be here soon.' The statement interrupted the resting of her body and mind.

'Do I need to go now? She's here isn't she?' As an afterthought, more through curiosity than need, she said, 'Can I see her?'

The second warder handed her the towel-wrapped infant, still attached to her by the cord. 'Here you go, Drummond, your daughter.' Jodie struggled into a half-sitting position and reached for the tiny bundle.

'She's got blood on her face. Is that ok?'

'Course it is. She'll be ok when she's been bathed.'

For the first time in her life Jodie felt the stirring of a strange, protective love.

'I don't want to go.'

'What d'you mean, you don't want to go?' The screw sneered at her, like a parent suggesting with those words, that question, of course she must go. No alternative. A must.

'I'm ok here, the baby's born. Everything's come away... why do I have to go anywhere?'

'You have to be looked over, Drummond. So does she. And that cord has to be cut. We're not qualified to do it.' The woman in charge, square jawed, stocky build with thick ankles overlapping her black lace-up shoes, held her stubborn ground.

'Besides, you'll only be there overnight. Then you can come back here,' she glanced around at the small, drab cell. 'Back to Hotel Splendide.' Another sneer on her face.

Hard bitch. Jodie clutched the living, breathing possession to her; felt the baby's fluttering warm movement, listened to her faint whimpering, a new-born shocked by her premature arrival into a harsh and unforgiving world.

'They'll take her away from me.'

'No they won't Drummond.' The other, softer woman spoke. 'Only for half an hour maybe,' she soothed. 'while they examine her... and you.' She gave a generous, almost kindly look at the tumbled, dishevelled young woman who half sat and half lay on the hard prison bed: who clutched possessively and protectively at her small, towel-wrapped bundle. 'They might even send you back this evening.'

The other warder humphed her derision and disapproval. What were they supposed to do with a baby here in prison anyway?

Neither of them accompanied Jodie to hospital, that duty was given to two nurses from the prison sick bay. Before she was put in the ambulance, one of them cut the umbilical cord

'We won't handcuff you, Drummond, you just cuddle that wee mite. Keep her warm.'

There was a flurry of snow in the air as they closed the ambulance doors on her and the baby.

The two left behind, tidied away the birthing items and the blood-soaked sheets.

'Wonder what she'll call her?'

'Don't know, don't care. Some daft name I expect.'

'Why d'you say that?'

'Because it's what they do nowadays, call their kids by football teams or towns and the like.'

'How d'you mean?'

The older prison officer flicked an unpleasant sneer onto her face. 'She'll probably call her something like Highbury or Arsenal. It's where she comes from isn't it?'

Her younger comrade laughed. 'Course she won't... she'll probably call her after her mother, or someone else in the family.'

'What family?' She's never had a visitor all the time she's been here.'

'Yes, but... Arsenal or Highbury...'

'Anyway, whatever she calls it, she won't be

allowed to keep it, not as a lifer. Drummond won't be leaving this place for twenty-five years. Less the six months she's already served,' she added.

26

On that cold December day, Jodie and her baby girl were taken to the Royal Derby Hospital, where they were both examined and put into a side ward after being cleaned up. The baby was given a lemon outfit, hat and tiny all-in-one suit, a donation from the hospital's charity shop.

'There,' said one of the prison nurses. 'Doesn't she look gorgeous in her new clothes?'

Jodie looked for *gorgeous* and saw only a tiny screwed-up, very red face. She said nothing, but held the baby close.

'You'll be kept in here for a few days, to make sure the baby feeds ok. Then you'll be returned to Foston Hall, to the sick bay. It's the only place we have that will serve as a mother and baby unit.'

'Then what?' she asked.

'I don't know, but I'm sure something will be worked out. You just rest now, Drummond. We'll come back later.'

Jodie lay back in the bed, cuddling the little one. She was tired but grateful to be free from the prison for a while.

As when she was in the Whittington, she looked around for a means of escape. No chance. The only windows were almost ceiling high, and just narrow strips. Not even wide enough to get a head through, she thought. In any case, it was the middle of winter out there, what was she thinking of? The little one would freeze to death.

The door opened again. This time it was a hospital nurse. She wheeled in a glass-sided cradle. 'Here we are,' she had one of those bright voices that suggested everything was always all right, and if not, it soon would be.

'This is baby's cot, she'll sleep by your bed so you can pick her up to feed her, give her a cuddle, whatever.'

She took the baby from Jodie and placed her, on her back in the cradle and wheeled it to the left-hand side of Jodie's bed. 'If she cries, you can put her to the breast, get her used to feeding even if your milk hasn't come through.'

Jodie looked blankly at her. 'Can't she have a bottle?'

'Oh no, m'dear. Breastfeeding's best for mother and baby.'

'Why?'

'Just because.' She was having no argument and giving no explanation. 'Here, shall we have a quick try now?' She picked up the baby again and handed her back to her mother.

'Let's pull your gown down and put baby to your breast. Either one.'

The whole procedure felt awkward and strange, but the baby turned her head towards Jodie's nipple and – amazingly – latched onto it. She suckled making strange little noises.

'Wow,' said Jodie. 'I never thought in a million years I'd ever being doing this.'

The nurse smiled. 'It comes so naturally, we're all part of the animal kingdom after all.'

Jodie could not quite see the connection, but looked down at her baby's head and kind of enjoyed the sensation of the infant being at her breast.

'Have you thought of a name for her?'

'Erm, no, not really... er, well, yes and no. I've sort of got two names in my head, but not quite sure yet which one to choose.'

'What are they?'

'Erm... either Ruby or Shannon.'

'Oh, Ruby's nice, not used much nowadays. Shannon is... well... a bit more popular. But I think Ruby's lovely. After all, look at her, she's a little gem.'

Jodie failed to enlighten the nurse as to why she toyed with the two names. Ruby was close enough to Reuben, if he was the father, and Shannon for Shane. She looked down at the baby's mass of dark hair. Yes, she was Reuben's daughter. Ruby she would be...

They were kept at the hospital for ten precious days, during which Jodie quickly learned her daughter's cries and frequently picked her up from the glass cradle to satisfy the infant's hunger. She grew to love the sensation of Ruby gaining strength and growth from her swollen breasts, and both mother and daughter became favourites among the staff who attended them.

Ruby was presented with more little outfits from the charity shop, and a beautiful crocheted blanket from one of the ladies who ran the shop. Jodie could not remember such kindness, not since her Mum had died. But the ten days had passed and Ruby was considered to have gained enough weight that mother and daughter could be discharged and taken back to the prison.

Jodie's hospital gown was replaced by prison clothes, a grey tracksuit and trainers. The only concession to them was a nursing bra.

Several of the hospital staff popped into her room to say goodbye to the baby and wish them both good luck in the future.

Jodie wondered what future... Her last view of the main ward outside her small room was of a huge Christmas tree, stacked with brightly-wrapped presents. Or were they just for show? Did it matter...?

'You can't keep her, you know.' Jodie faced the assistant governor across a wooden desk. A woman who showed no sympathy, her face grim and determined.

'What? What d'you mean, I can't keep her? She's mine.' Jodie drew the baby close to her, so close Ruby wailed a protest.

'Think about it, Drummond, you're in here for twenty-five years, no parole. How're you going to bring her up in prison? What about when she goes to school?' she added. 'To college, or university?'

'I don't know. But there must be something...'

'Like what? From here? Prison? Get real, Drummond, she has to go.'

Jodie could feel a molten anger rising inside her. The need to hit out and at the same time, to grab her baby and run. But to where? There was nowhere to go. For the next five minutes she raged and screamed, called the prison and the screws every foul name she could dredge up from the cauldron of her stomach.

Finally, two officers held her down, while the prison doctor was called. He injected something into her arm and ten seconds later she was unconscious.

It was dark when she awoke, back in her cell and on the hard prison bed. The moon reflected an eerie light through the reinforced window glass, flickering strange shafts of luminosity and shadow on the wall opposite her bed. She put her hand down, her left hand, to where Ruby's cot nestled beside her. There was no cot, no baby. She cried out, a strangled cry, 'Ruby. Ruby. Ruby...'

The doctor and a nurse came in and stood by her side.

'She's gone, Drummond. It's for the best.'

He gave her another injection before she had time or the strength to protest.

Next day she awoke, heavy from the drug-induced sleep. Her pyjama top was damp where her nipples had leaked. She felt for her breasts. They were bound, tightly. She knew that's what they did to dry up a mother's milk. Her head on one side, facing the wall and away from where Ruby's cot should have been, Jodie wept.

'Goodbye, little one. I hope they've found you the best parents in the world.'

27

Danny and Ray were excited. They had just received a phone call from the adoption agency. Danny had picked up.

'Mr Manning? Danny?'

'Yes.'

'I'm delighted to tell you your baby girl is ready and waiting for you.'

'She's waiting for us Ray. Let's go.'

Moments later, they rushed out to the car, armed with baby clothes and baby seat, a state-of-the-art stroller and a huge pink teddy bear.

Ray spread a huge smile across his face. 'Can't wait, can't wait.'

Danny sported a wide grin as well. 'Our little girl, Charlotte. Bet she gets called Charlie by the boys.'

'You don't mind that do you?'

'No, course not. Hope she gets to know her new name quite quickly. I think they said her mother named her Ruby. Don't like that. Charlotte's... much nicer.'

Danny drove, surprisingly swiftly out of London.

Probably because it was eleven in the morning and they had missed the rush hour traffic. It was one of those rare January mornings when the sun shone like springtime, a hint of winter's migration.

'How long will it take us, Dan?'

'About three and a half hours, maybe less.' As an afterthought he added, 'shall we drop in on the boys on the way back? Show them their new baby sister?'

'Brilliant idea. I'll call the school now. We can drop in on Ma and Pa as well,' he added. 'Maybe stay there overnight if you like?'

'Great idea, except we've brought no overnight clothes for ourselves.'

'Oh yeah... Never mind Mum's sure to have some of our things there, at least a couple of pairs of boxers.'

'Sorted. Clean underwear and no tops if she's sick down us.'

'Who? My Mum?'

'No, Charlotte you clown.'

They kept up their silly banter until they were past Kettering. Danny drew in at the next Motorway service station.

'Time for coffee.'

'And a pastry?'

Danny looked at his partner of eleven years and grinned. 'You'll get fat.'

'You mean chubby.'

'You're that already, Mrs Manning.'

'Yeah, but you love all my chubby bits.'

'Course I do, you old queen.' Danny resisted the urge to kiss Ray as they walked through the middle of the busy parking area towards the building. That could come later...

Another hour and they drew into the small car park at the back of the adoption agency. Danny pulled on the hand brake and switched off the ignition. 'Erm, we'd better take the baby clothes in and maybe the stroller. Or just the car seat, what d'you think?'

'I don't know, you're like a first time parent,' snorted Ray. 'Suppose you've forgotten when the boys were babies.'

'Well it is nine years ago since we had Simon.'

Mrs Neale came down the steps at the back of the agency to greet them. 'You've made excellent time. She's just been fed and looks all pink and lovely. All ready to meet her Daddy and Pops.'

Danny marvelled at the way she remembered their titles, and her efficiency as she divested them of the baby gear. She gushed over their choice of baby clothes as she peeked into the various bags.

'They are quite gorgeous and she will look stunning in them. I like the baby seat too, very snug looking.'

They followed her generous frame up the steps, through the glass double doors that opened into a spacious and colourful reception area. There were cuddly toys everywhere and the pastel painted walls were decorated with photos of babies and toddlers, some being cuddled by their adoptive parents, others by members of Mrs Neale's staff.

'She's through here with Pansy.' Pansy was one of Mrs Neale's assistants, a bright girl with coffee-coloured skin and a smile that displayed beautifully white teeth with a gap in front.

'Hi guys,' she greeted them, extending one hand while she cuddled the baby in the other.

Ray took a deep breath in, 'Oh my God, she is beautiful.' He touched the tiny face. 'Oh Danny, just look at her, have you ever seen anything so lovely?' He had tears in his eyes and Danny loved him for it. He swallowed away his own temptation to cry.

'Yes, she's perfect... can we hold her?'

'Of course you can, she's your daughter. Pansy give the baby to...' she laughed. 'One of them. They can take turns.'

'You first Ray, you're the one who'll be doing the necessaries most of the time.' Danny stepped back, and let his partner take the baby into his arms.

'What name did you say you were going to call her?'

'Charlotte.'

'Lovely, it suits her.'

Danny guessed she would have said that whatever name they chose.

She gave them ten minutes to cuddle their new daughter then instructed Pansy to take Charlotte into the changing room and dress her in her gorgeous new clothes.

'We'll just finish the paperwork then you two can be on your way. Are you driving back to London tonight?'

'No,' Danny answered. We're stopping off at the boys' school in Shrewsbury to introduce them to their baby sister, then probably staying over at Ray's parents' house, let them see their granddaughter.'

'Lovely idea.'

They made good time to Shropshire, with Ray sitting in the back next to his new baby daughter.

From time to time she regarded him, with her wide, dark eyes. And smiled. That melted him and he offered his finger to her tiny hand that she grasped, curling and uncurling her hand while holding her gaze.

'She can smile already, Dan. That's young isn't it?'

'What six weeks? Don't know, we'll look it up. We're here by the way.'

Danny drove in through the school gates and parked as near as possible to the main entrance.

'The headmaster has said as it's Thursday, the boys can have a long weekend furlough. They can come with us to your parents. Give them all a chance to get to know Charlotte.'

'That's decent of him. Quite surprised really,' said Ray. 'I always find him a stuffy old bugger.'

'Language, Raymond. In front of our daughter.'

'Oh sorry Charlotte. Smack Popsie's hand.'

They climbed out of the car, Ray releasing the baby from her seat and carefully carrying her into the school building, shielding her against a chill wind. Mr Starkey, the headmaster, came out of his office to personally greet them. He shook hands with Danny and gave a funny little bow to Ray. Secretly he never knew how to address Ray. Not Mrs Manning for sure...

'So, this is young Charlotte. The boys are so excited, especially as you're taking them to their grandparents tonight.'

'Are they here?' asked Danny, wondering if they might be out on the sports field.

'Oh yes, all packed and ready to go.'

On cue the two boys came rushing down the stairs, backpacks swinging.

'Dad, Pops,' at the tops of their voices, until they saw headmaster's frown of disapproval.

'Decorum gentlemen, decorum.'

'Sir.' Then ran towards Danny and Ray, ready for big hugs. They stopped short when they saw the bundle in Ray's arms.

'Is that her?' asked Alfie. His voice dropped to a whisper. 'Is she our baby sister?'

'She sure is matey poo. Come and say hello.'

Alfie peered over the baby blanket and sniffed her. 'She smells like talcum powder.' And 'Isn't she tiny?'

'Let me see her,' said Simon. 'Can we hold her?'

'All in good time, boys.' Headmaster interrupted the cosy family scene. 'Don't crowd her, you'll frighten her to bits.'

Danny thought it was more to the point that HM was the frightened one. Not used to babies. His charges were at least seven before he met them.

'Tell you what guys, let's all go to the car and drive to Gramps and Granny's, then you can cuddle her all evening if you want.'

They made a polite escape and were soon on their way to Ray's parents, with Alfie in front with his father and Simon in the back sharing the seat with Ray and the baby.

'It's like Christmas all over again.' Said a beaming Eleanor Chambers as she was handed her newest grandchild.

Hours later, as Ray and Danny fell into bed with baby Charlotte in her stroller next to Ray's side of the bed, Danny said, 'What a day and evening. I feel I've aged ten years.'

'Well you have since Alfie was a baby. Anyway,

at least Mum was here to give us a helping hand. Funny isn't it, no matter how old they are women always seem to retain that maternal instinct?'

'Yeah, well let's hope this young madam gives us at least a few hours' sleep before she needs a feed, or a nappy change, or another cuddle. She must have used up a month of those.'

They turned away from each other, Danny with his head under his pillow and Ray stretching out a hand to the baby.

'Night, best pal,' he whispered.

'Night to you too, Mrs Manning. Golden dreams.'

Next morning at breakfast Eleanor said, 'You too don't really have to go back to London today, do you?'

'Fraid so Ma, Danny's got a late afternoon meeting and we really ought to get this young lady into some sort of routine, else she'll be ruling all our lives.'

'True,' agreed Danny. 'And thanks Greg,' he turned to his father-in-law, 'for offering to take the boys back Sunday night, I'm sure they'll have a great time with you two for the weekend.'

'Can we go to the ice rink in Telford, Gramps?' asked Alfie.

'Course we can. And for giant ice-creams afterwards.'

'Yay!' cheered Simon. 'Ice and ice-creams. Will you come Granny?'

'I don't think so. Someone has to clear up the mess of five extra family members. No maids here you know, not like at your school.' She smiled as she said it, then turned to her son and his partner. 'Such a pity you have to leave so soon. I've hardly had time to get to know my granddaughter.'

'You will, Ma,' Ray promised. 'We'll be up again before you know it. Or you and Dad can always come down and stay with us.'

'True. Anyway, best be on your way. They said snow is forecast this afternoon... at least up here. Don't know about London.'

'Doubt it,' said Danny. 'Not very often you get snow in London, only a few flurries at best.'

Soon after breakfast there were affectionate farewells and 'be good for Gramps and Granny' to the boys. Everyone planted kisses on the baby's forehead and four came out to the car to say goodbye to three, or 'two and a half' as Simon suggested, followed by his amusing giggle.

Their journey back to London was fairly uneventful, a slight snarl up of traffic as they hit the North Circular, then a gradual smoothing out as they reached Highgate.

'She obviously likes car journeys,' said Ray. 'She's not made a murmur all the way.

It took them all of twenty minutes to unload the car and carry the baby in her seat inside. She woke when they put the seat on their sofa. Her eyes roamed the room, the ceiling and the glistening central chandelier that reflected the thin, watery sunshine from outside. Once she had made that visual journey, she turned to the two slightly anxious men who were her new parents. She regarded them for a few seconds before breaking into a shy smile and waving her tiny hands about.

'I think she likes her new home.'

'She'd better, there's no going back.'

Another small smile and a fist stuffed into her mouth meant, they thought, hoped, she meant to stay. A sharp wail and the smile disappeared.

'Time for her next feed,' said Ray.

'I'll put the kettle on, then go and put the car away.'

Charlotte Manning's new life had begun. Some two hundred miles away, a young woman in grey prison gear, topped with a padded jacket, wandered out into the prison garden. She walked towards the tool shed, and chose a large rake. Above her the sky was as grey as her track suit and nowhere near as warm. She shuffled her feet into small heaps of windblown brown lifeless leaves. With little or no enthusiasm, she attempted to rake them into one pile, ready to put into plastic sacks. Her pale face was as lifeless as the dead foliage; her body as barren as the blackened branches that had shed the leaves.

'Come on Drummond, put your back into it.' The new prison officer's voice reminded Jodie of a sergeant major shouting out orders in one of the military films she had watched since she had been in prison. She curled her lip, ignored the order and carried on raking at the pace she had chosen.

The officer touched her shoulder. 'I said move your arse.'

'No you didn't... ma'am, you said I was to put my back into it. Make your mind up... arse or back?'

She got pleasure seeing the anger swelling on the fat cow's face. What did she think she could do? Add another twenty-four years to her term? The other inmates stopped what they were doing to watch the clash between these two. Good to have a diversion occasionally. They were disappointed, however when prison officer Smyth with a 'y' apparently climbed down from the confrontation with a muttered 'suit yourself' and walked away. But not before she had shouted at the rest of them, 'And you lot, get on with your work.'

'Yes, officer Smyth with a y,' they shouted. More pleasure was gained when she reacted to their answer with a scowling face.

Two more officers joined her, diffusing what could have been a situation, and a clear sign there would be no more fun that day. Ten minutes later snow began to fall. Softly at first, with gentle, almost individual flakes, then increasing into a full-blown snow storm, causing prisoners and their guards to rush back inside and abandon their garden duties for the day.

A bell rang, summoning them to tea, the last meal of the day and not very interesting. Slices of bread, margarine and jam, with mugs of tea and maybe a slice of cake if the prison cook felt like getting her minions to bake some. There followed a general clatter of tin plates and mugs in the steamy atmosphere of damp clothing and the noisier one of some two hundred voices.

Jodie, as usual, chose to sit alone. She barely glanced at the others, except for a new inmate. Her swollen belly indicating she was not far off her time of giving birth. Jodie thought she looked young, too young to be in a women's prison. She shrugged her shoulders, not her problem. But she spared a moment's pity for the girl, knowing she would not be allowed to keep her baby. Her mind wandered back in time, remembering the sensation of breast-feeding little Ruby. She wondered how she was doing; if she was loved...

28 SIX WEEKS LATER

Tilda was home after her third operation and skin graft. Danny walked her up her house steps, almost a year since the explosion at the Teme Literary Festival.

'I won't ask you to close your eyes, sis. Don't want you to get vertigo or something,' Danny grinned. 'But I think you'll be surprised at some of the changes we've made.'

Matilda struggled to smile through her scars. She was a new, gentler Matilda, prone to emotional tears. She had suffered agonies after her sojourns in the burns unit of the Chelsea and Westminster Hospital. But, constantly visited by Danny and Ray and her stepfather, she bravely bore the pain, the indignity and the long days of lying still while her skin grafts became effective.

Alfie and Simon also visited, but not before Danny showed them photos of their aunt's horrific facial burns.

'I want you to see her without pulling shocked faces,' he explained. 'No shuddering, no pulling away, understood?'

'Yes Dad, we understand. Anyway,' Alfie said. 'She doesn't look so bad. She's kind of our Simon Weston.'

Ray smiled at his eldest son. 'Well said mate.'

But they waited until Matilda was home before they took Charlotte to see her. Danny fetched his twin sister from hospital, and Ray brought the boys and Charlotte by taxi to Matilda's newly decorated house. There were 'For Sale' notices up at both Mungo Dickson's house and that of the Braithwaite brothers. Danny was a little surprised that they were still for sale; he was tempted to put in a bid himself. He and Ray could always let them out until such times as the boys were old enough to leave home, but that was nowhere near in the foreseeable future. Something to think about anyway... Meantime, get Tilda indoors and comfortable.

She stood in the freshly painted hallway, where all doors to the downstairs rooms were open, revealing the newly decorated and refurbished rooms.

'It's... amazing Dan. What can I say?' and she burst into tears. Danny took her into his arms.

'Hush, lovely girl. Come on, let's get the kettle on, expect you could do with a cuppa.'

'I'd sooner have some bubbly,' she sniffed. 'I've had my fill of hospital tea.'

'There's Dom Perignon chilling in the fridge.'

She wiped her face – carefully, gently – with a tissue. 'That's better.' And managed a lop-sided grin as she mopped her tears.

'Unless you want to wait until the boys get here with Ray?'

'There's more than one bottle. You don't

honestly think your brother's turning meanie do you?' He got her seated in her new sitting room, furnished with new armchairs and small matching tables. 'I'll go pour us a glass each, while we wait for the invasion.'

'Ok, good thinking bro. Can't wait now to meet my new niece. Is she beautiful?'

'Perfect and a real little love.'

They barely had two sips apiece when the doorbell rang.

'That'll be them.' She sat up straight, an expectant look on her face and a niggle of apprehension in her stomach. *Please don't let me frighten the baby.*

The boys entered first and planted gentle kisses on her face.

'Oh good,' said Alfie. 'Champagne, can we have some?'

'Definitely not,' said their father. 'Not at over a hundred quid a bottle. You can have a small glass of Prosecco though, with some orange juice.'

Ray entered the room carrying their baby daughter. 'Hi Tilly,' he said. 'Look who I've brought to see you... Charlie, meet your aunt.' He offered the baby to Matilda. She hesitated, then held out her arms and cuddled the baby to her.

Aunt and niece solemnly regarded each other for a few moments. Danny hoped and prayed his baby daughter would not be fazed by Tilda's scarred face. Then Charlotte did something unexpected, she lifted her hand to Tilda's face and stroked it. She moved her mouth, almost as if she wanted to speak. Instead she gave a little gurgle and smiled. No one spoke or moved. It was a purely magic moment. And no one in that room, except maybe, for a small baby, knew that the child who gently stroked those scars was the child of the perpetuator of them. Matilda, speechless, drew a strange comfort from her niece's touch. Her pain disappeared and so did her feelings of rage against a woman called Jodie Drummond. She could see a way forward. To what future she did not quite know, only that there was a way forward, a future.

The doorbell rang again.

'I'll get it,' said Simon. 'It might be Grandpa.'

When he came back into the room, he was followed by Pam Clifton and her daughter, Amy.

'We saw you draw up in the taxi,' she said. 'And thought we'd like to bring Mrs Meadham some flowers... and a little present for the baby.' She looked embarrassed and Amy stepped from one foot to the other.

'Hope you don't mind Mum and me barging in...'

'No, course not,' said Ray. 'D'you want to see the baby?' He led them over to Matilda's chair. 'Here she is, Charlotte Manning, meet your auntie's neighbours.'

Charlotte looked up from the comfort and safety of her aunt's arms, stared at Amy... and let out the most piercing scream... of terror.

THE END

ACKNOWLEDGEMENTS

I am indebted to Geoff Thatcher, my partner and editor, for his tireless encouragement and support in helping me to shape these words into a finished novel, and pouring me the welcome glass of wine at the end of each working day.

ABOUT THE AUTHOR

Olga Merrick is a British author born in Middlesex, England and educated at Burlington School for Girls in West London and at The Open University. After a brief period as a teacher, she managed pubs in Hertfordshire, including a film-land pub and restaurant near Elstree film studios, then owned an Italian restaurant in Hay-on-Wye – the famous town of books – where she raised four sons and wrote stories to amuse them.

Today, Olga lives in Shropshire, England with her partner and their small poodle, Albi. Olga writes psychological crime thrillers with a distinctive British flavour and characters who are believable. Many of these are based on real people she has met throughout her life: these people inspired her to write her first novel, "Untouched Departures", the gruesome murders of a serial killer, first published as a paperback in November 2015.

Following the release of “A Rake of Leaves” in September 2016, Olga is writing two more crime thrillers for publication in 2017.

More titles from our authors†

READING BETWEEN THE LINES
an anthology of poems and stories
by John Cliff and Anna Newman

UNTOUCHED DEPARTURES
a psychological thriller by Olga Merrick

TALES OF ROMANCE
The Phantom Reborn and other stories
by Rosemarie David

FROM THE MOUNTAINS TO THE SEA
more tales of romance
by Rosemarie David

THE CHAMPAGNE WRITERS OF SHROPSHIRE
an anthology of poems and stories from Olga's
creative writers' group in Telford, Shropshire

Coming in 2017†

THE KILLING OF ELLIE SWALES
more psychological drama from Olga Merrick

SPARROWHAWK
another psychological thriller by Olga Merrick

† For further information about these titles, please email

chadgreenbooks@yahoo.com